THE FINA

THE FINAL RECKONING

Margaret James

This first world edition published in Great Britain 1996 by
SEVERN HOUSE PUBLISHERS LTD of
9–15 High Street, Sutton, Surrey SM1 1DF.
First published in the USA 1997 by
SEVERN HOUSE PUBLISHERS INC. of
595 Madison Avenue, New York, NY 10022.

British Library Cataloguing in Publication Data

James, Margaret
    The final reckoning
    1. English fiction – 20th century
    I. Title
    823.9'14 [F]

    ISBN 0-7278-5107-1

Typeset by Palimpsest Book Production Limited,
Polmont, Stirlingshire, Scotland.
Printed and bound in Great Britain by
Hartnolls Ltd, Bodmin, Cornwall.

Chapter One

It was no good. I couldn't sleep. I was tired – exhausted, in fact – but so wound up that lying down, closing my eyes and slip-sliding into oblivion, appeared to be out of the question tonight.

I was in the kitchen, making coffee by the light of the street lamp which conveniently stood right outside the window, when I heard the front door slam. A few moments later, Nick Singer came into the sitting room which we all shared. He switched on the overhead light, then flicked on the BBC World Service. The confident tones of some self-assured lady reporter rang out, piercing the quiet, North Oxford night.

It seemed Nick hadn't seen me standing in the kitchen, waiting impatiently for my watched pot to boil. For a few seconds, I observed him. He fiddled with the radio, retuning it to Radio Oxford. He glanced at the clock. He grimaced. He sighed. He did not look at all happy.

Nick is a physicist, a graduate of London University, currently working for his doctorate at Oxford's Clarendon Laboratory. He does mysterious experiments which go on for days and days and days, which generate stack after stack after stack of computer print-out. This piles up messily all over the house, collecting dust.

His subject – or so he'd informed my best mate Tessa

1

– is cryogenics. Whatever *they* are. I was always meaning to look it – or them – up in the dictionary, but so far I hadn't managed to get round to it. But, even if I had, we would never have built a normal conversation around Nick Singer's experiments. When asked about his progress, all he would ever say was either that it worked, or that it didn't work. Whatever that may have meant.

He peeled off his navy blue jumper and dropped it on the floor. Wearily, he rubbed his eyes. Perhaps, I thought, perhaps he would like a nice, reviving coffee. "Nick?" I began. "Do you fancy—"

"What?" Startled, he blinked. He glanced towards the kitchen door. "Is that Lindsay?"

"No," I murmured, "it's the Queen of Sheba."

He heard that. He managed half a grin. "So it is," he agreed, through a stifled yawn. "I didn't notice you, standing there in the dark. Why don't you put the light on?"

"The bulb's gone. Will you have a cup of coffee?"

"Please. If you're making it, that is."

"Sit down. I'll bring it in."

We sat on the hearth rug, warming our hands around our drinks. "Did it work?" I asked, politely.

"No, it didn't." Gloomily, Nick sighed. A frown creased his brow. "I've spent most of this term trying to fix that bloody apparatus. Last week, I honestly thought I'd got it sorted. But it's still not right. I don't know what's the matter with it this time." Still frowning, he glanced towards me. "You're up late," he said.

"Yes." I arranged my dressing gown so that it covered my cold toes. "I've too much on my mind to sleep."

I didn't know Nick very well. A newcomer to the rented semi-detached in Ferry Road, he had been in the house about five weeks. He'd replaced Alan, a freelance photographer who had gone off to Tibet or some such equally dangerous, insanitary and uncomfortable place, and let his room for the rest of that year.

I couldn't decide whether I liked Nick, or not. I certainly hated the mess he made, for Nick Singer was a squalor merchant *extraordinaire*. He seldom washed up, he never took his rubbish out to the dustbins, and yesterday he'd abandoned a fresh heap of his wretched computer printout all over the sitting room floor.

Along with the navy blue jumper, there were several hundred yards more of it there tonight, and I reflected – not for the first time – that among the dafter conventions of romantic fiction is that old chestnut of a plot in which the immaculately tidy, anally-retentive millionaire falls for the scatty slut whose skirt hems are constantly coming down, whose house is a tip, but whose heart is undoubtedly in the right place. The slut, in fact, whom he marries, and with whom he lives – happily, presumably – ever after.

In actual fact, in real life, the slut would drive the millionaire demented. You will have gathered that I'm a tidy person myself.

As for the man and his attitude towards me, I had come to the reluctant conclusion that as far as Nick was concerned, the human race consisted of a few laser-brains like himself, with whom it was actually worth holding a conversation, and morons like the rest of us, with whom it was not.

It would have been only fair, it would have been simple, natural justice in fact, if somebody as smart as Nick had also been a short-arsed, round-shouldered, repulsive little nerd. But he wasn't bad-looking at all. He was

3

tall, broad-shouldered and well-made. His permanently ruffled black hair, bright brown eyes and darting manner always put me in mind of a starling or blackbird, pecking for worms on a wet summer lawn.

His rather beaky nose and sharp, penetrating stare tended to reinforce this impression, especially when he put his head on one side and gave a person the most infuriatingly patronising smirk I have ever had the misfortune to witness.

Tessa, who shared the big front bedroom with her boyfriend David, confided to me that she thought Nick quite attractive. A definite eight out of ten, rising perhaps to nine on a particularly randy day. The numerous phone calls from various women, together with the fact that at weekends there tended to be some alien female friend of his around, either hogging the bathroom or helping herself to our cornflakes, sort of confirmed that other girls found him attractive, too.

But his manner put *me* right off. Soon after he had moved in, I'd asked – quite casually – what his research involved, and he'd muttered something about investigating the properties of various plastics at temperatures close to absolute zero. But then he'd gone on to add that there was no point in discussing it with me because, not being a physicist, I wouldn't understand anything he said.

Thus, roundly snubbed, I had since confined myself to general remarks about the weather, and reminding him that he was behind with his contribution to the milk bill. Enquiring tonight if his experiment had worked was an aberration. Well, I was tired.

Nick, of course, changed the subject immediately. "You look well shattered," he observed. A Londoner, his accent was pure *EastEnders*, almost aggressively so. "As if you ain't slept for a week, in fact."

I stifled a yawn. "I am a bit tired," I agreed. "But I can't go to bed yet. I have some things to do."

"Oh." He didn't ask, what things. Instead, for five minutes or more he sat motionless, holding his coffee cup as reverently as if it were a holy relic, and gazing into the glowing gas fire. No doubt he was doing some hideously complicated sum, right there in his clever little head. The proper study of mankind is Matter. But then he shrugged his shoulders again, and sighed. Again, he glanced at me. "I was sorry to hear about your mother," he said.

"Thank you," I murmured.

"She can't have been very old."

"Forty-eight." Now I sighed, too. "It was her birthday last month."

"What happened, then?"

I was tempted to reply that there was no point in discussing it with him because, not being a doctor, he wouldn't understand anything I said. But he was trying to be kind, so I didn't. "She'd been ill on and off for years," I began. "She blacked out regularly. She had headaches, blurred vision, and a lot of chest pain – which the doctor said was probably caused by a stomach ulcer. He prescribed antacids, and told her to drink plenty of milk."

I stared into the red glow of the fire. "So there she was, sucking her Rennies and drinking milk by the bloody gallon, and all the time her heart was getting weaker and weaker still. Last Monday, she had a massive coronary. She was dead before the ambulance even left the station. I've a good mind to sue!"

"Do what?" murmured Nick.

"I'm sorry?" Turning to him, I met his gaze. In his bright, brown eyes, I saw the mild interest of a well-disposed but basically uninvolved stranger. I looked away again. Tears welled up, threatening to spill over.

"Got any brothers or sisters?" asked Nick, then.

"One brother." Sniffing, I rubbed my eyes. "He works for a pharmaceutical company, in Toronto."

"What about your father?"

"My parents were divorced. My dad's just moved to Manchester, with a girl of about my age. I believe she's expecting a baby any day."

"I see." Nick stroked the rim of his coffee cup. "Is there anything I can do?" he enquired.

"Such as what?"

"I don't know." He arched one black eyebrow. "Drive you anywhere, maybe?"

"That won't be necessary." I blinked hard. "But thank you, anyway."

"No problem." He stood up. "Well, I need to get some sleep. Thanks for the coffee."

He left the room. I drank my coffee and let my mind wander again.

I found a seat by the aisle, facing the engine. I arranged myself and my luggage. The train shuddered, shook, then pulled out of the station.

There was nothing to be afraid of, I told myself briskly, firmly. I was only going home. After five years away from the place, the death of my mother and the obligation to sort out her affairs was dragging me back to the village where it had all gone wrong for me.

But now, the engine murmured, "Don't be afraid, don't

6

be afraid." In counterpoint, the wheels repeated, "Going home, going home, going home."

I hadn't eaten much breakfast, and by eleven o'clock I was very hungry. The woman sitting opposite me had brought her own little picnic of neat, triangular sandwiches and an orange, already peeled and in segments and hygienically wrapped in clingfilm, in a white plastic box. Her flaskful of aromatic coffee was making my mouth water. Such forward planning, I thought ruefully, as I struggled to my feet and began to make my way to the Railbar for some Travellers' Fare. Or is it Fayre, these days?

Whatever. There, mean little cans of mineral water, overpriced bread rolls and flabby-looking sandwiches in clear plastic coffins, their sell-by date today, were ranged, not particularly enticingly, on trays and shelves.

"Wicked," muttered an elderly man, as he parted with a cup of tea in exchange for a pound coin. He glanced in my direction. "Wicked," he repeated. "Bring me own next time." But then he winked, and grinned, and shuffled off down the corridor, slopping tea as he went.

"Daft old git," muttered the barman, but not unkindly. "Yes, madam? What may I get for you?"

I bought a rock cake and a packet of sandwiches. The mayonnaise on the sandwiches tasted as though it was made of vinegar and axle grease. The cake left a chalky deposit on my teeth. My travelling companion opposite smiled at me. She posted a delicate little homemade sandwich between two rows of gleaming false teeth.

We stopped at Moreton-in-Marsh for ten minutes or more, which unscheduled delay occasioned a bit of muttering from the pensioners across the way. I stared out of the window, taking in the bleak November countryside, watching the sheep patiently cropping the yellowing grass, and observing how the grey cloud was piling up in the east, threatening the first snow of winter.

"Going far?" asked the woman with the white plastic box, who had finished her picnic and now began to click her knitting needles. She was constructing some large, fluffy garment in a vivid shade of giblet pink.

"To Ledbury," I murmured. I didn't really want to get into a long and tedious conversation about it being nice for November, quite mild for the time of year. But the woman was pleasant, round-faced and comfortable-looking, so I exchanged a few more banalities and heard all about her son who was a tax inspector in Huddersfield before I finally lost the will even to pretend interest. I began to scrabble under the seat for my old black leather briefcase, which I'd bought at a car boot sale for fifty pence and of which I was rather fond.

"*You* don't happen to be with the Revenue?" enquired the woman, eyeing the case and squinting for the tell-tale ER embossed above the lock.

"I'm an accountant," I lied, opening my case and taking a folder from inside. "I'm seeing a farmer over Colwall way later this afternoon." Theatrically, I sighed. "He's in trouble with the VAT people, and these days his claims for EEC surplus subsidies are giving him no end of aggravation. That's without even considering the terms of his set-aside! The poor man's in a bit of a mess, I'm afraid."

"Oh, dear." The woman's needles clicked their sympathy. "You get on, then," she murmured. "I shan't bother you."

So, to the hypnotic rattle of wheels going over the points and the clicking of knitting needles, I began to re-read the details of the trial.

8

Chapter Two

As I read, the years seemed to slip away. Soon, I forgot I was on the train. I even stopped hearing the rustle of paper, the slurping of tea and coffee, the muted hum of querulous conversation.

I was a teenager again. A nervous, hyperactive child whose hormones were in ferment, and who – as my mother's cleaning lady would have put it – didn't know if she was coming or going, running around or standing still. I was, in fact, back at Brougham Gate.

Congealing blood might well be disgusting, but it also has a rather attractive texture. As I stared at the sticky, glossy puddle, the artist in me thought, what a lovely colour. What a marvellous sullen sheen, what a beautiful play of light. The great, spreading pool was crinkling at the edges now, and I wondered about touching its softly gleaming surface, as one touches new jam in an experimental saucer, to see if it has reached its setting point.

There seemed to be gallons of the stuff. "Who would have thought the old man had so much blood in him?" I murmured, remembering my A-Level set text, and thinking how clever I was to be so effortlessly apposite, on such an occasion as this.

I admit it. I was stoned, and I was also very drunk. This was hardly surprising, for we'd begun with a flagon of Bulmer's Strongbow, then downed a couple of cans of lager, and finally ended up swigging Louis Dyer's vintage *Haut Médoc* – straight from the bottle, naturally. Too plastered to see straight, nine times out of ten I'd missed my mouth, so streams of dribble had stained my school shirt a rich red-purple-blue.

That afternoon, I'd skipped double French, bunked off school early, and gone into town to catch the Hinton Frome bus. As we reached the outskirts of Hartley Cross, I tapped the driver's arm and got ferociously scowled at. But he did agree to put me down by the old water mill, which wasn't a scheduled stop. Here, there was less chance of anybody from our end of the village seeing me.

Well pleased with myself, I walked up Rackstraw Lane, which led to Brougham Gate, where Louis and Simon Dyer lived.

I'd finally found Simon in the rose garden, fast asleep in the dappled shade of an enormous *Boule de Neige*. "You look so lovely, lying there," I whispered, as I flopped down beside him. "*I will make thee beds of roses, and a thousand fragrant posies. I shall bring thee orient spice. Nutmeg, clove, and—*"

"Jesus-God-Christ!" Simon opened one reluctant eye. "Sod off, Lindsay," he muttered. He yawned, then he stretched. He licked his lips, then grimaced in disgust. "I need a drink," he said.

So, we went up to the house, collected some bottles and cans, then made our way to the barn. Here, as usual, casual swilling and snogging soon gave way to clumsy but energetic sex. Afterwards, Simon finished the last of the Médoc. Then he rolled us a joint, which we shared in companionable silence, since we were too exhausted by our recent exertions even to try to chat.

Looking back to that terrible summer, I just can't imagine what made a law-abiding, clean-living creature like me behave like that. Well, I *can* imagine. I was in love. Simon Dyer was the embodiment of every adolescent fancy I'd ever had, and given the chance I would have eaten him alive.

He was so beautiful! Finely-boned, slim and naturally graceful, with his smooth, honey-milk skin and red-brown curls framing an almond-eyed, heart-shaped face, he was, on reflection, rather too pretty to be a boy.

Not that he looked like a girl. He was much too angular, too narrow-hipped for that. He was, in fact, a dead ringer for Donatello's *David*. For Simon Dyer's body – admittedly almost permanently encased in torn jeans and an over-sized black tee-shirt – possessed the same languid grace, and the same androgynous charm, as the shepherd boy's. The same half-smile invariably played about his lips. I was flattered out of my senses to be liked – my God, to be *desired* – by such perfection as this.

"Darling, don't do yourself down," as my poor mother would have said. Believe me, I don't. I was attractive enough, and I knew it, although I accepted that, for some tastes anyway, I was a bit too thin. I liked to decorate myself, and to celebrate my eighteenth birthday I'd had my ears pierced yet again, a pretty golden ring put in my nose, and my hair razor-cut so short that it looked like suede. This last was a bit of a mistake, since I came out of *Fringe Benefits* looking more like a mean-eyed punk than the sex goddess I'd intended to be.

Since I had no curves, I looked good in jeans. So, I wore them all the time. I was forever painting my face, experimenting with this look or that, and I wore so much eye make-up that my father called me Queen Nefertiti.

Actually, I *did* resemble a tomb painting from the Valley of the Kings. My heavy black hair – which soon grew again – summer-dark complexion and more or less flat-chested figure saw to that.

Simon had stolen one of his father's very best bottles, but we had gargled it down as if it were Coke. Sitting, or rather rolling around in the barn, dangerously smoking Marlboro Lights and telling each other smutty jokes first heard in the bogs of our respective single-sex schools, we'd gradually discarded our clothes and got down to business.

When had Louis Dyer actually breathed his last? As I undid the last button on my blouse, as I wished I had a figure like Moira Douglas in the fifth year, 38C at least, lucky cow, *and* still growing? As Simon peeled off his Wranglers? As, suddenly desperate, he took me by the shoulders and pushed me back against a bale of hay? As we clung to each other, in a frantic but incompetent embrace?

An hour or so after we'd smoked the joint, Simon and I parted. Dragging on his jeans, my lover zipped himself decent, raked his fingers through his hair, and muttered that he had to check some fences – as the proprietors of a market garden and fruit farm, the Dyers had endless problems with marauding deer and rabbits – then see Nathan Casson about a job in one of the stables.

He took himself off. But I just went for a walk, or rather an amble, across the fields. That lazy euphoria one always feels after a combination of aerobic sex and too much to drink made me reluctant to go home to tell my mother about my early morning interview with the careers mistress, then start on my Business Studies course work before *Neighbours* could swallow up another half-hour of an unproductive day.

I was almost home when I realised I had left my school bag and brand new denim jacket in the kitchen at Brougham Gate. Looking for Simon, I'd naturally glanced into the house first, and been happy to lay my burden down on the great oak table by the scullery door.

"Shit," I muttered. I scowled my irritation. If I gave him a ring, would Simon bring my bag over later? Perhaps. It would depend on his mood. But if he *did*, my mother would know, or at any rate she would guess, what I'd been up to that afternoon.

I turned to go back for my property.

If I'd been sober, I'd never have thought the sight of Simon's father lying dead on the kitchen floor was even remotely interesting. Horrible, yes. Frightening, terrifying, certainly. But interesting, worthy of further investigation? No.

I began to investigate.

The first thing I noticed was the smell. Peering into the gloom, for here in the south-facing scullery beyond the kitchen proper, Louis Dyer's housekeeper always kept the green cotton blinds drawn close against the sun, I saw the source of it.

The old-fashioned roses were everywhere, heaped on the draining boards and piled high on the quarry-tiled floor. Their drowsy, decadent scents had mingled with the heavier, metallic smells of blood and corruption to produce a diabolical perfume which made me feel quite sick.

Choking back my nausea, I blinked. I turned back to the kitchen. Finally, I managed to make my eyes focus properly.

Louis Dyer lay on his back, his legs under the kitchen table. Above him, two fat bluebottles and any number of smaller flies droned in sleepily buzzing circles, round and round and round. The thing that had impaled him, its end protruding from his forehead just above his right eye, winked at me.

What was it – a chisel? A screwdriver? I observed that a wooden mallet lay discarded on a stool nearby. I was about to pick it up when I gagged and was sick in earnest. Suddenly terrified, I ran from the house, and kept running until I got home.

My mother found me in the bathroom, throwing up afresh. "What *have* you been doing?" she demanded, as I coughed and dribbled, then heaved again.

I tried to speak. I failed. "I'd wondered if you were with Simon," she continued, her voice carefully neutral, her manner deliberately correct. For, she didn't like Simon Dyer. He was a spoilt brat. An only child of a widowed father, he had too much money and too many things, including his own vintage Mini Cooper, which he drove like a fiend and which would probably be the death of him. He was a drug-addict, dipsomaniac and thoroughly bad lot. *Not* a suitable boyfriend for an ordinary girl like me. "Lindsay?" My mother was anxious now. "Have you and Simon—"

"Yes." But then, I grasped her meaning. "No!" I cried. "It's Mr Dyer. I th-think he's dead."

"What?" My mother stared. "Lindsay—"

"Mum, I saw him! He's in the kitchen at Brougham Gate, and he's . . ."

I couldn't say it again. I assumed he was dead. I was sure of it, in fact. But somehow, it didn't seem polite to be so absolute.

14

Levering myself up from a back-breaking crouch over the wash-basin, I caught sight of my reflection in the bathroom mirror. My cheeks were blanched, and my eyes black holes in the paper-white circle of my face. My school blouse, clean on that morning, was a rag. There were bits of straw stuck in the seams and button-holes, it was ripped all along one sleeve, and those streaky, purple-red stains had my mother gaping in horror and disgust.

"It's not blood," I assured her, quickly. "It's wine. Simon and I – we had a drink, you see."

"I see." My mother looked ready to pass out. "Lindsay?"

"Yes?"

"Did you have anything to do with it?" She was as white as the bathroom cabinet. "I mean, did you or Simon—"

"No! I found him, that's all. I just found him, lying there."

I felt my head spin. I needed to throw up again.

Meanwhile, my mother phoned the police. Half an hour later, I was explaining myself for the second, third time. "I went for a walk," I said, addressing the kind lady constable who sat beside me while a detective sergeant listened patiently. "Then I went back to collect my school bag. I'd left it in the kitchen, so I—"

"But Simon didn't go to the house with you?"

"No. I told you – he'd gone to check some fences. It's the rabbits, you see."

"Rabbits?" repeated the detective, conversationally.

"They've been getting into the broad beans. Mr Dyer hates them! He's tried everything. But they still—"

"Yeah, okay." The detective drew a deep breath. "Lindsay, after you and Simon parted company, what *exactly* did you do next?"

*   *   *

15

Many months, many statements, many interviews later, the case had finally come to court. The bald, undisputed facts were these. During the six months leading up to his death, Louis Dyer – a widower of fifty-two with a county-wide reputation as a ladies' man – had been having an affair with Jael Casson, a girl of my own age. Everyone in the village knew about it, and everyone disapproved.

What we didn't know, until Louis Dyer's solicitor told the police and it somehow got into the *Hereford Times*, was that the old man had intended to change his will, leaving the bulk of his not inconsiderable property to Jael, and thus effectively disinheriting his only child.

Louis had told Simon as much, and later telephoned his solicitor at home to confirm this, on the night before he died. But, as I informed the police, as I told them over and over again in fact, Simon had said nothing at all to me.

At some time between half past two and four o'clock that fine summer afternoon, then, Louis Dyer had walked into his own kitchen and been hit hard, on the back of the head. This blow had stunned, but not killed him. The piton hammered through his forehead just above his right eye, nailing him to the hard wooden floor, had done that.

The pathologist's report suggested that a person of unusual strength must have delivered the blows, both to the back of Louis Dyer's head and to the piton which had been hammered through his skull. Some time later, in the coroner's court, Dr Fenton had in fact produced expert witnesses – a mechanical engineer *and* a mathematician, no less – to pronounce on the exact degree of force required to inflict such terrible injuries to a man's head.

When questioned further, when invited to speculate on the size and age of the murderer, however, all Dr

16

Fenton would say was that he must have been a strong, fit, heavily-built man. He doubted if a woman could have done the deed. That let Jael off the hook, at any rate. The village gossips cast about them for a likely young lad.

After the discovery of his father's body, Simon had shut himself up at Brougham Gate. He did not answer the telephone, he would not come to the door, he refused to speak to the police. So it was inevitable, I suppose, that three weeks after the inquest had been opened and adjourned, Simon should be arrested and charged with murder.

Since he was remanded in custody and no application for bail was ever made, I didn't see him again until the trial, at which I was a police witness. Not a very important one, I must admit. I'd found the body. That was all. I'd been with the accused in the course of that fatal afternoon, it was true, but it seemed that after he'd left me, there had been plenty of time for him to have popped back to the house and bumped off his old man.

I was seventeen when all this began. Now I am nearly twenty-five, and that summer seems a whole long lifetime away. Since then, I've been to college, collected a degree in fine art, and begun to earn a modest but steady living. I can paint, I can draw – and so, although I shall never win the Turner Prize, these days I do quite well as a freelance artist in the commercial field, getting a regular trickle of commissions for magazine illustrations, letter-heads and greetings cards, and teaching GCSE courses at a local college. I shall never be rich, but provided I can wield a 2B and paint vases of roses and peonies to mass market taste, I hope to be comfortable.

I'd chosen to settle in Oxford because I had some friends there, and because I hate dirty, dangerous London

17

– which I need to be within easy reach of, all the same. I live in a pleasant, turn of the century semi-detached in North Oxford.

I am independent, I am confident, I am grown up. I am going home to Herefordshire to sort out my mother's affairs. But, I tell myself firmly, I will be back in Oxford well within the week.

Chapter Three

"You'll give yourself a headache, frowning like that," said a disembodied, female voice.

"What?" My concentration broken, I started. I glanced up from my sheaf of papers. "I'm sorry? Did you say something?"

"Yes, my dear, I did." All maternal anxiety, the lady with the pink knitting was looking earnestly at me. "If you're reading small print, you ought to be in a much better light. You could change places with me, if you wish."

Only an English, middle-aged mother, happily married and with grown-up children all doing well in the world, would have dreamed of addressing a total stranger so bossily – but so kindly, too. Looking up from my folder, I tried to smile. "Thank you, but I've almost finished," I said.

I opened a large, brown envelope now. Inside this was a bulky sheaf of newsprint, these individual cuttings held together by a rusty bulldog clip. The most recent of the cuttings was from the local paper. A short paragraph, it was brief and to the point.

Whilst in progress, the murder trial had been front page news in the national dailies. At its conclusion, however, when the majority verdict of Not Guilty was finally pronounced, it merited only a tiny mention on the back page of the local rag.

If Simon had been a Scot, if he had been tried in Edinburgh or Inverness, the verdict would have been Not Proven. I'm quite sure of that. No one in Hartley Cross, or indeed anywhere else, doubted Simon's guilt. But since there had proved to be insufficient evidence to convict him, no one made his or her views public, or at any rate not in print.

All the same, Louis Dyer had been a miserable old bugger, muttered the regulars, down at the Lamb and Flag. He'd been a rotten father to his motherless child. He'd knocked him about. He'd had his women parading all round the place. He'd refused to let him go to college because he needed Simon to help run the family business – and then had the face to imagine that buying his son a Mini Cooper more than made up for it all.

"Poor little thing," I imagined the members of the local Mothers' Union murmuring, as they sipped their tea and politely nibbled Mrs Sidderfin's excellent lardy cake. "Left all on his own, he was."

"Only six years old, wasn't he? When Celia Dyer died? After that, he'd nobody to give him so much as a cuddle goodnight."

"Then there was his dad. Being like *he* was, I mean. That didn't help."

"Well, Louis Dyer always fancied a drop or two."

"He liked a fight, as well. If he couldn't find one, he'd use that little lad as a punch bag."

"Then there was all the women."

"That Jael Casson! Only eighteen, forward as a showery summer . . ."

"I don't reckon they did anything, though. Not with Jael's dad and all her brothers, like – you know."

"They say Simon was carrying on with that Ellis girl."

"Young Lindsay, you mean?"

"Yes. Up to all sorts of tricks, they was! Well, after her dad left, she did go a bit wild. By all accounts."

By all accounts in the village, anyway. For, until Louis Dyer got himself murdered and his son was brought to trial, my own parents' separation and subsequent divorce, together with my apparently wild behaviour, had been the staple topic of gossip in every pub and tack room for five miles round about.

Village men frowned, and village women folded their arms across their solid fronts to declare that they'd never let a daughter of theirs go out looking like that. Whoever did I think I was? Pig-rings was for pigs, not human beings, and as for that shaven head – well!

I suppose I was ahead of my time. For almost everybody under twenty has a pig-ring these days.

The trial upset me, of course it did. I'd thought I was getting over it, but apparently I wasn't, for that autumn my mother decided the atmosphere in the village was bad for my nerves, and the sooner I left Hartley Cross, the better I would be.

Swallowing her pride, she spoke to my father and arranged for me to go and live in Worcester with him, until everything was back to normal again.

So, I stayed with my dad and his girlfriend until it was time for me to go away to college. I met my mother in town. Sometimes, she stopped over with a friend, and we made a weekend of it.

I missed her, naturally. But we rang each other almost

every day, my father and Louise were very nice to me, and I enjoyed living in the city. I never went back to Hartley Cross.

At Worcester Shrub Hill, I left the big Inter-City express and took a branch line train to Ledbury, a little country town which I found shivering in the cold of a wintry dusk. There were no taxis at the station, so I walked to the nearby market place, where I found a cab for hire.

Ostensibly for hire, anyway. The stout, balding, middle-aged driver sat dozing, taking forty winks in the front seat, his cigarette smouldering on the dashboard and the *Daily Mail* crumpled against the steering wheel.

I tapped on the window. "Are you for hire?" I enquired, as he opened his red-rimmed eyes.

"Depends." But then, waking up properly, he grinned at me. "Where do you want to go?"

"Could you take me to Hartley Cross?"

"You mean that place out Mortimer's Bridge way? Eight or nine miles, innit? That'll cost you!" Again the driver grinned, revealing nicotine-stained teeth. "Be a tenner or more, all the way out there. I ain't gonna get a fare back, see. So it'll be at least a tenner, all that way."

"That's okay." I grinned, too. Accustomed to paying London and Oxford prices, ten pounds for a cab to go all that distance seemed like a bargain. "Could we go now?"

"Ah." This was the Herefordshire *yes*, midway between the all-purpose Mummerset *aar* and the genuine, antique *aye*. The driver got out of his vehicle. He put my cases in the boot – no London or Oxford cabbie would have even dreamed of doing such a thing – then opened the passenger door for me. I got in, and soon we were heading out of town.

"Come far?" the driver enquired cheerfully as we bowled along, the question as inevitable as when the hairdresser asks what you're doing for Christmas or where you're going on holiday this year. "On the London train, were you?"

"Yes, that's right." I glanced out of the side window at the darkening countryside, which was brown and green and golden at the tag end of what I imagined must have been a beautiful day. "But I've come from Oxford."

"Oxford, eh? Nice little town, Oxford." Sagely, the driver nodded. "Decent shopping centre, all under cover, as I recall. Going to see relatives, are you? Friends?"

"Neither, really." I didn't want to talk. But the driver was a nice man. He didn't deserve to be snubbed. "My mother died," I explained. "I'm going home to sort out her belongings. To sell her house. All that kind of thing."

"Miserable business, that." The cabbie sounded genuinely sympathetic. "I remember when the wife's father passed on. That old fella's house – well, you've never seen anything like it! Never threw anything away, didn't old Ned Harris. Newspapers dating back to the war years, there was. Tins of Bird's custard powder all gone rusty, and packets of Cadbury's cocoa dried out hard as cement."

Ruminatively, the driver shook his head. "A proper old carry-on it was, believe you me. You got people to help you?"

"Oh, yes," I lied. "My brother lives locally, and my husband will be down at the weekend."

The rest of the journey passed pleasantly enough, the driver making non-committal chit-chat while I chipped in with the appropriate responses now and then. He was a man who liked to talk.

23

When we arrived at The Larches, the driver helped me haul out my luggage, then he manhandled it up the drive to the front porch. Fumbling in his pocket, he drew out a business card, which he handed to me. "You need a taxi, ring that number," he said. "Any time of day or night. Very reliable service. Always two or three of us on call, see."

"Thank you." I slipped the card into my bag. Then I paid him, tipping him three pounds, which seemed to astonish him. He'd tell his wife about it later. How he'd met this Oxford woman today, all airs and graces and more money than sense.

I stood in the porch for a long, lingering minute, gazing after the cab, which had long since driven away. From here, I could see the whole way down the meandering village street, taking in the general store, the neat cottage gardens on either side, and the Lamb and Flag right at the end, where the old turnpike road used to be.

I'd dreaded coming back. But now I wondered at myself. Why had I felt so threatened? Why had I wanted to re-read all that stuff, why had I spent two hours or more tormenting myself? It was all in the past. Ancient history. Nothing to do with the here and now, nothing at all.

The Larches looked just the same. Well – it was a bit shabbier, maybe. The rendered masonry displayed a few rather ominous cracks, the lintel above the front door was definitely rotten, and the window frames needed painting urgently.

It would have been so easy to rip them out, to replace all those crumbling wooden sashes with aluminium or PVC! But, like most of the houses in Hartley Cross, The Larches was Grade Two listed, and one simply couldn't do things like that, not to a Georgian gem mentioned by Pevsner himself, and regularly photographed by summer visitors in order to show the folks back home what English village cuteness was all about.

Although I hadn't been back since, well, since after everything happened, I'd seen my mother frequently, either in Oxford or at my brother's house in Colchester, for Gavin didn't live locally. No way, as he'd have put it. He was only a year older than me, but my parents had not been happily married, there had always been an atmosphere inside the family circle, and he'd left home at sixteen, declaring that nothing would make him return to that bloody place. Nothing, ever.

Last year, he'd emigrated to Canada. He'd said he was going for good, and I believed him. Not even the death of his mother would have persuaded him to return, and I knew better than to waste my breath asking him to come over and help sort through her old clothes.

I sighed. I remembered another occasion upon which I'd stood here in the twilight, hesitating to go inside. It was on the day that Simon had informed me, by letter, that he never wanted to see me again.

A few minutes before, as the taxi passed the war memorial, at that time of year rather festive-looking with its half-dozen poppy wreaths, vases of late chrysanthemums and Michaelmas daisies, I'd seen Jael Casson, pushing a pram. Or rather I'd passed Jael Taylor, for she was married now, and hadn't been a Casson for the past three years or more.

She'd noticed the taxi. She'd stared after it in surprise, her large, dark eyes wide with speculation and curiosity. Who could be inside it, she was wondering. Who had come all the way from Ledbury, in a Town and Country Luxi-Cab?

There were so many Cassons that I'd never been able to keep track of them all. Nowadays, no doubt, there were quite a few more. But I'd been at school with Jael, Simon had been in the same class as her brother Nathan, so I knew a bit about the family.

Their widowed father Saul had, in fact, worked for Louis Dyer as a nurseryman and driver for, since Louis was almost permanently disqualified, he had to have somebody around him who possessed a few essential skills. But why a devout, sober, God-fearing fellow like Saul chose to be employed by an old reprobate like Louis, I'll never know.

"*We* will look after Simon." A week after Simon had returned to Brougham Gate, Jael's brother Samuel – a dour, heavily-made young man who worked as a cooper in a small local cider factory, but who never touched alcoholic liquor himself – made this announcement from the steps of the Plague Cross, which stood in the yew-dark churchyard opposite our house.

It was a dull, wet Sunday morning. The few High Anglicans in the area were just coming out of Morning Service, and other Sabbath loungers and loafers were on their way to the pub for their first tipple of the day. Samuel, his sister Naomi and his brother Nathan had come from their own little chapel, where they and several dozen other like-minded worshippers praised the Lord in their own peculiar way. "*We* will see he strays not from the Path," cried Samuel, waving his arms about theatrically.

The villagers who heard this pronoucement shook their heads, and grimaced their indifference at the same time. Country people stick together, it's true. Simon Dyer might have been a violent criminal. He might have taken a life in a particularly horrible fashion. He was still one of them, however, and one of them he would remain.

But there was such a thing as going too far, and it looked like the Casson clan was about to do just that. Simon didn't need looking after. Not as such. Members of the WI would pop in now and again, to push a broom around, put his washing through the machine or take him a nice Victoria sandwich. But it seemed the Cassons intended to save his soul. To redeem a creature who had supped with the Prince of Darkness, not to mention broken most of the Ten Commandments besides.

The regulars at the Lamb and Flag supped their Old Peculiar and sighed. Angels knew their place. If the Cassons chose to rush in where those divine beings feared to tread, that was their look out.

Chapter Four

Although they were country people born and bred, the Cassons were not natives of Hartley Cross. But it was more than twenty years since they had left their tied cottage in the nearby hamlet of Ardisley Bridge, and gone to live in an ugly 1930s villa on the outskirts of an otherwise almost entirely Tudor, Stuart or early Georgian, picture-postcard village.

Saul Casson and his wife Dorcas, an unexceptional pair sprung from generations of ordinary rustic stock, had between them produced a large family of exceptionally good-looking children. Dark-haired and grey-eyed, Samuel, Daniel, Naomi, Nathan, Jael and Rebekah were quiet, obedient and hard-working, as well as honest, courteous and sober-minded. In fact, they were a credit to their mother and father alike.

In the enormous garden behind their house, Saul ran his own business. Businesses, plural, I should say. He grew fruit and vegetables for sale, he raised bedding plants from cuttings and seed, and he also turned his hand to vehicle repair.

A dab-hand at cannibalising insurance write-offs, there were always at least half a dozen of these sorry wrecks littering his untended front garden, lowering the tone of the village and generally upsetting the old age pensioners, who were anxious that Hartley Cross should remain the Best Kept Village in Herefordshire. It has held the actual title, on and off, since 1953.

"You'd think he could at least stick a few gladioli into them side borders," muttered old Mr Sidderfin, who was chairman-in-perpetuity of the local horticultural society, and who stoutly maintained that Saul Casson did what he did just to spite *him*. Neglected his front garden, I mean. That particular Sunday evening in June, he'd cornered my mother on her way home from church, and was enjoying a nice little moan before he went down the Lamb and Flag for his pint of best bitter and a bag of them there salt and vinegar crisps. "You'd think he could poke a few geraniums or lobelias into tubs!"

"He's too busy," murmured Harry Cox, Mr Sidderfin's equally ancient side-kick and long-standing best mate. "What with pottin' up his hangin' baskets for summer sale, and gettin' them old bangers up to the mark for the MOT, he ain't got no time for optional lobelias! Any road – he'd reckon plantin' flowers for pleasure was sinful, an' he wouldn't want to fall out with the Lord."

Harry Cox spoke no more than the simple truth. As everybody in Hartley Cross knew, Saul Casson was well in with the Lord, and evidently meant to remain so. A member of a fundamentalist Christian sect, every Sunday he and his brethren met in a plywood and corrugated-iron chapel, which stood in a field full of cow parsley and wild vetch a mile or two from Hartley Cross.

By the roadside was a weatherbeaten noticeboard, proudly proclaiming to any interested traveller or passer-by that the old shed which he could just make out among the stalks and brambles was in fact the Temple of Jehovah, the Dwelling Place of the Lord.

29

In order to get away from my mother, my father always went for a drive on Sunday mornings. Sometimes he took me with him, and then we would see the parade. A procession of Cassons, everyone wearing his or her very best clothes, they'd be trudging doggedly along the dusty road. Led by Saul, the rest of them would be in order of descending height, until the last child, who was always one of the older ones. He or she would be keeping an eye on Rebekah, the baby of the family, who had been born with Down's Syndrome and needed to be watched all the time.

"But you got to love her," murmured the villagers, one and all. "She might be mental, but she's a dear little thing."

Indeed, she was. But she was also clumsy and shambling, forever falling over, forever sporting cuts and bruises, forever accosting a villager to display her latest plaster, bandage or a fresh, strawberry-scarlet scab on her knee. Dull of eye and slack of jaw, her soft, blurred prettiness was destined to hint forever at a more defined and clear-cut beauty, which in her case could never be.

When Rebekah was fourteen or thereabouts, Dorcas Casson died. I don't remember how, or why. I don't even recall a funeral. Perhaps they buried her in the back garden, or beneath the foundations of the plywood church.

So now, Naomi and Jael took over all their mother's duties, which included teaching Rebekah at home. For Saul Casson refused point-blank to let his daughter attend a special school, along with idiots and defectives, as he put it. There was nothing wrong with *his* child, he maintained. She was just a bit slow.

As I have already mentioned, in addition to running his own concerns, Mr Casson also worked for Louis Dyer, as a general handyman and driver. Well, somebody had to drive Louis about for, if he wasn't actually drunk, he was often otherwise incapable. He had, in fact, been disqualified for dangerous driving so many times, that I suspect he had given up all hope of regaining his licence, at any rate for more than a few weeks at a time! But I also suspect that he didn't really mind. If he employed Saul, good old Saul, he could remain almost permanently smashed.

Theirs was a strange sort of friendship. But, in spite of the fact that they had nothing in common except that they were both widowers, Louis and Saul certainly *were* mates. Saul never got over Louis's death. Then, a year to the day after Louis Dyer was murdered, a stroke paralysed Saul Casson down his right side.

He made a partial recovery, however, and on his discharge from hospital he elected to move in with Daniel – who was, oddly enough, the least God-fearing of all his children. Indeed, Daniel was so unmindful of the Lord that he did the football pools and was known to bet on the dogs.

In Daniel's damp cob and thatch cottage, Saul was dutifully nursed by his daughter-in-law Rachel, a plain, sandy-haired woman for whom being married to tall, handsome Daniel Casson was hopefully some recompense for being obliged to look after an incontinent old man. Not to mention eternally having to mollify her three children, who complained that they couldn't bring their friends home any more, because Grandad dribbled like a baby and stank the place out. Grandad, for his part, grumbled incessantly about the noise made by the brats.

Finally, Daniel had decided enough was enough, and found old man Casson a cottage near the glebe, where he could live in tolerable independence, and stink and drool as much as he pleased.

At least, I thought, at least my poor mother had been spared all that. She had never—

"Lindsay?" My idle reminiscences were suddenly and violently disrupted, by a shrill and strident squawk. This was followed by what sounded like somebody trying to batter down the kitchen door. Startled, I shook my head. Then, "Lindsay, me dear – are you in there?" cried a voice from the past.

"Just coming!" I carolled, by way of reply.

I'd been sitting in the kitchen, familiarising myself with the sounds and smells of the house, and wondering whether or not I was glad to be home. I didn't want to talk to people. But I'd have to talk to this particular person, or she'd be calling out the police and fire brigade, to check I was okay.

So, very reluctantly, I levered myself out of my chair by the Aga, stumped across the flagstones, and opened the door. "Hello, Mrs Denny." Letting my mother's cleaning lady into the warm kitchen, I smiled in welcome. "How are you?"

"Not so good. Me rheumatics are giving me the holy habdabs this week. I can't bend down to tie me shoe-laces nor nothing. But I reckon I'll muddle through." Mrs Denny favoured me with her best censorious stare. "Well, now!" she declared. "*You're* not the girl you used to be!"

"Oh?" I frowned.

"Not a bit of it!" Mrs Denny pursed her lips. But then, she grinned. "You ain't got that thing through your nose no more. You ain't painted up like some circus clown, neither. In fact, you looks like a normal human bein' these days. I could've passed you in the street without gettin' the shakes and palpitations, and havin' to hold my handbag extra tight!" She met my gaze. "Well, me dear? You got it all sorted out, then?"

"Yes, I think so."

"You didn't forget to tell 'em you wanted *real* brass 'andles?" Mrs Denny's faded blue eyes were glistening. "*Your* Mum was a lady," she whispered, her voice growing tremulous now. "So, *she* wouldn've wanted none of that cheap alloy muck. That stuff with the yeller paint."

"I didn't forget," I lied.

For, of course I'd forgotten. I had made all the arrangements for the funeral by phone, asking the firm to provide their complete service, including their selection of a suitable coffin – or casket, as they insisted on calling it – from the middle of their range.

It hadn't even crossed my mind that people could choose the handles on their loved ones' coffins. I didn't really appreciate that coffins actually had handles, although I suppose if I'd thought about it, I would have realised that they must.

We made polite small talk for a few moments more, then I offered tea. But Mrs Denny said she had to be going. Our Alan would be wanting his supper. He was on lates tonight. "Will you be all right here, on your own?" she asked, as she pulled on her gloves. "If you like, you could come over to our place. I've got a nice stew on."

"Thank you." Touched by her kindness, I smiled my gratitude. "But I'll be fine. Honestly."

"Well, if you're sure."

"I won't be bored, or lonely. I've some phone calls to make, and there's an awful lot to do."

"I was going to say, I'll pop over an' give you a hand

with all that." Mrs Denny sighed. "Your poor Mum, she *was* a hoarder. There's boxes and boxes."

"I know." Resignedly, I shook my head. "I'll see you tomorrow morning," I told her, as she let herself out into the cold evening air.

The funeral was at eleven the following morning. Mrs Denny had promised to call for me, and she did, but by the time I'd put my coat on and my chaperone had agreed that since I was just a young girl, I did not really need to wear a hat, a dozen more lady mourners had arrived.

We trooped across the road to the church, in a black and grey flock. At the lychgate, Mr Michael Harrison was waiting patiently, to speak to me. "All ready, Miss Ellis?" he enquired, politely.

I assured him I was as ready as I'd ever be. So, if everything was in order, could we begin?

I was relieved to see that Harrison Brothers had been as good as their word. They had really done their stuff this time. The coffin was of plain, limed oak, with gleaming brass handles. It also sported a few little curlicues and swirly bits, indicating it wasn't a cheap job, and thus enabling Mrs Denny and the rest of the village women to hold their heads up high.

The flowers were beautiful. The choir was mercifully absent. I supposed all its infant members were at school.

For most of the service, I was miles away. In Oxford, in my agent's office in Wardour Street – anywhere but in a cold village church on a chilly autumn morning. Only the occasional cough, or the infrequent sniff or mutter, brought me back to where I actually was in real space and time.

Eventually, we stood around the open grave. As the

34

coffin was lowered into the cold earth, as the rector intoned the old-fashioned words and phrases in his usual sing-song monotone, the villagers stood nodding their agreement, their heads bowed in silent respect. Afterwards, these middle-aged and elderly village ladies, most of whom loved funerals and were most definitely on kissing terms with all the undertakers from the city, took me in hand.

They came back home with me. They put the kettle on to boil, then from their shopping bags they produced ginger cake, banana bread and chocolate sponge, each individual offering wrapped in cling film and ready sliced for tea.

Plastic boxes full of neat little sandwiches, mince pies, iced biscuits and sausage rolls complemented the funeral baked goods. The table spread, we all sat down together, and ate. Well, *they* ate . . .

"Come along, Lindsay," exhorted Mrs Sidderfin, sliding a slice of her special chocolate gateau on to my plate. "Feed your face."

"I only want a cup of tea," I began. "I—"

"Not on a diet, are you, love?" Round, comfortable Mrs Harry Cox placed a cheese and cucumber sandwich next to the chocolate cake. She eyed me up and down. "Well, no. Course you're not. You always was one of Pharaoh's lean kine!"

"I'm sorry?"

"Them in the Bible story, as ate and ate, but never grew fat. Come on, now. Get that sandwich down you, there's a good girl."

So, with twenty sharp, beady eyes fixed upon me, their owners all anxious that I should not waste away, I had no choice but to comply.

Later, some of the younger villagers looked in, had a cup of tea and a piece of cake, and paid their respects to me. Girls I'd been at school with, most of whom had babies or toddlers in tow, kissed and hugged me, saying how sorry they were about my mum. "How are you coping, like?" they demanded. Did I need anything?

But Jael did not come. None of the Cassons came, which rather surprised me, had me wondering what I'd done to offend them. If anything. But then, I told myself, they were a funny lot. I needn't waste time speculating on their motives. My mother hadn't been a particular friend of theirs.

As I ruminated, however, Tracy Freeman handed me an envelope. "Rachel give me this, in the playground," she explained. "Asked me to pass it on. Since I was calling in, like." She hitched her baby higher up her hip. "She says they were all very sorry to hear, and if there's anything she can do, you only got to say."

"That's kind of her." Opening Rachel Casson's envelope, I drew out a card which was all sticky with that odd, translucent glitter which seems to be used especially on messages of condolence, and liberally bestrewn with bright orange roses. Involuntarily, I blinked. "I'll give her a ring this evening, I expect," I murmured, inconsequentially.

I wanted them all to go! I needed to cry, but I'd never have done that with so many people about. For me, grief is a private thing.

But, even as I willed them to get their coats on and go home, one of the older women was opening the ancient, long untuned piano. She struck a rousing chord.

As I reflected that Simon Dyer had never even sent a card, the village ladies drew me into their circle. As they began the first hymn, they fussed and clucked and patted my hands, and tried to comfort me.

Chapter Five

After I'd finally seen the last of the village ladies off home, after I'd washed and dried every cup and saucer and plate in the house, vacuumed up the cake crumbs and thrown the scraps on to the back lawn for tomorrow's dawn chorus to feast upon, I went up to bed.

But I'd been unable to sleep. So, after dozing off and on until five o'clock in the morning, I got up, went downstairs, and made myself a cup of industrial-strength black tea. Sitting there by the Aga in my dressing gown and slippers, I did some preliminary sketches for a series of greetings cards, but my heart wasn't in it, and everything ended up in the bin.

I made myself more tea. As I sipped, I read a few chapters of a novel, which I certainly didn't take in. Then, I tried to make sense of my mother's house and contents insurance policy. By nine o'clock I'd developed a fearful headache, so although the sorting and sifting and packing were beckoning inexorably, I decided I had to get out for a bit of fresh air and exercise, which I hoped might clear my head.

The Larches is directly opposite the church, and beyond that is open countryside. I didn't particularly *want* to walk through the churchyard. I certainly did not *intend* to check up on my mother's grave. But, all the same, my footsteps somehow led me there.

A dozen or more wreaths, crosses and other floral tributes had been neatly arranged, covering the fresh wound of damp, brown earth. Bright yellow chrysanthemums, white carnations and purple freesias lay, miserably bedraggled, their petals nipped and scorched by the cold, frosty air. There they would lie, dying and decomposing, until the sexton collected them up and burned them.

I know people like to send flowers. I know it's the done thing here in Hartley Cross, that it's a mark of respect, of friendship – all that. But, all the same, I wished I'd said, no flowers.

I was about to walk on when I noticed them, a few splashes of red, dotting a wreath of white lilies. At first, I thought these must be stray petals from the spray of red roses which lay adjacent. It was only upon closer examination that I realised they were gouts of bright, fresh blood.

I shook my head in disgust. The local foxes had no finesse! Evidently, a neighbourhood Mr Tod had taken a pigeon from Mr Sidderfin's dovecote, then carried it into the churchyard, where he'd eaten what he fancied of it in comfort and tranquillity, as he reclined upon my mother's grave. Looking more closely, I observed that the poor creature's bones and wings and feathers were still scattered all about.

I left the churchyard, crossed the glebe, then made my muddy way down Ruddle Pit Lane. On my left-hand side, the boundary wall of a pretty half-timbered cottage was low enough for me to see into the well-kept vegetable garden alongside. There, a young woman in a bright blue anorak, jeans and sturdy wellington boots was busy weeding a row of Brussels sprouts. "Hello, Jael," I said.

39

"Hello." Glancing up for the briefest possible moment, Jael carried on with her gardening. "I heard you was back," she murmured, as she dislodged a lurking snail and tossed it into the bucket by her side.

"How are you?" I enquired. I hoped, cheerily.

"Fine," she replied.

"What about the baby?"

"He's fine, too." Straightening up, Jael finally condescended to give me her attention. "Sorry I couldn't make it yesterday," she muttered. "The thing is, I had to take our Michael along for his jab. The clinic's in Ledbury, see, and Wednesday afternoon's the only time I can have the car."

"Don't worry about it." Encouragingly, I smiled. "Mrs Denny and most of the WI were there, anyway."

"So I heard." Suddenly, Jael grinned. "I'll bet you had a proper carry-on with that lot. Afterwards, I mean."

"I'm sorry?" I hadn't actually caught what she'd said.

"Them old biddies likes a nice funeral. Gets 'em in the mood for a bit of singin' and dancin' – all that sort of thing. Did Mrs Sidderfin fetch you round some of her special chocolate gateau?"

"Yes, she did," I replied. But then, I realised what was happening. I could even *feel* it now! Like the Lady of Shalott's curse, the idiot gawp had come upon me and had stuck, like a custard pie lobbed by a practical joker, all over my face.

For Jael was still beautiful. So absolutely, astonishingly lovely that in her presence, all I wanted to do was stare and stare. She was sheer perfection, pure and simple and, as an artist, I could never get enough of that.

What must it be like, I wondered later, to look as astonishing she did? She must dread breaking a nail, cutting herself, or bruising a knee! More serious accidents, illness or injuries didn't bear thinking about. For, afterwards, even Jael Casson would be spoiled. She'd be ordinary, damaged. Just like the rest of us, in fact.

Although Jael and I were exact contemporaries, we had never been friends. I didn't dislike her, it wasn't that at all. But, even as children, we'd never shared a confidence, lent or borrowed pencils, or dug our grubby fingers into the same bag of cheese and onion crisps. The fact was, Jael had no friends.

We weren't jealous of her. Well, not exactly. But, as I'm sure you've noticed, teenaged girls are gregarious creatures, who tend to go around in boringly homogeneous groups. In fact, one of the great myths of our time is that plain and pretty girls hang around together, that a gorgeous blonde's best friend will always turn out to be some mousy little fatty with braces on her front teeth and a squint in both eyes. It's just not true! Take any group of teenaged girls, mark them for general desirability on a scale of one to ten, and you will find the whole lot of them will be within a point or two of one another.

Yes, there will be blondes and brunettes, there will be a mix of tall and short, fat and thin, but every girl in that group will be just about as attractive – or not – as all the others. So poor Jael, at ten plus plus and then some, never belonged to a group, or even had a friend.

When boys entered our field of vision and became trained in our gunsights, however, everything changed. Jael was the first item on every boy's shopping list, and the rest of us were obliged to queue for her rejects.

Some rubbish they were! But, in the conceited way of most males, especially those whose huge feet, crooked teeth and dandruff would have repelled anybody not already in oestrogen-powered overdrive, every man Jack of them fancied his chances with Jael, and gave the rest of us an excellent reason to hate her . . .

"You staying long?" she demanded then, as she picked up her bucketful of snails. "I mean here, in Hartley Cross?"

"No. Not for long." Brought sharply back to the present, I managed to wipe the idiot stare off my face. "Only until I've sorted out my mother's things."

"Right." For a long moment, she seemed to consider. Then, she made up her mind. "Will you come in and have a cup of tea?" she invited. "Or coffee, if that's what you prefer?"

I was going to demur. To say perhaps another day, because just now I had to get back. But then, "Come in," she repeated, almost pleading now. "Come and have a bit of a chat! The babby's no company. Neil never gets in until well after seven, and . . ."

She trailed off, embarrassed. Poor thing, she hated to be asking a favour. But she was bored, she was lonely, and in her circumstances any company would be better than none. So, "I'd love to," I replied.

I followed her into the house.

"Sit down, then," she said, as she took my jacket and hung it on a shiny brass hook. Brightly, happily, she smiled. "Right! Do you want tea, or coffee? I got some nice filter stuff. Or there's instant decaffeinated. Neil has that at bedtime, but our Naomi drinks it morning, noon and night."

"I'll have the same as you," I told her.

"Well – I always has tea, meself."

"Tea will be fine."

So, whilst Jael busied herself at one of the cabinets, hunting for her good china, I gazed all around. Obviously, the cottage kitchen was very recently fitted, with brand new units in pale golden pine, and up-to-the-minute appliances of all kinds. Jael must be very proud of it, I decided, for no stray crumbs littered the work surfaces, no half empty cereal boxes sat on the dresser, and no bits and pieces of crockery lay on the draining rack waiting to be put away.

Indeed, the only evidence that this room might actually be used for cooking and eating in were some pretty china jars labelled Tea, Coffee and Sugar – which I wouldn't have minded betting were only for show.

Jael filled the kettle, then placed it carefully on the spotless ceramic hob. Frowning, she flicked an invisible speck of something undesirable off her pristine toaster, which sat neatly beside it. "You got a microwave?" she enquired, as she eyed her own complacently.

"No," I replied. "I've never thought of it, actually."

"Oh, but you should! They're wonderful things." Compassionately, she smiled. "I dunno how I'd manage without mine, what with Neil coming in at all hours, and the babby on solids, too."

"It must be indispensible," I agreed. But then I smiled, too. Confronted by the squalid reality of the kitchen in North Oxford, in which Nick Singer's everlasting fry-ups scented the stagnant air, Tessa's breakfast dishes sat festering day in, day out, and David's horrible washing soaked in the chipped enamel sink, poor Jael would probably faint dead away.

But anyway, she was quite childishly delighted to hear I wasn't as mod-conned as she was. So much so that she spent the next ten minutes extolling the virtues of her

43

washing machine, tumble-dryer and sandwich toaster, none of which looked as if they were ever used at all.

She made a pot of tea and eventually placed two steaming mugs before us, setting them down as carefully as a Brownie taking her Hostess Badge, or a little girl playing house. She asked a few general questions about my job, and then observed it must be very useful to have a nice little talent, like. When I admitted I was neither married nor engaged, she looked almost smug.

"But then," she reflected, "old Simon was the one for you. We all said so. Right from when you was both kids, you was sweet on him. Yeah, we all saw you and Simon bein' together one day."

"*Did* you?" Caught off my guard, I stared at her. I felt my face begin to burn. My scalp prickled, and my hands shook. My tea slopped on to the table and, to my astonishment and distress, the tears welled up in my eyes.

But, even as Jael gaped at me, even as she was reaching for kitchen towel to mop up the spillage, and asking if I was all right, did I want a paracetamol – there was a lot of that 'flu going around – a burbling and grumbling came from somewhere inside the house. This was followed by a grizzling wail. My hostess excused herself, to see to the baby, leaving me alone.

I stared down into my mug. Why had Jael mentioned Simon? What business was it of hers, whom I liked or didn't like, who was the one for me?

But then I reflected that here in the village, everyone was his brother's keeper. In a city, everybody is an individual. Here in Hartley Cross, however, we were all part of one great, amorphous whole.

This innate clannishness had, of course, caused the

police endless trouble and aggravation, for during the murder investigation Simon's friends and neighbours had told them virtually nothing. Nothing of value, that is. The whole community had said no useful word, had closed right in on itself, not so much to protect Simon – although there was, of course, an element of this – as to protect itself.

During the trial, Simon himself had exercised his right to silence. Few witnesses were produced by either the prosecution or the defence, and the bulk of the material evidence, such as it was, came from the pathologist and the two forensic scientists who had poked and prodded Louis Dyer, largely to no avail.

No incriminating fibres, mysterious stains or tell-tale finger prints had been found on or anywhere near the corpse. The coroner's verdict had been murder, right enough, by a person or persons unknown. But that was as far as it went, and was probably how it would stay.

On returning to Hartley Cross, Simon had inherited his father's property. Now, at Brougham Gate he remained.

"He's nodded off," said Jael, coming into the kitchen and sitting down again. Reaching for her mug, she sipped her stone cold tea. "I like him to have a couple of hours in the morning," she explained. "He's cheerful for the rest of the day, then. So, if I feels like a walk up the playing fields after lunch, he'll sit there in his push-chair, look all around – happy as Larry, he'll be. But if he ain't had his sleep, he just moans and cries, and I can't do nothing with him then."

"It must be very difficult," I murmured.

"It is. But Neil – well, he's ever so good!" Jael's beautiful grey eyes grew dreamy. "*He* can get him off to sleep in five minutes flat! Play with him and keep him occupied all day long. He's got the magic touch, our Rachel says."

"Really?" I was curious to see this Neil. This super-hero, who'd blown into town one fine summer's morning, and swept the local beauty off her feet. All I knew about him was that he worked for Baines Brothers, as a slaughterman.

Once again, I glanced round Jael's pristine kitchen. He must be collecting decent bonuses, I reflected, to be paying for all this. "I've never actually met Neil," I began.

"No, I suppose you haven't." Jael still looked a bit muck struck. "Well, you must," she said, firmly. "You'll like him a lot. Everybody does."

"Everybody?"

"Almost everybody." Jael grinned. "He don't get on so well with our Samuel. But there again, I reckon nobody gets on with that old misery! I daresay them poor beasts he has dealings with down Baines Brothers don't take to him much, neither."

But then, Jael grew serious. "Actually," she murmured, "he's really good at his job. He's careful, he's quick, and he's kind. Mr Geoff Baines was up here last week with some pork chops for the freezer, an' he told me so himself."

"Oh." I was beginning to feel a bit sick. "I see. Well, I think I ought to be going soon. Thank you for the tea."

"It's a messy job, I admit." Jael hadn't heard a word I'd said, for now she was warming to her theme. "But somebody has to do it, and it's better for the beasts if that somebody's got a feelin' for them, don't you agree?"

"I suppose so," I muttered, reaching for my scarf and gloves. "Thank you for—"

"Then again, Baines Brothers is a smallish place. Not one of them great big factory abattoirs! So, it's all local trade. The farmers bring the beasts fresh in every morning, still in their family groups – an' by the time they realise somethin's up, Neil and his mates has them stuck and in the cutting rooms, dead as doornails, with no screamin', cryin' nor nothing."

Jael wasn't just talking for the sake of it. For, even I knew enough about the meat trade to be aware that this insistence on quick dispatch of livestock is of the essence. A beast which is already stressed and trauma-tised, backing away from the knife and rolling its eyes in terror, will be tough. Chemical changes in its body will render the meat dark red and chewy, commercially less desirable. An animal which dies quickly, however, makes good eating. Jael's Neil might well have been a humane man, considerate, kind and all the rest of it – but his working practice still made good commer-cial sense.

Not that this fact was stopping the trend towards factory abattoirs, huge, windowless death-houses on industrial estates, to which unfortunate creatures were driven in enormous lorries. By the time these poor things were ready for the stunner, they would be screaming in terror and die very hard indeed.

I sighed. It was enough to make a person turn vegetar-ian. As I had, after finding Louis Dyer's corpse.

"You actually seen old Simon yet?" asked Jael, as she freshened my cup.

"No." Once again, I felt the blood rush to my face. "No, I haven't seen Simon at all."

"Will you call on him?"

"I might." Feeling rather faint now, I took a biscuit

from the proffered tin. I realised my hand was shaking. "W-what's he doing with himself these days?"

"This and that." Jael shrugged. "He's got a little business going. Antiques, bric-à-brac – all that sort of thing. Our Nathan gives him a hand, now and then."

"You mean in the evenings? At weekends?"

"Well, I suppose you could say he's part-time, really." Again, Jael shrugged. "A couple of months back, he got laid off at the Metal Box. There's nothing else going at the moment, so he's glad to pick up a few quid, helping Simon out."

"Yes, I suppose he would be." So these days Nathan Casson was part of the black economy. "What are his prospects for getting another job locally?"

"Practically non-existent, I'd say." Jael sighed. "Well, you know what it's like. Or p'raps you don't? You ain't been back here for five years or more."

"No," I agreed. "But—"

"Why didn't you come back? I don't mean to live. But you could've popped over to see your mum now and again."

"My mother preferred to visit me." There didn't seem to be any point in telling Jael that, after I'd settled in Oxford, my mother had become so neurotic that she'd practically forbidden me to come back to Hartley Cross. It hadn't seemed worth arguing the toss about, so I'd agreed to see her when she chose to come to me.

"She liked to come over to Oxford," I told Jael. "She always stayed at the Randolph – that's a big hotel in the city centre, always full of people and noise. Well, it made a change for her, I suppose. How are the others?" I enquired, changing the subject, I hoped permanently.

"Dad's not too good." Jael freshened her cup. "Well,

he *is* getting on a bit now, so I suppose that's only to be expected. Samuel's living in Telford. He give up the cooperage last summer, see. Now he drives them big lorries for Howarth and Son."

"What about Naomi and Rebekah?"

"Naomi's married. She lives in one of them new Association houses, what they've built over on the Glebelands estate." Disgustedly, Jael sniffed. "They calls 'em houses, anyhow. Little boxes, they oughter say! Them city people, they come out here, buy up all the decent places – I tell you, if Neil hadn't got some money off of his poor old mum, God rest her, I suppose *we'd* have ended up in one of those."

"What about Rebekah?"

"She's not up to much." Jael shook her head, and sighed. "A year or two back, her social worker got her a place at some college specially for people like her. In the West Country, it was. Nice place. Landscaped, near the sea. But she fretted awful. So she come home. She lives with Dan and Rachel most of the time."

But then, suddenly, Jael smiled again. "Now and then," she continued, "Simon has her for the day. He's good with her, old Simon. Patient, lets her toddle on at her own pace – he don't even mind her dribbling, and that."

"I see." I looked down at my hands. "Look, Jael, it's been really nice to chat, and thank you for the tea. But I do have to get on."

"Yeah, I suppose you must." Jael stood up. She helped me on with my jacket. "But you *will* pop round another time?"

"Of course," I replied, lying through my teeth. It had been a horrible mistake, I realised that now, even to have considered talking to Jael, let alone joining her for tea. For

49

here, in her immaculate kitchen, memories had begun to scratch at my skin.

Not painfully. Not yet. But I knew that if I stayed in Hartley Cross, these scratches would become cuts. That I would soon find big, red wounds opening all over me, and I would bleed to death. Just as Louis Dyer had done.

I would go back to Oxford tomorrow, I decided. I would not see Simon Dyer again.

Chapter Six

So much for good intentions, I thought, as I walked along the old turnpike road, passing the Malt House and Vineyard Cottage – both recently gentrified, I noticed, presumably by the same sort of city people who were buying up so much of the attractive property in Hartley Cross. So much for firm and decisive action, I reflected, as I passed the former village school – these days a weekend retreat owned by some prosperous Birmingham businessman – and turned into the drive which led to Brougham Gate . . .

But there was no going back now, so I strode purposefully up to the front door. Then, I rang the bell.

As I waited, I gazed all about me. Well, I decided, he couldn't have inherited much ready cash. This ruinous house, which I remembered as a beautiful Tudor mansion, all pale grey timber and rosy red brick, looked like an enormous great chicken coop in the last stages of decay.

One of the tall, barley sugar chimneys had come tumbling down, and lay in pieces on the gravel sweep. A previous winter's gale had blown huge numbers of the roof tiles on to the drive, and there they still lay, broken and jagged, waiting to trip somebody up. Where the upper storey of the house had been rendered and painted a soft russet, the plaster was stained and sodden, bulging away from the walls.

51

Here and there, great lumps of it had come away completely, leaving the brickwork beneath rawly exposed. At the gable ends, the lovely Tudor mouldings were spotted black and green with all manner of lichens and moulds.

The half-timberings themselves were growing every sort of fungi. Yellow mushrooms and orange toadstools adorned all the great oak beams, and I thought, these moulds were just like costume jewellery – but of the cheapest, tackiest kind. They were now haphazardly pinned upon an elderly dowager's once splendid finery.

After a wait which seemed like all eternity, but was probably only a minute at the most, I finally heard somebody coming along the passageway. I knew that shuffling tread so well! There was still time to run away, I told myself. There was still time to hide . . .

But then, Simon opened the door. Or rather, he tugged until it yielded, scraping it without ceremony across the flagstones of the entrance hall.

"Hello, Lindsay," he said. He looked neither pleased nor displeased, neither delighted, nor appalled. "I heard you were back."

"I–I thought I ought to drop by." My heart was in my mouth. But, all the same, I managed to smile at him. "H–how are you?"

"Oh, not so bad." Miraculously – wonderfully – he smiled, too. "Getting along, I suppose. As, of course, one does."

I had half-expected to see him grown prematurely old. Haggard, I suppose, with guilt and regret. But Simon Dyer's looks had, in fact, improved. The pretty boy's face had become more angular, it's true. But the slight, insubstantial teenager's body had filled out, had hardened, so that the boy was now a fine-looking man.

He'd continued to smile at me, and now he spoke again. "Have you time for a coffee?" he asked, pleasantly. "Or maybe a cup of tea?"

"I'd love one," I replied.

I meant it, too. Also, I needed to make sure I wasn't dreaming. For I appeared to be having a normal, rational conversation with this man! He, in turn, looked almost pleased to see *me*.

I would not deceive myself, I decided. As soon as I'd set eyes on him again, I knew. Simon Dyer still had my heart in his keeping! So, filling myself to the brim with tea, so that I sloshed when I walked, seemed a small price to pay for an hour of his company.

But then, as I followed him into the damp, chilly house, my second self made her voice heard, and asked if this was such a good idea after all. As we made our way down a dark, narrow passage, I became aware of the spiders of memory crawling up my spine, and as Simon led me into the kitchen where ancient, rusting pans and other medieval-looking implements dangled from equally rusty hooks, I began to wonder if I might faint. Or be sick, at any rate. For, over there, was where Louis had . . .

No. I wouldn't think of Louis. Instead, I concentrated on externals, commenting to myself on the state of the kitchen, for here the walls were literally running with damp, and black spots of mould had spread to form whole islands of corruption on the flaking plaster beneath.

Involuntarily, I shuddered. Seeking comfort and reassurance, I turned towards my host. "Shall I take your coat?" he enquired, courteously.

"No!" I crossed my arms against my chest. But then, I forced a smile. "What I mean is, it's rather cold in here.

I don't suppose you'd notice. Living in the place, that is. But I—"

"It's cold because the Rayburn's on the blink," interrupted Simon, calmly. "I keep meaning to get Nathan or Daniel Casson round, to have a look at it."

Then, turning away, he filled the kettle. He put it on the hob of a brand new calor gas stove, which stood next to the enormous stone sink into which one could have tipped a whole hundredweight of King Edwards, and still had room to spare.

I noticed then that the cooker was filthy. Brown grease and bits of decaying food clogged all four burners, and when Simon lit the jet, a stink of rancid fat fouled the air.

Opening a cupboard, he began to scrabble around inside. "Do you mind having coffee?" he asked, eventually. Apologetically, he shrugged. "I knew I had some tea in here somewhere, but I'm afraid it may have gone off. It looks a bit green."

"Coffee will be fine," I assured him.

"Right." So, as the kettle grumbled and rattled on the hob, Simon rooted around in another cupboard, found a jar of cheap instant coffee, and poked a spoon inside. Eventually, he managed to dislodge a few powdery grains. "It gets so damp in here," he muttered, hacking at the cake of dark brown decaffeinated, which had set into a concrete-hard mass.

The kettle boiled, and Simon made us two mugs of scummy, tan-coloured broth. "I *might* have some milk," he murmured, gazing all around, as if he were expecting Daisy the Cow to come lumbering in any minute.

"It doesn't matter," I said. "I actually prefer it black."

"So do I," said Simon, gratefully.

So this is what happens, I thought. This is what you get

when you let a man live entirely on his own. He reverts, and although he might be only twenty-five, he'll start behaving as if he's seventy-five, and has never boiled an egg or sewn on a button in the whole of his long, inadequate life. I put my disgusting drink to one side. "What are you doing these days?" I enquired.

"I run an antiques business. From one of the barns." To avoid meeting my gaze, perhaps, he drained his cup dry. "You know. Victoriana. Glass. China. Welsh dressers, wardrobes, all that kind of thing. We do quite a brisk trade, especially on Saturdays and Sundays in the summertime. Naomi comes over sometimes, to make teas. Then we have a sort of little café going, as well."

Haven't you got a proper job? I thought, but didn't dare to say. "You see quite a bit of the Cassons, do you?" I enquired.

"Oh, yes!" Again, he smiled. "Daniel and Rachel come over all the time. Naomi makes me cakes. Jael sorts out my washing, and Nathan does deliveries for me. I don't drive these days, you see."

Disqualified, I thought. Like father, like son. Glancing quickly at Simon's complexion, I discerned a few broken veins. His eyes were bloodshot, too.

He looked back at me. "It *is* nice to see you again," he said, complacently. "You look so well!"

"Do I? I don't *feel* well." I shook my head. "I've a cold that's been hanging around at least since September, and I can't seem to relax at all. Even though I'm so tired I feel I could sleep for a week."

"You're bound to be a bit stressed at present." Simon sighed his sympathy. "I was very sorry to hear about your mother."

"Thank you."

"It must have been an awful shock. But you'll get over it."

"Perhaps."

"You will." He gazed deep into my eyes. "You got over that other business, didn't you?"

"I think so," I lied. "I can't forget what happened, of course. But I don't have bad dreams any more."

"That's good." Simon cleared his throat. "May I say something about all that?"

"About your father, you mean?"

"Yes." Still, Simon's gaze held mine. I didn't speak again, so he continued. "You remember, don't you, that Dad was on the point of changing his will? He was going to leave everything to Jael. Or at any rate, that's what he said."

"I remember."

"So I had motive, didn't I?"

"But nobody thinks you – that you actually killed him," I lied.

"Don't they?" Simon shrugged. "The police were quite certain it was me."

"Perhaps." I had to look away. I reached for my bag. In fact, I was about to get up and make a run for it, but then I thought, maybe Simon is right. Perhaps it *is* better to face it now. To clear the air, and let us both get on with our lives . . .

"Simon," I began gently, "we were in the barn for the whole of that afternoon. Thirty minutes, you'd have had. Half an hour, to find your father, to attack him, to – do that other thing, and to clean yourself up again. You were drunk, you were stoned, and I can't see how on earth you—"

"Who else had any reason to want him dead?"

"*I* don't know!" Helplessly, I shrugged. "But your father did have the odd enemy or two."

"Did he?"

"Oh, Simon! Come on!" We were grown up now, and plain speaking was the thing. "Your dad wasn't a saint! He was knocking off half a dozen women from the village. He bought that field from poor Roy Barlow, then flogged it to a developer for ten times what he paid old Roy.

"Dave Norland threw him out of the Lamb and Flag three times a week at least – but Louis certainly got his own back! He gave Flora Norland a lift home from Worcester – driving whilst disqualified, I might add – took her to the Old Rose at Ardisley, got her pissed, then screwed her."

"Yeah, okay." Simon shook his head. "So what you're saying is, my father's killer could have been a disgruntled husband or lover, a ripped-off sheep farmer, an outraged father—"

"Precisely." Firmly, I changed the subject. "I heard you often have Rebekah over nowadays. How is she getting on?"

"She's okay." Simon shrugged. "She has her ups and downs, of course. She had pneumonia a couple of months ago, had to go into the County Hospital, in fact, but she made an excellent recovery. The doctors were very impressed. It seems her lungs are in very good nick for somebody with her – er – condition."

"Did she ever learn to speak?"

"No. Well, that's not quite true, she *can* talk a little. She knows a few words. She certainly understands what's going on." Simon frowned then. "You stayed away so long," he murmured, not looking at me.

"I had nothing to come back for," I said.

"You weren't curious to see me?"

"Simon, you were the one who broke things off!" How could he say such things? "*You* didn't want to see *me*!"

"I was upset." He looked up, and met my gaze. "Understandably so, I think."

"Perhaps." I reached for my scarf. "I must be getting on," I muttered.

"Of course," he agreed. Courteously, he handed me my bag. Then he saw me out.

As I walked down the drive, I replayed our conversation in my mind. I hadn't known what sort of reception to expect, and I had steeled myself against abuse, against even having the door slammed right in my face.

But my former lover had been polite to me. Pleasant, solicitous, and kind. He hadn't asked if I was married. Or even if there was someone special. But perhaps he hadn't needed to. He must have seen that I was still in love with him.

The point at issue was, of course, did he still love *me*?

Chapter Seven

"But we're never going to get all this lot sorted out!" complained Mrs Denny, as she surveyed the boxes and boxes of letters, papers, books and other odds and ends, which I'd collected from every room in the house, then dumped on the floor of the dining room. "Never, in a million years."

I nodded in agreement. "My mother *was* a bit of a hoarder," I admitted. You're not kidding, I thought. But why she'd felt the need to keep quite so much waste paper – why she'd imagined she would one day need *my* old school exercise books and files full of biology course work, for example – was a mystery indeed. I was tempted to lug everything out into the garden, pile it all into one gigantic heap, and make a roaring great bonfire of the lot.

"So, what are you going to do with all the furniture, then?" asked Mrs Denny, as she prised open the first of the dozen black plastic sacks which we would certainly fill that day. Covetously, she stroked a little Pembroke table, upon which she'd expended God only knows how much elbow grease in the course of the past however many years. "What's going to happen to this, f'example?"

"I'll sell it, I expect." I reached for a rubbish bag, then began to stuff handfuls of old letters inside. "I'll get a dealer to come over from Hereford, and give me a quote for the lot."

"You don't want to keep none? But it's ever so nice, some of it!" Evidently disgusted, Mrs Denny shook her fiercely-permed head. "None your old Utility stuff here!" she cried. "None of your modern rubbish! That there sideboard, look – your Mum got that off her Gran. She had it off of *her* mother, back in the First World War!"

"I never knew that." Glancing towards the heavy Victorian horror which had occupied that corner of the dining room ever since I could remember, I grimaced in distaste. "Would *you* like it?" I enquired, somewhat dubiously.

"Me?" Mrs Denny flushed quite pink. "I couldn't afford it," she muttered. "It's a valuable antique, that."

"I meant, as a present." I was blushing myself by now. "As a sort of keepsake. To remember my mother by."

"Well, I dunno about that . . ."

"You were very good to her, after all. She'd have liked you to have it."

"Well, that's ever so kind of you." For a long moment, Brenda Denny considered the matter. But then, delightedly, she grinned. "I'll have a word with our Alan, shall I?" she suggested. "See if he can borrow one of the firm's old vans. To pick it up in, like?"

"You do that," I replied. "I expect I'll keep the little table, too. For myself, that is."

In actual fact, the Pembroke table *was* rather nice. The sort of thing people lug along to the *Antiques Roadshow*, I suppose, to be told they own a charming Edwardian copy of a Georgian original, worth about two hundred pounds. If, on the other hand, it had been genuine, it would have been wise to insure it for at least twenty thousand quid . . .

"*Now* what're you laughing at?" asked Mrs Denny, as I shook my head and smiled, but only to myself.

"N-nothing," I stammered, caught out.

"Right then. We'd better get on." Mrs Denny tore another plastic bag off the roll, and blew it open wide. "There's floods in the city," she said chattily, as we began to pack old magazines and newspapers inside. "Some of them as lives down Hunderton way's had to be 'vacuated. Or so our Alan says."

"Where do they go?" I wondered, aloud.

"To stay with relations, I suppose." Resignedly, Mrs Denny sighed. "They open up church halls and that, don't they? Like in Sarajevo, sort of thing?"

Not quite like in Sarajevo, I thought, but didn't like to say. Could Mrs Denny be hinting that I ought to open up The Larches, I wondered, as a shelter for the flooded out or otherwise dispossessed?

"When will you need to go and see to Alan's dinner?" I asked, hoping it would be soon, so that I could have a break from all this.

"I left him a plate on the hob. He knows how to warm it through." By now, Mrs Denny was getting properly stuck in, and seemed in no hurry at all to get away. "Give us another of them old sacks, there's a love. You going to take all this down the recyclin' place, or what?"

We worked on steadily. By midday, however, I'd had more than enough of dust and musty old magazines, so I sent my helper home for her lunch. After I'd eaten a sandwich myself, I caught the bus into town, fed the ducks on the Castle Pool, then decided to have a wander round the shops.

I'd go into Marks & Spencer, and buy myself a nice big bagful of their delicious vegetarian ready meals. Then

I'd have a look in the Society of Craftsmen shop. Then I'd – well, the possibilities were legion.

I never visit Hereford without feeling as if something precious has been forever lost to me, without experiencing a pang of homesickness and regret. I was born there, you see, and lived in the city until I was at least six years old. Until my father inherited some money – rather a lot of money, in fact – from a spinster aunt, and decided to become a country gentleman.

Captivated by the charms of Hartley Cross, he'd bought The Larches, a ramshackle Georgian box urgently in need, as the estate agent no doubt put it, of sympathetic restoration and repair. Or of razing to the ground and starting again! But once my father had set his heart on anything, he would never be told what to do, and in spite of my mother's strident objections, he proceeded to pour his money straight down the drains of that wretched place.

So, did we live there happily ever after, in rustic peace and rural tranquillity? Of course we didn't! In fact, I can date the absolute breakdown of my parents' already overstressed marriage, from our move there.

I strolled through the Cathedral Close, made my way down Church Street, and came out into the hustle and bustle of High Town. Although I'd already been wondering if I might see somebody I knew, I was nevertheless somewhat startled by the sound of a man's voice loudly calling my name.

"Lindsay?" he repeated, as I stared all around me. "No, over *here*!" he cried, sounding amused but patient all the same. "In the bloody *van*!"

"Sorry!" Walking over to the battered old transit, I gave Nathan Casson an apologetic grin. "I didn't see you at first."

"Lost your specs again, eh?"

"I don't wear glasses!"

"Then perhaps you oughter." Nathan grinned back at me. "Hop in, then."

I did as I was bidden. "What are you doing in town?" I enquired politely, as he revved the engine.

"I give Jael and our Reb a lift." Letting off the hand-brake, Nathan eased the transit into the stream of traffic heading down towards Eign Gate. "Reb needs some new clothes, 'parently, so Jael said she'd help her pick some out. They'll be hours yet, in and out of them women's shops."

"So you're just driving around?"

"Yeah, that's right. Just killin' time." Sighing, he shook his head. "Got nothing else to do, have I? Do you want a lift home?"

"Well, I was going to get the three o'clock bus." I smiled my appreciation. "It's kind of you to offer," I continued, "but I've lots to do at home, and if I hang about here until the shops close—"

"I'll run you back now, then." Increasing his speed, Nathan moved out into the middle lane, which would take him on to the ring road and out of the city. "Like I said, I got nothing else to do."

"But will you let me pay for your petrol?"

"If you insist." His grey eyes twinkling, he glanced towards me. Cheekily, he grinned. "But perhaps I ought to pay *you*?" he suggested. "After all it ain't often *I* gets the pleasure of a lady's undivided attention, and exclusive company!"

"Oh, Nathan!" I laughed, too. "I can't believe that!"

"It's true!" he insisted. "Women these days, they just don't want to know. You takes a girl to the pub, look – an' she's eyein' up all the other blokes as soon as you walks in the door! Take her to the flicks – an' she's oglin' Mel Gibson or that Arnold Shwassenegger from the time she gets her Butterkist 'til it's time to go 'ome again."

"What a rotten shame." I shook my head, in mocking sympathy. "Poor old Nathan."

"Tragic, innit?" Lugubriously, he sighed. But then, he grinned again. "I hear you're living down Oxford way these days?"

"That's right," I agreed.

"You're a painter, Jael says."

"I wouldn't call myself a painter. Well – I don't paint *big* pictures, anyway. I design greetings cards. Theatre programmes, letter-heads, promotional leaflets for tradesmen – all that sort of thing."

"Oh. Right." Sagely, Nathan nodded. "You seen old Simon since you got back?"

"Yes, I have. I called round for coffee yesterday, as a matter of fact."

"How do you reckon he's looking?"

"Fine. Well, considering." I managed a careless shrug. "He says your family has been very good to him."

"Yeah, well, we keeps an eye on the bugger." Nathan shrugged, too. "Our Dad and his, they was always mates. Old Mr Dyer, he done a lot for us, especially after our mum died. We got a sort of obligation, if you know what I mean."

"Yes," I agreed. "I do see that."

"You got over it all, then?" Nathan looked serious now. "I mean, all that business before you went away – you put it all behind you, sort of thing?"

"Oh, yes," I replied. "I think so."

"Made a new life for yourself, eh?" Nathan's expression

relaxed again. "I see you ain't married," he observed. "You engaged or living with, or anything?"

He wasn't being impertinent, or nosy. This is what country people always want to know, for it is how they define you, by your marital status – or lack of it. "I've had a few friends," I told him. "But there's no one special. Not just at the moment, anyway."

"So we're both on the shelf." Again, he nodded. "It ain't that we ain't had offers, mind," he observed. "Choosy, we are. Eh?"

"That's right." I was glad he was driving. For now I could turn to look out of the side window, and Nathan couldn't see my face.

So I was choosy, was I? Bitterly, I sighed. I didn't know about Nathan, but in my case failed relationship after failed relationship had made an emotional mockery of the past five years. In the course of those, I had been accused of every fault and failing known to mortal man, from mere unwillingness to commit myself, to being in urgent need of long term psychiatric care. The plain fact was, the only man I'd ever loved – the only man I feared I ever *would* love – didn't want me. Unless, unless – but was I fooling myself again?

I wished I knew. Watching the bleak autumn landscape go by, I could not help but reflect on the dreariness and desolation which made it permanent winter in my own heart.

Nathan seemed to sense my mood. Or perhaps he was simply thinking of his own concerns, and that was why he'd fallen silent, and didn't speak to me again until we reached the outskirts of Hartley Cross. "You staying here the rest of the week?" he enquired, as we drove past the war memorial. "Or have you got to get back?"

65

"Get back?" I repeated, uncomprehending. For I was miles away.

"To Oxford, like."

"Oh, I see what you mean." I forced a smile. "I thought I'd go on Monday morning. On the eleven-fifteen, from Ledbury."

"Right." Nathan pulled up in front of the shop, where he could turn round easily, to go back for his sisters again. "I'll take you into Ledbury," he told me, as he let me out of the van. "Well – you don't want to go payin' Luxi-Cabs' prices, when you can just give me my petrol money and the price of a cup of tea!"

"But I wouldn't dream—"

"Monday morning it is. Half-past ten. Yeah?"

"Okay. Thanks, Nathan."

"You're very welcome," he said. Then, in a cloud of foul exhaust fumes, he drove away.

I watched him go. He waved, I waved back and then, turning towards home, I walked slowly up the narrow village street.

I'd always liked Nathan Casson. He was a year or two older than me, and more than twice my size, but, all the same, he had never bullied or talked down to me, nor done Tutankhamun impressions as I and my Middle Kingdom haircut walked by.

For a few years, he and Simon had been best friends, becoming known as William and Ginger to Louis Dyer, and them-two-little-buggers-as-is-always-up-to-no-good, to everybody else. They no longer stole chewing gum from the post office or pinched Mr Sidderfin's Victoria plums, it's true. But I supposed they probably still had an occasional pint together, down at the Lamb and Flag.

*   *   *

Mrs Denny was not at all impressed by my insistence that I had to go back to Oxford, where the next few months' rent and the following summer's holiday in Italy were sitting by my drawing board, in the shape of a commission for a set of Wild Flowers and Grasses of the Pembrokeshire Coastal Footpath greetings cards. She was only slightly mollified when I promised to come back the following weekend, in order to "get it all ship-shape and Bristol-fashion, like." Mrs Denny had never approved of leaving a job half-done.

As I assured her that next Saturday we would definitely get the rest of the papers and my poor mother's clothes sorted out, *definitely*, I was reflecting that I would have returned anyway.

If only to call on Simon again.

The journey back to Oxford was uneventful. Well, you can't call an overheating engine and the subsequent two-hour wait at Charlbury, nor loss of current to the buffet car, so no hot drinks were available – Great Western apologises, ladies and gentlemen, but you'll have to do without your mud brown coffee and your orange tea – *events*. Not exactly.

I finally got home at half-past four in the afternoon. I sorted through my post – no cheques, alas – then went upstairs and forced my way into my room. The obstruction lying behind the door turned out to be not a body, but a vast heap of Julia Wakeman's clothing. I'd give Tessa a piece of my mind, I resolved, as I ground my teeth in rage.

Julia Wakeman is an absolute pain. A former girlfriend of Alan the photographer, she is a student of some sort, apparently based in London. This doesn't stop her coming to Oxford every so often, however, and dossing down on any available floor.

Whilst I was away, she had borrowed *my* room – then proceeded to make herself thoroughly at home. Evidently the sort of person who never went out anywhere without first trying on and discarding almost every garment she owned, she had used the floor as her wardrobe. To this compost heap of discarded clothing, she'd added a sprinkling of dirty coffee cups, take-away pizza boxes and used cotton wool balls.

I heaved her stuff out on to the landing, and repossessed my room. But, even so, it took me at least half an hour to clean up the mess. How can people *bear* to leave Tampax wrappers, and worse, just lying about on the carpet? Not to mention their laddered tights, old lipsticks, and items of personal mail?

Just as I was hoiking a pair of black nylon knickers from their hiding place under my bed, I heard the front door slam. Going to hang over the banister, all ready to give the slut who'd fouled up my room something to think about, I saw Nick Singer dump his rucksack on a chair in the hall.

He looked up, met my gaze, and grinned at me. "Hello, stranger," he said. He raked his messy hair out of his blackbird eyes. "We weren't expecting you until Thursday."

"Evidently not." I didn't smile back. "Just how long has Julia Wakeman been occupying my room?"

"Since Saturday evening, I believe. I can't tell you the exact moment of her arrival. I was out." Still Nick grinned. "She's staying the rest of the week, I think."

"Well, she'll be sleeping on the sofa in the living room tonight." I nudged the heap of her belongings a bit further along the landing. "Or out in the garden shed."

"Oh. Right. Do you fancy a cup of tea?" asked Nick, as he shrugged off his grubby old donkey jacket and dropped it in a crumpled heap on the floor.

"No, thank you," I replied. "I have work to do."

I retreated into my haven. As I closed the door, I wondered if I'd been a bit short with Nick. After all, it wasn't his fault the mucky cow had taken over my room, and left sticky rings all over my drawing board.

I'd have words with Tessa later.

I worked solidly for the next few days, scurrying out of my burrow only to grab a cheese sandwich or take a quick shower. Sometimes, Tessa came and stood in the doorway, leaning against the jamb, to make conciliatory noises and ask if we were still best mates.

"I didn't think you'd mind that much," she murmured, as she watched me work, but didn't dare try to see what I was actually doing. For, rule one with me is that everything's private – until it's finished, that is. "Poor kid, she's ever so cut up about that guy from Trinity. He messed her about something chronic. It's really sad."

"Maybe it is," I agreed. "But that doesn't give her the right to turn my room into a rubbish tip."

"I suppose not." Tessa shrugged. But then she shook her head at me. "It's not healthy though, is it?" she demanded. "Being as tidy as you are, I mean."

"Isn't it?" Carefully, I drew the outline of a leaf. "Who says?"

"We all do, really. As a matter of fact, Nick thinks you're anally repressed."

"Does he, indeed?" Bloody cheek, I thought. "I won't tell you what I think about Nick," I said.

*   *   *

For the rest of that week, I continued to work steadily. Only occasionally did I lose concentration and resort to introspection, and allow myself to see a picture of Simon Dyer on the screen inside my head.

I wished he'd gone to seed! Why wasn't he prematurely bald? Why wasn't he thickening round the waist, why wasn't he coarsened and lumpish? That would have made things so much easier for me!

The weekend arrived at last. Firmly turning down Tessa's oft-repeated offer to go with me to Hartley Cross and help me sort out the rest of the stuff, I packed a case, told Tessa that under no circumstances was Julia Wakeman to re-colonise my room, and found my car keys, which for some reason were hanging on a hook by the kitchen door.

I supposed this meant that, whilst I was in Hereford-shire, somebody had been driving my car. Not bloody Julia, I hoped. Grimacing, I went out to look for it.

I eventually discovered my ancient Renault 5, which didn't really enjoy long journeys but would co-operate if I talked to it nicely, sulking in the drizzle a couple of streets away. The plan was, I told it, to drive it to Hartley Cross and collect my mother's old letters and diaries and the little table, which I'd keep in my room in Oxford.

"None of it's heavy," I continued. "Just a bit cumber-some, that's all." Then I bit my lip. Talking to a car, for God's sake, *and* in public. I was heading for the edge, most definitely.

I'd got up early, and by half-past seven I'd been ready to leave the house. I meant to be in Cheltenham by nine, and back home again by eleven. So now, I slung my bag in the back, fastened my seat-belt and checked the mirror.

The person who had borrowed poor Flora had been

smoking pot. Or perhaps the nasty smell was just body odour. Or those vile French cigarettes. In any case, to let out some of the fug, I left the driver's side window open, and would keep it open until I was out of Oxford.

But, when I turned the keys in the ignition, nothing happened. Or not much happened, anyway. The engine coughed, spat and expired. I tried again. Cough, spit, choke, horrible smell of burning, nothing. I drummed my fingers on the dashboard, and sighed.

Then, in my rear view mirror, I saw somebody coming in my direction. Homeward bound after a heavy all-night session with his thermometers and test tubes – or so I imagined – Nick Singer was sauntering down the road, no doubt looking forward to one of the revolting fry-ups of bacon, eggs and greasy fried bread slices which appeared to form his staple diet.

He'd obviously heard me trying to get the engine to fire. Drawing level with the car, he stopped. "Do you have a problem?" he enquired.

"It looks like it," I murmured. I glanced up at him. As usual, he was a mess. His hair was ruffled and spiky, looking as if it had been cut with blunt nail scissors by a blind chimpanzee. Resembling nothing so much as bedraggled blackbird's feathers, in this early morning light it was as purple-black as the circles under his eyes.

On his top half, he wore a baggy green jumper, the cuffs of which were frayed and shredded beyond repair. He had no coat, and although the day was cold and a sleety drizzle was falling steadily from a goose-down sky, he'd been strolling along as if this chilly November morning were a mild summer afternoon.

As he looked at me, a weary grin spread across his beaky features. As if I were a moron who needed special help and encouragement if I were to have any hope at all of making myself understood, he raised his eyebrows in gentle enquiry. "Well?" he prompted.

"It won't start," I muttered, in reply.

"Dear me." He shook his head. "Is there any petrol in the tank?"

"Of course there is!"

"Are the plugs okay?"

"Yes!" I glared at him. "It may look like a rust-heap to you, but I do in fact look after this car! The oil was changed last month. The spark-plugs are brand new. All the electrics—"

"I could have a look, if you like."

"You're not in a rush?" I enquired, sarcastically.

"No." He pushed damp hair back from his forehead. "Got all the time in the world, in fact. Could you release the bonnet?"

I did as he asked. He got down to work. Humming and tutting, he checked all the obvious things, fiddled with various wires and cables and bits and pieces of engine, then straightened up. Wiping his oily fingers on his already filthy jeans, he pursed his lips. "Do you always leave your car out here in the street?" he enquired.

"Yes," I replied. "Why?"

"I think somebody's been messing about with it. Well, I know they have! You'll need to call the breakdown people. Have them take it to a garage. The engine will need to come out, you see."

"What?" I stared at him. "Seriously?"

"I'm afraid so. It's completely buggered."

"Great. Fantastic, in fact." Heavily, I sighed. "Now I'll have to get the bloody train."

"Train? Where were you going?"

"To Hartley Cross. I want to bring some of my mother's things back to Oxford."

"What sort of things?"

"Personal stuff. Letters. Books. A little table."

"You can't bring a table back on the train!" For a long moment, Nick looked at me. "Listen," he said. "I could drive you. If you like."

"*Could* you?" I stared back at him. "But what about your experiment? Can you leave it?"

"I shouldn't, but I must." He frowned. "I thought – I hoped – I'd finally got it sorted. But I spent most of last night fucking things up again. So, I need some time to think about it. A long drive would give me a chance to let my mind wander a bit."

"Not too much, I hope," I said, nervously.

"Don't worry." Once again, he grinned. "If you're that bothered, you could drive while I ruminate. I'd lend you the car, but it's not insured for anyone but me. So although we could be very wicked and let you drive it, I wouldn't be happy about letting you actually take it away."

"That's okay." He was already putting himself out, and I was already more than grateful. "Will you stay the night?" I asked. Then I blushed. "What I mean is, will you—"

"If I'm invited." He shrugged. "But if you drive up, I won't mind coming back here later today. Look, the thing is, you can't lug all that stuff on to a train. I'll bring it back for you."

The drizzle had intensified and was now a downpour. He was getting soaked to the skin, but didn't seem to notice. "Nick," I began, "you'll need to get some breakfast."

"I had some toast and coffee, at the lab." He nodded

down the road, towards his own parked car. "Well, then? Shall we get moving?"

"I think you ought to get out of those wet things," I replied. "Before you catch your death."

Chapter Eight

Although he was obviously dead beat, Nick did not let me drive his ancient Ford Escort after all. It would be a right bugger, as he elegantly put it, if somebody ran into us, if we had even a bit of a shunt. Even if it wasn't my fault.

I wondered which he was more concerned about, his motor or me, and was about to remark that with a somnambulist at the wheel, a shunt was more or less a racing certainty – but then I reminded myself that he was doing me a big favour, and shut my mouth again.

In any case, I reflected, in the event of any accident we would be well-cushioned by all the mess. For this car was a gigantic mobile handbag, laundry basket and litter bin combined, and the squashy plastic bags full of – dirty washing, perhaps – by which I was surrounded, would certainly protect *me*.

"I'll sort your car out when I get back," he told me, as we drove towards the bypass, as he yawned and fidgeted and rubbed his bloodshot eyes. "I've got this mate at Pembroke – he's just bought a second hand Range Rover. It needs a bit of work, few new parts and that. So, when we go to get those, we'll take your old Renault to Jack Finnegan's place, up Blackbird Leys."

"How will you get it there?"

"We'll borrow Jack's pick-up. Or tow it. All right?"

"Well, I . . . you don't have to, you know."

"I know I don't *have* to." Glancing momentarily at me, Nick Singer grinned. "But I will, anyway."

At my suggestion, we went by the scenic route, through the Cotswolds and into Gloucestershire. At my absolute insistence, we stopped in Tewkesbury, where I bought my driver a coffee and a fat jam doughnut, which he consumed in about three seconds flat in as many voracious bites. "Would you like another?" I asked, offering him the greasy paper bag.

"But don't you want it?"

"*I* had a proper breakfast." Primly, I smiled. "So I'm quite happy to wait another hour or two for my lunch."

"Well, in that case . . ."

Nick took the second doughnut.

Sugar frosting his mouth, smears of jam blobbed on his chin, and that silly grin spread all over his face, now he looked about eight years old. "So what did you have, then?" he demanded.

"I'm sorry?"

"For this proper breakfast of yours?" He narrowed his eyes at me. "Bacon and eggs, two sausages and a tin of baked beans, yeah? All washed down with good old PG Tips?"

"Certainly not." I grimaced in disgust. "I had muesli, an orange, some wholemeal toast, and a glass of lemon tea."

"Yeah?" sniggered Nick. "I was asking Tessa only last week where she kept her rabbits. I'd noticed all them bags of bran and oats in the cupboard, see. But that was actually your health food, eh?"

"It may look as if it comes from the pet food counter, but that sort thing is much better for your heart." I regarded

76

him coldly. "Okay, so you find the idea of eating oats and bran flakes wildly amusing, but at least *my* breakfasts don't foul up *your* environment!"

"What's that supposed to mean?"

"As well as being bad for you personally, *your* fry-ups fill the kitchen with fumes, and make the whole house smell like a greasy spoon."

"So how would you know?" Nick was still grinning at me. "I bet you've never been near one of them places! Let alone set foot inside."

"What? I'll have you know—"

"Time to press on, I reckon." Squashing his polystyrene cup into the paper bag, which he then screwed up and lobbed neatly into a nearby litter bin, Nick wiped his mouth on the back of his hand. He turned the key in the ignition and reversed out of the parking space. We drove out of town.

We didn't speak much after that, Nick because he was so tired – or so I presumed, anyway – and myself because I was thinking about Simon Dyer, and what I wanted to say to him when we next met. Now and again I made some remark which required comment or an answer, but this was mainly to reassure myself that my driver wasn't actually asleep.

Then, as we crossed the county boundary into Herefordshire, Nick seemed to wake up. He began to talk to me, inviting me to observe the way that stupid bastard in front was weaving about all over the road, or to agree that old geezers in their nineties should not be driving Morris Minors on the public highway, but be locked up in twilight homes for the brain-damaged. Or rather, brain-dead.

Evidently, he'd got the better of his own fatigue.

We drove into the village just as the clock in the

church tower was striking noon. As we made our way up Rackstraw Lane, Nick stared at the pretty Tudor cottages on either side in exaggerated disbelief. "What a place!" he exclaimed. "It's just like something out of a Christmas pantomime! *Jack and the Beanstalk*, or something like that."

We turned into the main village street. "Look at that black and white bugger over there," he continued. "The one on your left, with the tall, twisty chimneys and thatched roof. It don't look real." Glancing towards me, he grinned. "I keep expecting to see old blokes coming out the doors, all dressed up in smocks and gaiters and that. Churls, is that what you call 'em? Churls, and varlets. Or is it knaves?"

"Oh, for heaven's sake—"

"Wenches, too. You got much in the way of wenches here?"

"You must have been to villages like this before." I don't like people making fun of me and mine, and now I gave him my steeliest glare. "You've been to Woodstock, haven't you?" I demanded. "To Minster Lovell, and places like that?"

"Well, yes. I suppose. But this is different." We drove on up the narrow street, and he continued to stare. "It's sort of like – fossilised. Preserved. It must have launched a million biscuit tins and chocolate box lids! I wonder what the jigsaw rights are worth?"

Jigsaw rights, indeed! I'd had enough. "Look," I said crossly, pointing. "A telephone kiosk. A post office. A war memorial, a minimart—"

"A *what*?" he exclaimed, laughing.

"A shop, for God's sake! Slow down a bit, we're here."

We drew up outside The Larches. Reaching behind me, I hefted my overnight bag from off the back seat. "All right," I conceded, "I admit this place does look a bit like a backdrop for *Dick Whittington*. But that's only because it's old. Ordinary people live here! They eat cornflakes, drink coffee, watch the rugby on a Saturday afternoon. Just like you, in fact."

"*I* don't watch rugby," he countered. "I play it, though," he added, "if that counts for anything?"

"You know perfectly well what I mean!" I scowled at him. Why did this man make me so angry? "Come in and have a cup of tea," I muttered. Then go straight back to Oxford, I thought, uncharitably.

The house smelled musty, unused and unloved. In my absence, Mrs Denny had been in and out, had flicked a duster and vacuumed all around. But, child of wartime austerity that she was, she had also turned off the central heating. Consequently, the pervasive odour of damp old house completely overpowered the lighter scents of the various aerosol sprays, the *Mr Polish, Brita Sheen* and *Supa Sparkle*, to which Mrs Denny was almost religiously devoted. Thanks, I supposed, to the commercials on ITV.

"This is a bit of all right." Standing in the hallway, Nick Singer stared – rather rudely, I thought – all around. "You never told me your family was lords of the manor round here."

"What?" I was looking through the letters, which Mrs Denny had laid out in a neat fan, on the highly-polished table in the hall. "Oh, I see what you mean. Don't be silly, we're not."

"No?" My companion merely grunted. He peered up the stairs into the twilight, which enshrouded the first floor landings dismally. "Why's it all dark?" he enquired.

"Mrs Denny drew the curtains, I expect. As a mark of respect."

"Oh. Right." He had the grace to look abashed. But only for a moment. "Who's this Mrs Denny, then?"

"My mother's cleaning lady and general help."

"Yeah?" He sniffed. "My mum does a gaff like this," he observed. "It's in Spitalfields. It's not as big as this place. But it's classy, all the same."

"I'm sorry?" I was trying to make sense of a letter from the Inland Revenue, which I supposed my mother's solicitor would eventually need to see. "What do you mean, exactly, your mother does a gaff?"

"She's a char." Nick stared into the dining room, then turned to scowl at me. "Where's this table, then?"

"Table?"

"The one you want taken back to Ferry Road."

"It's in the drawing room. But look, you don't have to go just yet! At least have a cup of tea and something to eat." Encouragingly – I don't know why – I smiled at him. "I daresay Mrs Denny's got some milk and biscuits in."

It was, alas, quite the wrong thing to say. "She's such a treasure, my little woman," muttered Nick, his scowl now as black as his raven hair.

In the kitchen, we found a lardy cake neatly wrapped in plastic film, and a note addressed to me.

'Dear Lindsay,' it read, 'I got you in some milk. It's in the fridge. Mrs Sidderfin hopes as you will like the cake. Our Alan says he will come for the sideboard this weekend. I left the electric going, but I think having the central heating on is a waste if you're not here. Yours, B. Denny.'

As Nick stared down at the note, I filled the kettle, then put it to boil on an emergency electric ring. "If you want to use the bathroom or anything," I began, as he now turned to scowl at the big red Aga which I'd been wondering if I could sell to a private buyer, "it's upstairs on the left. The books and papers I want you to take back to Oxford are in the bedroom directly opposite."

"Right." Taking his cue, Nick slouched out of the kitchen. Presently, I heard him stump upstairs.

When he came back down again, he was still scowling. "How many bedrooms you got up there?" he demanded, almost incredulously.

"Ten altogether," I replied. "Why?"

"I just wondered." He dumped a box of papers on the kitchen table. "But there was only you and your Mum living here, right?"

"Yes. But—"

"If I'd been her, I'd have turned the place into a hotel, or something." He shook his head. "All this space! I dunno – it don't seem right to me."

Of course I understood what he meant. Of course, in a country in which thousands of people are actually homeless, to have had one woman living all alone in a great, rambling Georgian mansion does look rather bad. "I do take your point," I began. "But my mother wasn't well. She—"

"Yeah, I know." He looked directly at me then, holding my gaze. "I'm sorry," he said. "I didn't mean to be horrible."

"I'm sure you didn't," I agreed. "I've made the tea."

"Great." Then, suddenly, he was grinning again. "You got any ghosts here?" he demanded. He reached for the milk, tore the corner of the carton, and poured. "Any spooky green spectres or sobbing white ladies, anything like that?"

"No. Sorry to disappoint you." Feeling the tension between us evaporate, I smiled too. "Right, then. Have a piece of cake and a drink, then we'll bring the rest of the boxes downstairs. After that, we'll have some lunch. Mrs Denny's left cheese and things," I added slyly, just daring him to make some snide remark about "little treasures" for a second time.

We piled up boxes in the hallway, we packed the few books, which I wanted to keep, in a small oak wedding chest, and we made a quick inspection of the rest of the house – just to check everything was okay, rather than because I wanted to give Nick a guided tour. I only realised afterwards that he might have thought I was showing off.

I needn't have worried, however. As far as Nick Singer was concerned, good humour seemed to have gained the upper hand, and hopefully meant to hang in there for the rest of the day. "This would be an ace haunting ground for a white lady," he observed, somewhat wistfully or so it seemed to me, as he gazed round my mother's oak panelled bedroom, with its yellow silk curtains, solid antique furniture, and heavily-draped bed. "If there *was* such things, of course."

"Don't you believe in ghosts, then?" I teased, knowing perfectly well what the scornful answer would be. "Or spirits, or demons, or sprites?"

"Do what?" He looked at me as if I were insane. "Of course not," he replied.

"Well, aren't you a miserable old cynic!"

"What?"

"Don't you believe in anything supernatural? In any phenomena which can't be explained rationally?"

"Course I don't." Nick grinned. Then, he went to stare out of the window, at the church over the way. "Well, okay. There *are* things – phenomena, if you like – the apparent existence of which I personally cannot explain. Not that I've ever met any poltergeists or doppelgangers, you understand."

"But?" I prompted.

"But as for your crop circles, your ley lines and your energy fields, your flying saucers, and your aliens landing in the back garden, to take Mrs *Sun* Reader from West Hartlepool on a shopping trip to Mars, followed by tea with Elvis in a distant galaxy where the bug-eyed monsters all speak perfect English – I ask you!"

He turned to glance at me. "Why *do* all aliens speak English?" he enquired. "Is it the *lingua franca* of the whole bloody universe?"

"I suppose it must be." I found I was grinning, too. "After all, God *is* an Englishman!"

"True."

"Anyway, perhaps these aliens don't actually speak *any* language."

"Oh, right. They communicate through the subconscious, yeah?"

"Perhaps." It didn't seem such a ridiculous idea to me. "Do *you* think in any particular language?"

"Yeah, course I do. *I* think in English! When I read, I'm saying every word inside my head." He made his idiot face. "My lips move, too. I'm a moron, me."

"Really? There was I thinking you were the great white hope of the Clarendon Laboratory."

"What?" He narrowed his eyes. Then, he frowned. "It's all right for you," he muttered. "I was the first person in my family even to go to college. My mum and dad still reckon I'm stupid, to be scraping by on a SERC grant, when I could be in business with me Uncle Norman. Flogging dodgy camcorders and what have you, down the Mile End Road."

"I see." Glancing at my watch, I saw it was just gone half-past one. "Come back downstairs now," I said. "I'll make us some lunch."

"Or we could go down the pub?"

"I don't think so. I want to get on. As for you – if you *do* decide to drive back later today, you'd better not get plastered on the local Old Peculiar, had you?"

"So I'm an alcoholic, eh?"

"You are?" I grinned. "Sorry. I didn't realise. I never deliberately mock the afflicted, you know."

He made no comment. I felt I was learning fast.

We had our lunch, then Nick announced that he was going out for a walk. "I need a bit of fresh air," he observed, "and that's one thing you got plenty of round here."

"It does rather depend where you go," I told him. "I mean, it's not so fresh by the pig farm, down the end of Ruddle Pit Lane. In fact, it stinks." I looked up from the pile of my mother's correspondence. "Don't get lost, will you?"

"Might I?"

"It's a possibility."

"You'd better come with me, then."

"I haven't time."

"Oh, come on. You can spare half an hour." Narrowing his eyes, Nick peered at me. "You're looking a bit peaky," he observed. "A spot of exercise would do you good."

"I suppose it might." I considered my options. "I don't want to have to come looking for you, do I?"

"No. But if you send me off by myself, I'm bound to get lost. Got no sense of direction whatsoever, me. So?"

"I'll get my coat," I replied.

Nick had not brought any sort of jacket with him, let alone a coat. His tatty green jumper was hardly weatherproof. "Would you like to borrow a mac?" I enquired, as I pulled on my thick, winter gloves.

"One of yours?" He grinned. "The sleeves would be up to my elbows."

"There's an old waxed jacket of my dad's in the gun cupboard. You're welcome to wear that."

"It's all right." Nick's grin broadened. "I know my place. I don't want to dress up as the local squire."

"As you wish." I opened the front door. "Don't blame me if you get cold."

We strolled down the village street. Pushing his hands deep into his pockets, Nick gazed about him. If he starts going on about varlets and churls again, I thought, I shall just ignore him.

But he didn't say anything at all. Instead, he appeared to be deep in thought.

Meeting Mrs Sidderfin, I thanked her for the cake and then introduced her to Nick. "My car broke down," I explained. "So Nick very kindly drove me over. He's going to take some of Mum's things back to Oxford tonight."

"Oh, ah?" Mrs Sidderfin regarded my companion critically, storing him on her personal database so that she could tell the WI all about him, when the ladies met at the church institute the following Tuesday afternoon. "You want to wear a coat this weather," she said. "You could catch your death in this damp! I was saying to

Brenda Denny only the other day, it's chilly afternoons like this . . ."

Then she was off, jabbering away about nasty bugs and things that settled on one's chest, while Nick nodded wisely and agreed that you couldn't be too careful these days. You couldn't indeed.

"There was no need to wind her up like that," I murmured, as Mrs Sidderfin – having run out of steam, asked was that the time, and exclaimed really, she had to run and get the tea on – said goodbye, then stumped off up the lane.

"Wind her up?" repeated Nick. All injured innocence, he gaped at me. "Whatever do you mean?"

"You were laughing at her. You—"

"Does that whatsitsname, minimart, sell papers?" he interrupted. "Might they have a *Guardian* or *Independent*, do you reckon? Or is it too late in the day?"

"Why don't you go and look?" I didn't want to go into the village stores, not with Nick Singer anyway. "I'll wait for you outside."

As I'd anticipated, he came out again grinning, with the *Sun* under his arm and a packet of Doritos open in his hand. "It was this or the *Telegraph*," he explained, "and I couldn't be seen reading that fascist rag."

"Didn't they have anything else?"

"No. But they don't stock the *Guardian* anyway." He munched on a handful of Doritos. "There's no call for that sort of thing round 'ere, me dear," he added, taking off Mrs Joby quite magnificently.

We crossed the glebe, then walked back through the water meadows. I'd left the lights on at home, and it was comforting indeed to see their golden glow beckoning to us, through the winter trees. For the first time, I wondered about actually keeping The Larches. I could work from home, and maybe in summer I could take in paying guests. Perhaps Simon and I . . .

Simon. Soon, I would see him again. For a moment I forgot all about Nick, walking by my side. When I heard him cough, I wondered who it was.

He coughed again. "I think I got one of Mrs Hayseed's bugs," he said.

"It's the cold night air," I told him. "It's settled on your chest. You're not long for this cruel world."

"I dare say you're right." He sighed. "But there's a slender chance I could die happy. If my experiment works, that is. Or I make it with somebody like this."

"I'm sorry?"

"Coming towards us now."

I looked, and saw Jael, looming like a spectre through the dusk. Hatless and coatless, she was running. A plastic carrier bag swung from her grasp. She'd presumably had to dash to the shop, and left her baby at home. "Hello!" Politely, I smiled. I didn't expect her to stop.

"Hi, Lin." Breathless, distracted, she raced past us. I doubt if she even registered Nick's existence.

But he registered hers all right, and as she disappeared into the gloom, he groaned. "Well, you might have introduced us!" he cried.

"She was in a hurry." His mock-tragic expression made me laugh, and I shook my head in teasing sympathy. "We'll have to try and catch her again. When she has more time."

"I'll put me name down on the list." Staring into the empty dusk, Nick whistled softly. "Talk about gorgeous. You never told me there was class like that hereabouts."

We arrived back at The Larches just as the last of the

light faded away. After debating the issue inside my head, I decided not to repeat my offer of overnight accommodation. Nick was touchy enough about my stately home already, and I didn't want to give him any more opportunities to sneer or condemn.

Not only that. Although we lived in the same house in Ferry Road, and there was never any question that we were anything other than fellow tenants, I had a feeling that if I suggested he should stay, Nick Singer was quite vain enough to imagine I was making a pass at him. I didn't think I could cope with that.

"Will you be okay to drive?" I asked, hoping he would take the hint.

"Yeah, sure." He grinned. "Make us a cup of tea, lady, and I'll be on my way."

He left about half-past four, just as it grew properly dark, assuring me that he was quite wide awake enough to drive, and that he could certainly find the way. He promised to return the following Saturday, to help me shift the rest of some heavy bedroom furniture, clear out one of the attics, then take me back to Oxford again. He took my little table and a carload of other stuff away.

I'd wanted to be by myself for a while. But, when Nick had gone, the house seemed so big, dark and empty, that I was almost afraid. I wondered about ringing a couple of the WI ladies, and asking them to come round for cards and tea. But then I realised it was Nick I wanted, to keep me company. In an odd sort of way, I was already missing him.

Chapter Nine

All day Sunday I sorted and sifted, and all day Sunday I thought about Simon Dyer, too. He must have heard I was back at The Larches. It was his turn to call on me. Surely he would come, I reasoned, if only out of common courtesy?

But then I brought myself up short. So who was I fooling? This wasn't the nineteenth century, this wasn't Regency Bath, in an age when the etiquette of paying calls was taken more seriously than that of paying debts, when any casual morning visit would be ticketed and docketed and punctiliously returned! If Simon wanted to see me, he would come and look for me. If he didn't . . .

"I'm not going to make a thing of it," I told my reflection in the bathroom mirror, that Sunday evening. "If he hasn't called or rung by Tuesday, I'll simply go and see *him*. I'll take him a jar of jam or something. Bake him a cake, maybe."

Monday morning dawned on a hard, white frost. In the garden, sick-looking Brussels sprouts plants stood miserable and yellowing, summer bedding plants finally gave up the ghost, and the primulas in the rockery looked dead as the proverbial doornail. But these would recover by lunchtime. They always did.

I spent the morning in my mother's dressing room, going through the drawers of the desk there, torn between taking everything I found straight to the dump, and sorting through it conscientiously. She had been an indefatigable letter-writer, and the mountain of correspondence which this had generated in reply rustled and tumbled in a paper sea which pretty soon came frothing up to my knees.

In the end, I simply bundled the letters wholesale, discarding their envelopes in order to reduce the bulk. I'd take these over to Mrs Denny's grandson, I decided. A keen stamp collector, Damien Denny would be delighted to receive them, and was more than welcome to them all.

I listened to *Woman's Hour*. I wondered about making myself some lunch, but then I saw that the sun had come out, so I decided to get some exercise instead. I pulled on my wellingtons and found my mother's old Burberry. I set out, deliberately walking away from the village, away from Brougham Gate, and out into the countryside beyond.

The two men working in the field by the river glanced up as I walked by, but it wasn't until after I'd reached the stile into the next meadow that one of them called out to me. "Lin'sie?" The mellow burr of rural Herefordshire was so noticeable, even in a single word. "Well, don't speak to *us*, then!"

"Sorry!" I walked back, to find Nathan and Daniel Casson grinning at me.

"What's the big hurry?" asked Daniel.

"There isn't one. I didn't recognise you, that's all." I shrugged. "You were too far away for me to see your faces, and—"

"Like I was sayin' to her only last week – needs glasses, she does." To show he was joking, Nathan winked at me. "Been to see our Jael, have you?"

"No. I'm just out for a walk."

"Call in on your way back, eh?" Daniel pushed his knife into his pocket. "She gets that fed up, stuck indoors with the babby all day. She'd welcome a bit of company."

"I might drop by." I looked at the pile of osiers which they'd cut from the willows along the bank. "Have you two taken up basket-making, then?"

"Nah." Nathan grinned. "We sells 'em to those hippy types, as lives up in them caravans and tent affairs, on the Links. They makes baskets, an' that."

"Why can't they come down and cut their own sticks?"

"Dunno." Daniel shrugged. "They're too stoned, I suppose."

"They ain't local," put in Nathan.

"They comes from the cities." Daniel made his spaced out face. "Peace! Love!" he intoned. "They's mad as hatters. But they pays well for the osiers, so who're we to complain?"

"Well, quite." I remembered now, my mother had told me that there was a hippy encampment on Links Farm, full of people pursuing the good life. Or at any rate, eating magic mushrooms and baking hashish brownies all day. I shuddered. Life in a damp bender, with dogs and children running wild all over the place – no thank you, that was definitely not for me!

"So you'll pop in an' see our Jael?" asked Daniel, as he began to tie the bundles of springy canes together.

"I expect so," I replied.

So I more or less had to, after that.

On my way home, I made a circuit of the glebe, a route which would eventually take me past Jael's little cottage. Perhaps, I thought now, it *would* be nice to call in and see her. We could have a chat and a coffee, maybe.

Indeed, I did see her, long before she saw me. She was gardening again. From the road I observed her, bobbing about, trowel in hand, putting her flowerbeds to sleep for the cold winter days ahead.

I stopped by the low brick wall. "Jael?" I called, but not too loudly, in case the baby was asleep in his pram, round the side of the house.

She did not seem to hear me. I was about to call again but then, as I watched her, she crouched close to a patch of low-growing rock plant. Her lips were moving now. Apparently, she was talking to the evergreen, whispering to it tenderly.

Oh dear, I thought. She *is* lonely, poor thing! I imagined Nick Singer coming across this scene. He'd have a fit. "It's Cold Comfort Farm!" he'd exclaim, laughing his silly head off. "There's the fair Elfine. Chatting to the sukebind, yeah?" In spite of myself, I smiled.

"Good afternoon, Jael!" My tone light and deliberately cheerful, I grinned at her. "A nice day for it. Whatever it might be!"

"What?" Straightening up, she blinked at me, for the feeble autumn sun was right in her eyes. "What do you mean?" she demanded, I thought rather angrily.

"You seemed to be talking to yourself." I kept my own voice carefully neutral. "So I wondered if you were thinking aloud, maybe. I do it all the time myself, and—"

"Oh. Right." Jael frowned. But then, diffidently, she smiled. "I was miles away," she admitted. "It's our Naomi's birthday on Saturday, see, and I was wondering about givin' a little party for her. Deciding who to invite, like." Awkwardly, she fingered her trowel. "Would *you* like to come?" she asked. "That is, if you're around?"

92

"I – well, yes. I would." I returned her smile with interest. "Thank you."

"Bring that chap of yours too, if you like."

"Chap?" For a moment, I was mystified. How did she know, *what* did she know, what had Simon said to her?

But then, realisation dawned. Mrs Sidderfin had been spreading the gospel again. "Oh, you mean Nick," I murmured. "He's not my chap."

"No?"

"He just lives with me."

"Oh, yeah?" Jael grinned. "Well, excuse *me*!"

"I mean, he lives with me and three other people, in a rented house in Oxford. Jael, he's just a friend! He drove me over last Saturday because my own car broke down, and he'll be coming back to fetch—"

"Yeah, okay." Still, Jael grinned. "Well, if he's here this Saturday, he can come along to Naomi's party. We could do with a few extra blokes, and if he's not attached to you, so much the better. He can give old Naomi a birthday twirl."

"Oh. Right." I wasn't at all sure about the wisdom of letting a sarcastic cleversticks like Nick Singer loose on the Casson family. But then, I told myself, he's singular, they're most definitely plural, so if he gets too lippy, one of Jael's brothers can easily sort him out . . .

"Jael," I said then, foolishly thinking that now things seemed so easy and friendly between us, I could mention it without giving offence, "you *were* talking to that little plant, weren't you?"

"What?" The frown returned to crease her face. She bit her lip. "No, I bloody wasn't!" she muttered. "What do you take me for? A mental case, or summat?"

"No, of course not. But—"

"You imagine things, you do."

"Maybe." I shrugged. "Sorry, Jael."

"That's all right." But she would not look at me.

"I'll see you on Saturday, then."

"Yeah, okay."

So, the cordiality between us fast cooling, we said goodbye. I took myself off down the lane.

Whilst I was still at school, I recalled, a witch had lived in the village. She'd died when I was about fourteen, and her cottage had been demolished – but the farmer who owned the land had never since tried to sell it, or even use it for casual grazing in spring. He simply left it alone. So, her garden was still there, a secret, overgrown jungle largely inhabited by the progeny of her many cats, who regarded it as their own happy hunting ground.

Poor Mrs Samson had been a harmless enough old biddy, a rural eccentric who'd been tolerated and left to her own devices largely because it was rumoured among the credulous that she could cast magic spells. She did *some* good in the community, for Mrs Sidderfin and Harry Cox swore by her recipe for herbal cough drops, which they sucked all winter, and which made them smell of mothballs and nasturtium leaves. But they never got coughs or colds.

Mrs Samson's main claim to fame, however, was that she'd been an enchantress, enchanting – or singing to – all her plants, especially before pulling up or snipping off even the tiniest piece of one, explaining why she wanted it, and thanking the plant for its co-operation, for passing its power on to her – which, of course, it did. Consequently, she'd occasionally been called in to give an ailing house plant a good talking to. To tell a row of recalcitrant spinach seedlings to buck up their ideas.

Today, I had seen Jael enchanting that clump of wahtever it was. I *knew* I had. I wished I knew why.

Simon did not call. But, strangely enough, I found I did not fret about this. Not at all. The ice had been broken. There was time enough now, I reasoned, for both of us to come to terms. To decide what we might or might not say.

I worked steadily all that week, clearing out the room we'd grandly called the old nursery, and sorting through my own books and toys, my Rupert Bear annuals, my Lego and my collection of china horses and bears. These last – once treasured so devotedly – could, I decided, go to the Brownies' Bring and Buy.

I parcelled up my mother's clothes, to send to the charity shops in the city. Mrs Denny clucked and muttered furiously about this, asking wasn't there anything I wanted to keep for myself? It was all nice stuff. No rubbish there! So, to mollify her, I unpacked a bundle or two, then offered her the pick of anything she wanted.

After much tutting and frowning, she chose a Windsmoor skirt, which I was one hundred per cent certain would never fit her, and a raincoat from Marks & Spencer. "What about these jumpers and cardigans?" I enquired. Thinking, well, at least they would stretch.

Mrs Denny considered. Then, "I'll take that pinky-grey one," she declared, pointing to a rather threadbare Pringle garment which I remembered from the mists of distant childhood, and which I'd last seen worn for turning the compost heap.

"Something else?" I suggested, encouragingly.

"No thank you, dear." Mrs Denny shook her sausage

curls. "The rest of the stuff – well, it's all very nice, I'm sure. But it's not really me." Shoving her booty into a plastic carrier bag, she grinned. "Right, now. Shall we get on? Them kitchen cupboards haven't been turned out since Adam was a boy. There's digestive biscuits in there, sell-by date March 1992, I noticed yesterday."

A week of my own company, together with that of Mrs Denny, plus any of her mates from the WI who felt like dropping round, had the most unsettling effect on me. My friends in Oxford already thought I was dull and staid – but now, almost overnight it seemed, I became middle-aged.

I grew interested in the detection and treatment of stubborn biological stains. I gave the bath an energetic scrubbing with *Miracle Lime Off*, then went down to the minimart for more cleaning fluids, there to ponder the relative merits of *Super Shine* and *New Wonder Sparkle*, the first of which contained Revolutionary Bio-Beating Enzymes, but sadly lacked the other's Eco-Friendly Solvent Power.

If Tessa could see me now, I thought, as I scoured the kitchen sink to a blinding snowy whiteness, then stood back to admire my work. Then, I shook my head. I ought to get back to Oxford pronto, I realised, to see people of my own age. People who left tea bags festering in the plug hole, whose coffee mugs were sand-blasted once a year, and whose rooms were mucked out only when the rats and mice threatened to move in . . .

So, I'd cleaned, I'd organised – I'd even done a bit of work on a commission – but, as Friday morning dawned crisp and blue and golden, as I sniffed the deliciously scented air, as I decided that this might indeed be the loveliest place on earth, I was wondering if I really wanted to come and live in this back of beyond, in this middle of nowhere. Talking to the trees and the flowers has its own peculiar appeal, I dare say – but by Saturday morning I was talking to the walls as well. Desperate for some rational company, I thought I'd even be pleased to see Nick Singer again.

At half-past twelve, he arrived. "Well? How's it going?" he demanded without preamble, as he sauntered into the kitchen where I was making a pot of tea. He'd only walked straight through the rose garden, that's all, so now he deposited great gobbets of mud and muck on my nice clean floor. "Got everything sorted?"

"No." If he wasn't going to waste any time on hello and how are you, then neither was I. "There's loads of stuff I haven't even looked at yet. Do you want a cup of tea?"

"If there's one going."

I poured. "I've written to my dad," I continued, "to suggest he comes over on Monday. Lots of bits and pieces here are his, after all." I offered Nick a biscuit. "But I doubt if he'll bother. He'll just tell me to get a skip and dump the lot. Then sell up."

"Does he have an interest in the house, then?" asked Nick, pushing shortbread into his face.

"Is it his, do you mean?" I shrugged. "I don't actually know. When my parents split up, the deal was for my mother to stay here with the children, for my father to pay maintenance and so on – the usual arrangement, I believe.

"But about ten years ago, my mother inherited quite a bit of money from her own parents. She might have bought my dad out. I'm seeing her solicitor next week, to find out exactly how things stand."

"So you're not coming back to Oxford today?"

"I'm not sure." But then, realising what I'd said, I blushed red. I should have rung Ferry Road. Thinking only of my own concerns, I'd messed Nick around without even considering it. He might have a test tube on the boil at this very moment! His experiment might be at its most critical stage yet, and here was I . . .

"I'm sorry." I bit my lip. "I ought to have called you, to say there'd been a change of plan."

"Yeah, you ought." He frowned. But then, suddenly, he grinned at me. "Well, never mind. I had a nice trip through the Cotswolds. But I went by way of Cheltenham this time. That route you took me before was a bit of a detour, to put it mildly. Do I get a sandwich, and another cup of tea?"

"Of course." I got up. "Come through to the drawing room, it's warmer in there." Leave mud everywhere, I thought shame-facedly, you've every right to do that.

But now, to my surprise, Nick bent to loosen his laces. He jerked off his boots and threw them outside. "Sorry about the mud," he said. "I'll brush it up later, when it's dry."

We sat on the drawing room sofa, companionably drinking tea and eating cheese sandwiches, while my visitor told me the news. Julia had gone back to London, Tessa had got plastered down at the Bricklayer's Arms and tearfully confessed to Nick that she'd begun an affair with a married man, and my agent had phoned repeatedly, five times in one day. The answering machine was getting well hacked off. Why hadn't I told him where I was?

"I'll ring him on Monday," I promised. "Er – Nick?"

"Yeah?"

"What are your plans for the weekend?"

"Drink my tea, get in the car and drive back to Oxford, I suppose." Indifferently, he shrugged. "There's a match against Keble tomorrow. I'm a reserve. If things are all right at the lab, I might play."

"You . . . you don't fancy a lazy weekend, then? Out in the sticks?"

"Stay here, you mean?" Again, he shrugged. "I dunno. I haven't brought a sleeping bag or anything."

"But there are loads of blankets and quilts and things." Sorry for the inconvenience I'd caused him, and wanting to make amends, now I warmed to my theme. "I know – you can have the Red Room! There's a four-poster bed in there. A great big thing, all tented and billowing, like a ship! You can have breakfast in bed, with all the Sunday papers—"

"Yeah? So what we gonna do tonight?" he cut in, unimpressed.

"We could go to a party!"

"Oh?" Non-committal, he sniffed. "Whose?"

"Jael's."

"So who's this Jael?"

"An old school friend. You saw her last time you were here. She was dashing home from the shop."

"You don't mean that bird with the black hair and great long legs, in the red jumper and jeans?"

"That's the one."

"Right. I'll definitely stay." Nick beamed at me. "Do you reckon I'd be in with a chance there?"

"Well, actually – no." I grinned, too. Holding up five fingers, I ticked off points. "She's married, you see. She has a gorgeous new baby. Her husband's a slaughterman at the local abattoir. Nobody messes with Neil Taylor, because he—"

"You don't say," he interrupted, yawning.

"I'm afraid I do. Oh, and she has three big, strong brothers, too."

"Oh, well." Regretfully, Nick shook his head. "Her loss."

"Absolutely," I agreed.

"What else you been doing with yourself this week?" Nick took the last biscuit. "Apart from clearing up and sorting out?"

"Well, as it happens, I've actually done some work of my own. Watercolour sketches mostly, for birthday cards and things."

"Oh. Right." He looked at me. "I'd forgotten you did all that sort of stuff."

"My bread and butter. How's the experiment?" I enquired, then I wished I hadn't, because he frowned.

But it wasn't bad news. "I can't quite believe this," he replied, eventually, "but I think we're actually getting somewhere. I've made a few adjustments to the apparatus, and now the computer's spewing out some very interesting stuff. My supervisor thinks we're on to something, definitely."

"That's good."

"It might be." Nick sighed. "But when I was in the library yesterday, having a look at some articles in *Physics Review*, I came across something which inclines me to suspect that either I'm buggering it up again – or that the Canadian bastards who lead this particular field have been massaging their results."

"Which is more likely?"

"I dunno. I've fucked things up, I suppose." Once again, he sighed. "Well, that's the more obvious explanation, anyway. But even if *I'm* right, it's not for a mere postgraduate to go hacking his way through the groves of academe, slashing and burning everything in sight. I mean, I can't write a paper accusing two Nobel laureates of fiddling their figures. No one would publish it if I did."

He pushed his plate aside. "I'll leave it for a few days. Something might occur to me. So how do I go about making an impression on your mate Jael, without getting my face smashed in?"

"Don't waste your time." I laughed. "*You* might think you're subtle, but if you get any ideas of that nature, she'll know what you're thinking almost before you know yourself."

"How will she know?"

"She's a witch." I handed him some lardy cake. "Her dad's a Bible-basher, and the whole family spends every Sunday on its knees, sure enough – but *she's* into the Old Religion. Herbs, spells and wort-cunning. All that."

"I see." Nick grinned. "So where's her warts, then?" he enquired. "Where's her pointy hat?"

"Mind your own business and drink your tea." I glanced through the window. "Look," I went on, "it's a lovely afternoon. Let's go for a walk. Blow the cobwebs right away!"

So, I put on my wellingtons, Nick reluctantly accepted the loan of my father's old Barbour, then we set off. We left the village, crossed some fields, then walked by the river. Hanging over a little stone bridge, I watched two water rats busying themselves amidst the reeds. Crumbling some stale biscuits, which had been lurking in the depths of my jacket pocket, I dropped them in the water. "Here, ratty, ratty!" I cried.

As they swam towards the floating crumbs, I turned to Nick. "Look at that!" I beamed, delighted. "Aren't they sweet?"

"Sweet?" Watching the little creatures collecting bits of

biscuit, and carrying their spoils away, he shook his head. "Those buggers carry Weil's disease," he muttered. "You know what that is? They bite you, you're a dead man. Or woman in your case, naturally."

"Oh, Nick!" I made a face. "Is there no romance in your rational, scientist's soul?"

"None at all," he replied. "Come on."

We left the bridge, crossed another meadow, then started to climb our little local mountain, a thickly wooded scarp left over from some ice age or other, from the summit of which we would be able to see into three counties.

"This way." I pushed through some bracken, and found the path again. "Not getting tired, are you?"

"No. Only scared to death." Nick came up behind me. "I reckon this is a plot," he muttered. "You've brought me up here to do away with me. I've seen that film."

"Which film is this?"

"*The Wicker Man*. Some stuff with Britt Ekland in." He narrowed his eyes at me. "When we get to the top, there they'll be. All the villagers, in their Sunday best. Ready with the bonfire, to—"

"To do you to a turn, for Sunday lunch? You do talk some rubbish." I smiled my encouragement. "Nearly there," I promised.

"Oh, God," he groaned

"Come on." I laughed at him. "Tell you what – I'll race you to the top."

"There." I spread my arms wide. "Over to your right is the rest of Herefordshire. Down here, it's Worcestershire. Gloucestershire's on your left hand side."

"Yeah, very interesting. They all look the same to me."

"Of course they don't! Look, there's Hereford itself.

You can see the cathedral tower, and all the church spires."

"Yeah, so you can." Suddenly, Nick shuddered.

"Are you getting cold?" I asked.

"No, not really."

"Then a fairy tapped you on the shoulder. Or somebody's just walked across your grave."

"Here we go again." Nick shook his head. "Sometimes, I wonder about you. I mean – you don't really believe in all this fairies and witches nonsense, do you?"

"Of course," I teased. "My spirit guide is with me as we speak. My aura glows all round about my head."

"Yet you don't *look* bonkers."

"I'm not."

"You must be." Theatrically, he sighed. "You'll be telling me you believe in crystal healing next."

"But I *do* believe in crystal healing." It was fun to wind him up. "In reincarnation, too."

"Holy Moses."

"Who was he? An aromatherapist?" I laughed at his frown. "Don't worry. I'm not going to bore you with details of my own past lives – nor suggest that *you* were once a white friar. Or a black monk. Or even a pig farmer, in Warwickshire."

"That's a relief." He grinned. "Me poor old grandmother would turn in her grave if she thought we'd had people like that in the family."

"She can rest in peace," I told him. "But, joking aside, I do sometimes wonder – is the idea of reincarnation really so far-fetched?"

"It's bloody ridiculous."

"But couldn't we somehow inherit the *remembrance* of past lives? Lives our ancestors actually lived? I mean

– if we inherit blue eyes, big feet, a tendency to be musical or asthmatic, why shouldn't we inherit memory, as well?"

"Because there isn't a gene for memory. Not as such. That's why."

"But—"

"As far as we know," he interrupted, "memory doesn't work like that. What I mean is, it's *not* like having blue eyes. Or asthma, or musical ability."

"But couldn't we inherit tapes? Or even loops?"

"You mean, information loops? Like the Muzak in shopping arcades?"

"Yes."

"So we're born at one point on the tape. Listen to the Whitney Houston. Get on to the Diana Ross – and before we know it, we're back to the original Des O'Connor or Frank Sinatra again?"

"Yes. Why not?"

"I suppose it might be possible. Although I can't see *how*." He shrugged. "Why would be need that sort of inheritance, anyway?"

"Why do we need tonsils? Or adenoids?"

"Well, if you're that Radio 4 presenter bloke—"

"Be serious."

"Yeah, okay. But I know what's coming next. Now, you're going to say, what about instinct? Animals know how to look after their babies, birds build nests, perhaps they've inherited memory loops, too? Maybe that's exactly what instinct is? well, I can't actually prove you wrong."

He shuddered again. "I *am* cold now," he muttered. "I expect you are, too. Shouldn't we be getting back?"

"Do you believe in God?" I asked, as we slipped and

slithered down the muddy path. It was actually harder to descend than it had been to climb the hill. "Nick?"

He looked at me. "What is this?" he demanded. "The Spanish Inquisition?"

"No." In actual fact, I was trying to decide just how much he was likely to get up the noses of the Casson family tonight. "I wondered, that's all."

"It depends what you mean by God," he said. "If you mean the Lord God of Israel, as quoted in the Holy Bible – no, I don't."

"Why?"

"Think about it." We were negotiating a very slippery bit just then, and he took my hand, I assumed to steady himself as much as to help me. "Lindsay," he continued, patiently, "you're a clever girl. Reasonably observant. Quite well informed. You must have noticed that the people who believe in that sort of God are among the most dangerous human beings on the planet."

"Why do you say that?"

"They have a monopoly on revelation. They know the answers to everything. Most of them seem to believe they're entitled to thump anybody and everybody who doesn't agree with them."

"Mrs Sidderfin goes to church. I can't imagine her thumping anyone."

"Maybe not." Nick was well into his stride by now. "But to go back to belief and disbelief, look at this this way. Once you accept the existence of *one* supernatural being – even one as great and grand and respectable as the bloke in the Book of Genesis – what's to stop you accepting any silly fairy story? Any load of old crap?"

"I bet even you used to believe in Father Christmas!"

"No. In *my* family, that wasn't actually encouraged." He

105

shook his head. "I can't *believe* parents actually tell their kids there's a real Father Christmas! Who lives in Lapland with a thousand non-union elves, turning out Barbie dolls and Power Rangers by the score. Who—"

"Oh, I see!" I burst out laughing. "*You* were never taken to visit Santa Claus. It's scarred you for life!"

"What? Oh – yeah. That's exactly right." Now, Nick laughed, too. "I said you was clever, didn't I?"

"We ought to get a move on." I eased my fingers from his grasp. "It'll be getting dark soon, and we don't want to be stuck out here in the wilds, in the middle of the night."

"Not with all them ghosts and witches about," agreed Nick, solemnly.

Chapter Ten

We arrived back at The Larches desperately in need of caffeine and carbohydrate, but otherwise refreshed and relaxed. I filled the kettle, opened the biscuit tin, and dropped tea bags into the pot. "One lump, is it?" I asked, as I reached for a couple of mugs. "Or two?"

"Three." Nick was already at the biscuits. "In a mug," he added, spraying crumbs.

We drank our tea. "That's better," said Nick, taking another custard cream, which he disposed of in one voracious bite. "Have a digestive?"

"No, thanks." Getting up from the kitchen table, I walked to the window. It was pitch dark now. The sky was that heavy, velvety black one never sees in a town, where there's too much artificial light for it ever to be properly dark at all. Soon, I thought, it will be the witching hour . . .

I stared out into the night. Growing increasingly nervous – jittery, even – I didn't need to wonder why. For tonight, I would see Simon. Talk to Simon. Perhaps even dance with Simon, too! I rehearsed imaginary conversations now, deep inside my head. Holding me close, Simon told me how much he'd missed me, how happy he was to see me. That I hadn't changed a bit and – best of all – how miserable he would be if I went away again.

Having nothing much to do – except the everlasting sorting and packing, of course, of which I was heartily sick and tired – I decided to go and ask Jael if she needed any help with the food for the party. I make a very mean blue cheese dip. I'm a dab hand at a sweetcorn vol-au-vent or stuffed tomato, too.

But, in spite of having conceived a violent *schwärm* for Jael, Nick declined to come with me, saying he had a few articles to read, and that he wanted to do a sum. So, I went to fetch my boots. To save time, I decided to get into my glad rags there and then, so now I changed into clean jeans and a clingy black top. Then I did my face. Ten minutes later, I was ready to leave.

"Will you be able to find the house?" I asked, as I shrugged on my new scarlet puffa jacket, then picked up a bottle of Australian white.

"I expect so." Nick glanced up from his reading. "But fill me in again."

"You cross the road here, walk over the glebe, and it's the little black and white cottage on your left, half-way down the lane. We passed it this afternoon, in actual fact."

"I'll find it." Nick scribbled a note to himself. "See you later."

"Hello," I said to the pretty, dark-haired woman who opened the door to me, who was Jael – and yet not Jael, for she was too dishevelled-looking, and much too fat. A rustic Venus, I thought, gone spectacularly to seed.

"Hello, Lindsay." Wiping her hands on her apron, Jael's sister Naomi grinned in welcome. "I thought you'd be our Neil," she said. "He took the babby up Daniel's place, see.

But there again, Jael did tell 'em not to hurry back!" She stood aside, to let me enter.

Right behind Naomi stood Rebekah, who was sucking her thumb and regarding me anxiously. "Hello, Reb," I said. Encouragingly, I smiled. But I got no response whatsoever, until Jael came up and carefully removed the thumb – whereupon Rebekah began to cry.

"Now, you can just stop that!" rapped Jael, giving her little sister a warning shake. "Goodness, it's only Lindsay! You remember Lindsay, don't you? She lives in that big grey house, near the shop."

"The one opposite the church," I prompted.

"You remember, Reb," urged Naomi. "I'm sure you do!"

"Nuh." Rebekah pushed her thumb back into her mouth. Balefully, she glared at us all.

"She *does* know you," murmured Jael, glaring back. "When Nathan mentioned he'd given you a lift last week, she asked if you was that lady in the red coat, with the shiny black hair."

"I'll let her come to me then, shall I?" I suggested.

"That'd be the best way." Jael took her sister's arm. "Come on, Reb," she said, more kindly now. "There's still lots of things to be done. We needs your helpin' hands!"

Rebekah grinned. Then, meekly, she followed her big sister into the kitchen, where preparations for the party were well under way. But, instead of helping, "I want my tea," she announced, imperiously.

"You'll 'ave to make it yourself, then." Jael filled the kettle. "Here you are. Make a cup for everybody, eh? No, plug it in over there – we ain't got room on this side today. Now, you just watch yourself. We don't want no burns or scalds, do we?"

Jael had always been protective towards Rebekah. They all were, in fact, for, if anything could be said to unite the Cassons, it was their attitude towards this youngest, damaged one.

Recently, so Mrs Denny had informed me, the local social services department had suggested finding Rebekah a place in a sheltered housing complex, on the outskirts of the city. But the Cassons would have none of it. Instead, they did as they'd always done, taking it in turns to have her to stay with each of them. Muttering and grumbling about bloody interfering busybodies, they'd refused to have anything to do with social services from that moment on.

As I watched Rebekah getting on with making our tea, measuring milk into four earthenware mugs and carefully warming the pot before pouring boiling water on to the leaves, I wondered privately if her own little bolt hole in a sheltered housing complex might not have been quite a good idea.

She might have learned some skills and gained some independence then. As it was, the poor thing was shunted around from spare room to spare room in half a dozen separate homes. As far as I knew, she had no little space to call her own. She lived out of suitcases, and did as she was told.

I made my blue cheese dip. Then, I chopped some carrots, cauliflower and peppers into bite-sized pieces. Rebekah ate a few, then began to arrange the rest in little pyramids, in a pretty glass dish.

"You don't eat 'em like that," scolded Naomi, as her sister helped herself to more carrot matchsticks and cauliflower bits. "Look, they're for a dip. You spikes 'em on a cocktail stick, then bungs 'em in that pot of goo. Lin, if you've finished, could you keep 'er occupied for ten minutes? While Jael and me gets on?"

So, whilst the two big sisters baked and boiled and fried, I sat down at the kitchen table and entertained Rebekah. Well, I did my best.

"She likes to do things with her hands," said Jael, handing me paper, crayons and some sharp, kitchen shears. "Likes to cut out, too. Get her to make some of them little men, in rows."

But, afraid my charge might cut herself, I showed her instead how to make origami swans. As she folded and pleated the paper, her features grew fierce in concentration. But then, when her efforts proved successful, her little face positively glowed. "Do you want to draw a picture next?" I enquired, as the fifth paper swan took shape under her stubby but nimble fingers. "Or shall we make some little paper boats?"

"You draw summat," she replied.

So then I drew poppies and buttercups and roses and honeysuckle, all of which she recognised. She then proceeded to inform me, very gravely, that we couldn't see any of them just now, because it was winter time, and all the flowers were asleep.

"Do you like flowers, Reb?" I asked, as I coloured in a fat, pink rose.

"Yeah!" She grinned at me.

"What sort do you like best?"

"Daf'dills. But I dun like roses!" Snatching up a brown crayon, she scribbled all over my pretty pink rose. "Dun like roses at all!"

"Reb!" Jael was furious. "That was a nasty thing to do! Now, you say sorry. At once!"

Rebekah merely grunted.

Jael shook her, and told her to apologise, again.

Rebekah began to cry.

"It doesn't matter." Quickly, I dropped the crayons back into their tin. "Look, I know what we'll do."

So, we mixed up some cochineal and made Rorschach blots, Rebekah becoming more and more imaginative as time went on. "That's a tree!" she cried, turning an amorphous mess this way and that. "Look, Nay! A big tree, with apples and pears and plums on!"

"So it is." Indulgently, Naomi nodded. "Do us another, then. What about a nice, big house this time?"

But, just as suddenly as she'd decided she didn't like roses, Rebekah grew bored by ink blots, too. Instead of reaching for more paper, her thumb went back into her mouth. "Nuh," she muttered, frowning. "Don't want to no more."

"She's getting a bit tired." Stroking her sister's thin, straggling hair away from her forehead, Jael kissed Rebekah's puffy cheek. "She needs a little nap now. Could you go and snuggle her down, Lin? Only I got my hands full in here."

So I took Rebekah into the sitting room, where she lay down on the sofa. I covered her with a blanket, gave her one of the baby's soft toys to cuddle, then drew the curtains and turned out the light.

"You're very good with 'er," observed Naomi, as I walked back into the kitchen.

"Do you think she really remembers me?" I asked.

"Hard to say." Naomi shrugged. "I was talking about our Dad yesterday. Remembering how he was before he was took sick. I could have sworn she understood what I was on about!

"But then she starts moaning and crying, saying he hit her and pushed her, which he never did, I'm sure. He'd give the rest of us a clout, I don't deny it – he wasn't

112

slow to get his temper up when one of *us* was bad! But he'd never have thumped little Reb. Never."

"She gets confused, that's all." Jael dabbed at the corner of one eye. "They reckon she's low grade, them assessment people. She'll never amount to much."

"Poor little Reb." Naomi shrugged, at the hopelessness of it, I imagine. "Drew the short straw there, she did."

"She's lucky to have all of you, though," I observed. "She may be disdavantaged. But she'll never have to rely upon the tender mercies of the Welfare State."

"Yeah, I suppose." Gloomily, Jael sighed. But then, she grinned. "Well, ladies – I think that's just about it!"

It was indeed. The table was laid with buffet food, the glasses were set out in sparkling rows upon the highly polished sideboard, and the sitting room furniture was pushed aside, for dancing I supposed. As Jael had said, there was nothing else to do.

I glanced at my watch. It was only seven o'clock. Should I hang around, I wondered? But then I thought, other people would not start arriving until about eight, at the earliest. More to the point, Jael and Naomi still had to have baths, to get into their party gear. So I went back to The Larches. I'd make Nick Singer some tea.

As I walked across the glebe, I could see the lights of The Larches coming nearer and nearer still, and for a moment I was fourteen again, coming home from a Guide meeting to hot milk and ginger biscuits, by the drawing room fire. My poor mother! Every so often, the fact that I would never see her again hit me so hard that the tears came into my eyes.

Still sniffing a bit, I walked up the drive. I found my

key. Turning it in the lock, I squared my shoulders, then went inside.

"Oh – hello, you." Nick had just made a pot of tea. He'd evidently done his sum, too, for screeds and screeds of paper covered in mystic symbols were now spread all over the kitchen floor. Learned journals lay on the table, all of them open, several with blocks of type highlighted in yellow marker pen. Well, I reflected, he'd certainly made himself at home.

"So, how's it going up at Cold Comfort Farm?" he enquired, as he opened a carton of milk. "All the Starkadders present and correct?"

What did I tell you? What did I say, only a few pages back? I shrugged off my jacket. "Oh, you mean the Cassons," I murmured. "I think they're okay."

"Jolly good show." He poured me a cup of tea, and grinned. "How's the gorgeous Elfine?"

He was so predictable it was sad. "If you mean Jael," I muttered, "she's fine."

"Excellent." Nick grinned. "I can't wait to meet the rest of the family!"

"But they're all perfectly ordinary," I protested. "They're—"

"Nobody's ordinary in this place," he interrupted. "You yourself talk to the water voles, and—"

"They were water *rats*, actually."

"Whatever." He passed me the biscuit tin. "You don't get that sort of thing in Hackney. Nor do you meet many sex-starved hill farmers, who've been had up for buggering sheep."

"What *are* you talking about?"

"While you were out, I read the local rag. I tell you now, I was well shocked! There was this fellow on page sixteen,

114

he's been had up on six counts of interfering with ewes – *and* he's asked for several offences of a similar nature to be taken into account!"

"That's all quite hilarious, isn't it?" I glared at him. "I suppose you think slashing horses is funny, too?"

"No. It's not funny at all. I don't find the idea of assaulting sheep particularly amusing, either." Nick shrugged. "It was just the way it was reported which made me laugh. The act described is disgusting. Poor sheep."

"Quite."

"It'll need to see a good psychiatrist now. If it's to have any chance of leading a normal, sheepish life."

I narrowed my eyes at him. "You don't like the countryside, do you?" I asked

"Well, to be honest, I do find it a bit creepy." Reflectively, Nick stirred his tea. "It's so dark at night. It's not very much lighter during the day."

"Not at this time of year, no." I looked at him enquiringly. "Are you coming to this party?"

"Are you sure I'm invited?"

"Yes, of course."

"I haven't brought my glad rags."

"That doesn't matter," I told him. "I don't suppose anyone will notice. But it won't matter if they do. They're only a bunch of sheep-shagging peasants, anyway."

To my surprise, he had the grace to blush.

Jael opened the door to us. She had changed out of her jumper and jeans into a black jersey dress. The fabric was a cheap polyester mix, the cut was indifferent and the garment draped very badly but, all the same, she looked wonderful. Sensational, that's the word.

Even Nick Singer thought so. He, in fact, was gobsmacked. I laughed to myself, then looked around the place, to see who else had come.

Rebekah was up again, but when Nick entered the sitting room she hung back, hiding behind Daniel and Naomi, and peering like a frightened rabbit from behind two solid rocks.

Nick grinned at her.

She ducked behind Naomi's shoulder. But, when she peeped out again, he winked – and she thought this was hilarious. She giggled almost coquettishly. Then, feeling braver, she came out from behind her relations, and said hello.

"This is Neil." The voice behind me was soft and shy, not like Jael's normal speaking voice at all. "Lin?"

I turned, and saw my hostess with a tall, heavy, fair-haired man of about thirty, who had a glass of lager in his left hand, and was holding out his right to me.

I took it, and felt my fingers enclosed in as firm, as hard a handshake as I've ever been anxious to escape in all of my life. But, on the whole, Neil Taylor looked so ordinary, so uninspiring, that I was quite taken aback. What had a creature like Jael Casson ever seen in *this* blank sheet of a man?

"Hello, Lindsay." His voice was low, soothing – caressing, almost. His smile was kind. Remembering how he earned his living, I couldn't decide if I liked him or not. But then, I realised, the fact that I was undecided was a big point in his favour. For I'd been determined to hate him on sight.

I took our coats and went to hang them in the downstairs cloakroom. In the darkness of the hallway, I listened to the hum of voices. Then, my heart did a somersault.

116

Simon was already here! He was in the kitchen, talking to somebody.

I smoothed my black top, then flicked back my hair. Then, taking a deep breath, I opened the kitchen door. I went inside.

Nathan and Simon, together with Nathan's black labrador, sat round the kitchen table. They'd evidently been there some time, for empty beer cans littered it, and crisp packets lay empty in pools of Special Brew.

"Lindsay!" Turning to see who had come in, Nathan gave me a great, beaming smile. "You're looking lovely as the dawn! Well, then? Going to give us a kiss?"

Obviously, he was drunk. Absolutely wrecked, in fact – I doubt if he could have stood without support. But Nathan was always a cheerful inebriate, so although his father preached to him of hell fire, and his brothers and sisters no doubt worried about his liver, nobody really minded his intemperate ways.

This evening, he was grinning from ear to ear. "Here, Simon!" he cried, or rather slurred, "don't Lindsay look gorgeous tonight?"

Simon said nothing at all. He would not even look at me! He simply stared down into his drink. Then, heavily, he sighed.

"Miserable bugger," observed Nathan. Casually, he belched. "So how you getting on with the old house clearance, then?"

"It – it's coming along," I murmured, willing Simon to look up, to smile, to say something – anything – to me. "But as you can imagine, there's still a lot to do."

"You want a hand, you give me a call." Nathan patted his lap. "Make yourself comfortable for a few minutes?" he invited, leering encouragingly.

I looked at Simon. He was staring fixedly at the puddles on the table. "G-good evening, Simon," I began.

No reply.

"Simon?" Encouragingly, I smiled.

He grunted something then. But he did not look up. Nor would he speak to me.

"Cat's definitely got his tongue tonight," murmured Nathan. "Don't take it personal, Lin. He ain't said two words to me for a week. Here – did you bring that fella of yours along tonight?"

Suddenly, I could bear it no longer. "J-Jael asked me to fetch some plates." I stammered. "So perhaps I'll see you later." With that, I snatched three plates from the drainer, and then I fled.

I stood in the hallway, breathing hard. I didn't think I'd ever been so completely humiliated – well, not for a long time, anyway.

It wouldn't have hurt him, would it, just to have smiled at me? To have said hello? But then, I sighed. It was par for the course. The fact of the matter is, I'd completely forgotten how horrible Simon Dyer could be. How off-hand, how dismissive, how downright cruel. Especially to me! For, in the old days, before – before it happened, he could keep up that sort of cold-shoulder treatment for hours. Days, even, whilst I pleaded and wept and begged him to tell me what I'd done.

I was shaking violently now. So, leaving the plates on the hall table, I went upstairs to the loo. Sitting there in the cool, forgiving darkness, I permitted myself a tear or two, letting them trickle down my cheeks and splash on to the floor.

But then, I pulled myself together. Simon would cheer up. Nathan would see to that! I repaired the damage to my face, raked my finger through my hair, then went back to join the fun.

The sitting room was a seething mass of Cassons and their friends, all squirming and writhing to old Beatles hits.

"Here she is, then!" As soon as he saw me, Daniel pounced, dragging me on to the floor. "Where'd you get to?" he demanded, breathing beer fumes into my face. He hugged me round the waist. I supposed his wife Rachel must be upstairs, feeding the latest addition to their already enormous family.

Nick had his work cut out, for he was showing Rebekah how to do the twist. For her part, she seemed to have decided he was nice, so was consequently all over him, hugging and squeezing him, slobbering in his ear and planting great, smacking kisses on his face.

Since Rebekah tended to dribble and her nose ran more or less constantly, she was always somewhat damp. So, the objects of her affection tended to get a bit clammy themselves. Everyone was kind to her, of course, treating her like the overgrown toddler she was, and not expecting any social graces of this poor, backward child.

But, as I watched them, I realised Nick was being more than kind. He was being courtly, too. Although he was quite obviously dying to dance with Jael, towards whom his glance was drawn repeatedly and so longingly that it was almost comical to see, he seemed to appreciate that it would upset Rebekah dreadfully if he left her for anyone else.

So he stayed with her, letting her tread on his toes, half strangle him, then wipe her nose on his shirt front, and bearing all this with exemplary fortitude and magnanimity. I was proud of Nick Singer that night.

119

Eventually, however, Jael decided she'd had enough of John Lennon twisting and shouting. She put on some Jennifer Rush and then, kicking off her black stiletto heels, she began to slink and sway.

Soon, she was giving Nick the sort of smouldering glances which would probably have got her laid right there on the Axminster, had her hefty-looking husband and brothers not been standing by.

Somebody turned the lights down low. Jennifer moaned and throbbed insistently. Jael moved in for the kill. Nick's expression was unreadable.

But then, "I don't like this song!" As Jael put her hands on Nick's shoulders, as she tossed her long, black hair and pulled him into her embrace, Rebekah's wail cut the tension like a knife. "Nick! Dance with *me!*"

"Come on, Reb." Samuel's deep baritone was soothing, placatory, calm. "You've had him all night! Now let old Jael have a—"

"Nick!" cried Rebekah, bursting into tears. "Nick!"

"We'll all dance together." Unwinding Jael, Nick crossed her arms against her chest. He selected a new CD, of music with a thumping, regular beat. He turned the volume high. "Right, then!" he announced, "if you'll all hold hands, I'll teach you the horah!"

"The what?" muttered Daniel, who liked to rock and roll.

"It's very easy." Taking Rebekah by the hand, Nick demonstrated the basic steps. Rebekah cottoned on straight away, and soon she was beaming with pleasure.

"Attagirl." Nick grinned at her, then all round the room. "Come on, you lazy buggers!" he cried. "You need some exercise, too!"

His enthusiasm proved to be infectious. Soon, all the

Cassons and their mates were stamping and whooping like crazy, Jael's husband especially making the floorboards vibrate and the rafters ring.

Woken from their drunken slumbers, I suppose, by the God-awful racket coming from Jael's little sitting room, Nathan and Simon appeared in the doorway. Too far gone even to stand up straight, let alone dance, Nathan grinned and shook his empty can in time to the music. Simon just stood there, however, Mr Glum incarnate.

But *I* was feeling much better now. All that exercise had released my inhibitions, and the lively company of the Cassons and their friends had cheered me up. As Nick grabbed my hand and swung me round, I heard myself laugh out loud.

I glanced towards Simon Dyer. He had turned away. Okay, I thought, be like that. But you've blown it tonight. You'll have to break my heart another day.

It was nearly eleven o'clock. Long past Rebekah's normal bedtime. As the music wound down, as everyone collapsed into chairs or subsided on to the floor in giggling help-lessness, she tugged at Naomi's hand and whispered that she was too sleepy to dance any more. "I'll take her up," offered Daniel. "Okay then, Reb. Say good night."

So, Rebekah did the rounds of the room. She gave all her brothers and sisters a kiss. Hugging Nick, she dribbled something into his hair.

He kissed her, then handed her over to Daniel once again. "All the best then, Reb," he murmured. "Mind how you go."

Naomi and Daniel helped their dozy little sister up the wooden hill, and soon we heard the sort of noises only to be expected when an over-excited child is being put to bed. In the smoky sitting room, Nick was being made much of, patted and clapped on the back, for the Cassons had decided he was all right.

"You want a beer?" enquired Neil. Encouragingly, he grinned. "Nah, don't drink that canned rubbish. Horse piss, is all that is! Look, I got some bottles of special brew in the kitchen. I'll fetch 'em in."

"Have summat to eat, as well," added Rachel, handing him a fat sausage roll.

When Rebekah had gone to bed, however, Nick seemed to deflate. He flopped into an easy chair. He rubbed his tired eyes. "I think it's time I hit the sack," he yawned, blearily.

"Already?" I grinned at him. "But you can't go yet! The night is young!"

"Well, *you* don't have to leave." He nodded towards Naomi's husband, who was opening a bottle of vodka. "Things'll get interesting now the babies are in bed."

"Maybe." I glanced towards Simon. He caught my eye, but then he looked away. Sod him, I thought. "I'll come home now," I said.

"I enjoyed that," said Nick, as we set off down the lane.

"So did I." The night air was chilly, but I was sticky and sweating still. I wanted to get home, take a hot shower, then go to bed. "What was that dance you taught us? It looked like something out of *Zorba the Greek.*"

"Yeah, I suppose it must have done, a bit." Nick shook his head. "God," he sighed, "she's so beautiful! Does her husband realise, do you reckon? Does the jammy bugger know just how lucky he is?"

"I expect so." I grinned. "You almost got lucky yourself this evening. She was making quite a play for *you* tonight!"

"Exactly. She was playing." Nick scowled. "That's all it was – showing off."

"Poor Nick." I tucked my arm through his. "Don't be cross with her," I whispered. "She didn't mean any harm."

"I suppose not." Again, Nick yawned. He really was exhausted, I could see that now.

"You get off to bed," I told him, as I opened the front door of The Larches. "Go on, get your head down, have a good eight hours tonight."

To my surprise, he didn't argue. He collected one of the plastic carrier bags which littered his car, then went upstairs as meekly as a lamb.

I was quite tired, too. So, after checking on the Aga, I banked up the fire in the drawing room and went to bed myself.

I read until I dropped off. I woke at eight the next morning, chilled to the bone. My duvet had slid off in the night, it's true, but I'm such a restless sleeper that it often does that. I was cold because the house was like a tomb.

I could hear someone banging about downstairs, but it took me a good thirty seconds to realise it must be Nick. A couple of minutes later, he tapped on my bedroom door.

"Hang on," I muttered, shivering. Getting out of bed, I reached for my dressing gown, put it on, then opened the door, which I closed firmly behind me. "G-good morning," I managed, my teeth chattering.

"Good morning to you!" He handed me a steaming mug of coffee. "I think your central heating's buggered," he announced, cheerfully.

"I'm sorry?"

"Your boiler's on the blink."

"Oh, shit."

"Here, watch your language."

"What? Well, I like that! *You* can talk!" I looked him up and down. Wearing jeans, socks and at least three bulky sweaters, he looked like a bear in clothes.

He hadn't shaved, of course. But, since he was so dark, designer stubble actually suited him. In fact, in that cold early morning light, he looked attractive rather than otherwise, and I could see what Tessa meant when she'd said he was a definite eight out of ten. Married man, nothing. Perhaps Nick was next on her list, after all . . .

In spite of myself, I smiled.

"What are you grinning at now?" he enquired.

"Nothing." I sipped some more coffee. "I'd better get Mrs Denny's Alan over," I murmured.

"If you like." Nick shrugged. "But I could fix it for you easily."

"What did you say?"

"I could sort your central heating out."

"I thought you were a physicist. Not a plumber."

"You thought right. But I do understand the ins and outs of your average domestic central heating system." He eyed me narrowly. "So should you!"

"Well, I don't. I gave up science at fourteen."

"Shame on you." Sighing, Nick shook his head. "Got a torch?" he enquired.

Chapter Eleven

I had a quick wash – well, a lick and a promise, really – then put on jeans, two jumpers and an ancient cardigan which had belonged to my dad. Then I went downstairs to prepare breakfast, for my visitor and for me.

As I made toast and brewed fresh coffee, I was singing. In spite of the fact that I was half-frozen, I was feeling quite cheerful this morning. For I had, at last, worked out exactly what was wrong with Simon. As well as with me.

How could I have been so stupid? Of course, I should have explained! For, I could imagine what had happened, I could just *hear* the bloody Cassons, winding Simon up and teasing him without mercy, in their ham-fisted, rustic way. "Oh, she's got a new friend now," Jael would have told him, winking at her sister conspiratorially. "She's goin' around with this student fella. What's that? Oh, yeah – *I* reckon it's serious! What do you think, Naomi?"

Bitch.

On Monday, I decided, I'd go to up Brougham Gate, see Simon, and put everything right.

"I think I'll have a potter around the stables this morn-ing," I told Nick, as we ate our toast and he read the sports section in the *Sunday Express*. "Nick? Anybody at home?"

"You're going pottering around the stables." Looking up, Nick grinned. "Potter off, then. I'll wash up."

"May I finish my coffee first?" I sat back in my chair. "I was talking to Mr Sidderfin last week," I continued. "I asked him if he knew anybody who might like to lease some stabling and one of the paddocks from me. Well, it would bring in a bit of cash. But *he* reckoned I ought to let a developer look the stables over. To see about converting them to houses, or flats."

"Oh." Nick glanced up from his perusal of the football results. "You sure you want a load of yuppies and week-enders out there in your back yard?"

"I was thinking of low-cost housing for local people, actually. Young married couples. People sharing, and that." I shrugged. "Personally, I don't reckon we'd get planning permission. But I'm going to have a look round anyway. To see what I think."

So, whilst Nick cleared away the dishes and fixed the central heating – the problem was something to do with the pump, apparently – I walked round to the stables, where I'd once kept my own ponies and dreamed my equestrian daydreams of Horse of the Year Show glory. Where I had, in fact, spent most of my waking hours, when I was thirteen.

So it wasn't until an hour or more later, when I was walking through the terminally neglected rose garden, taking a short cut to the back kitchen door, that I saw the mess. It was all over the lawn, glistening red and creamy white in the early morning sun.

Gagging, I turned away. In fact, I almost ran. But then, a horrible fascination drew me back again. I went closer. Then, closer still.

The carcases of at least five chickens lay there, scattered randomly. Their wings were torn off, their breasts were slashed and gnawed, and their yellow claws scrabbled pointlessly at the sky. The sight was absolutely revolting – but then, I realised, curiously pathetic, too.

With an effort, I swallowed my bile. Resigned to the fact that I would have to clear up this bloody carnage, I walked right up to where the poor, dismembered creatures lay.

"Foxes." The very word is like a knell, striking dread and loathing into the hearts of all true countrymen. Especially those with chickens to protect. It's only ignorant city dwellers who think foxes are cuddly little beasts, all sweet and adorable with their cute, pointy faces and dainty little toes. These unfortunate victims of Reynard's capricious cruelty had quite possibly come from Mr Gregson's poultry farm, down at Harewood End.

I'd ring and ask him, I decided. But I needed a cup of coffee first, and a little sit down, for I was starting to feel sick all over again.

When I entered the kitchen, Nick was still tinkering with the boiler. So, after making coffee for us both, I sat at the kitchen table and washed half a dozen of the little china cottages which formed part of my mother's collection of Coalport and Staffordshire pastille burners. They were probably worth quite a bit now, I thought, as I lowered one into the luke-warm suds. Despite the fact that most of them were scorched, chipped or otherwise damaged, probably beyond repair. As were so many of her things . . .

I sighed. She'd been such a magpie, my mother! A jackdaw in human form. When we'd first moved to The Larches, she'd hated the place. But this rotting, crumbling, decaying old house had then become her nest, and she had filled it almost to overflowing.

"Right, then! The bugger should be working properly now." Nick tossed the antique spanner, which was all I'd been able to find him in the way of tools, on to the kitchen table. Then, theatrically, he flicked a switch. "Stand well clear," he advised, taking a few paces backwards himself.

The boiler gulped, spluttered, then juddered alarmingly. A snake-like hissing was succeded by awful clanking noises, which echoed all round the room.

"Oh, God!" Grabbing my arm, Nick dragged me bodily across the kitchen. We took cover beside the huge Welsh dresser, where we crouched fearfully.

There was a bang, a whoosh, then the roar of a rushing, gurgling torrent surging through the pipes, as cold water flooded the system again. Glancing at Nick, I saw he was grinning. "You did that to scare me!" Furious, I glared daggers at him. "*I* thought it was all going to blow up!"

"So did I!" A picture of wide-eyed innocence, Nick gazed artlessly back at me. Or tried to, anyway. But then, he laughed. "Well, to be honest, I didn't reckon it would actually explode. But that old boiler's in a disgusting state. It's held together by cobwebs and rust. You ought to get a new one."

"I can't afford it. Anyway, I may be selling the house." I stood up again. Reaching for a towel, I began to dry my hands. "I'll tell prospective purchasers that the boiler needs replacing, naturally."

"Naturally." Nick picked up his spanner. "I ought to check the water tank now."

"The one in the loft?"

"You mean you have others?"

"No." I suppose I'd asked for that. I walked towards the kitchen door. "Come on," I muttered. "Stop trying to catch me out, and get yourself upstairs."

Standing on a stool, I pushed open the trap door, then yanked the loft ladder down. "You should pull that out diagonally," said Nick, as it descended with a series of clunks and clanks. "Jerk it like that, and one fine morning the hinges at the top will break clean away."

"Is that a fact?" I regarded him coldly. "I never realised the angle of extraction was so important," I observed, more than a little sarcastically.

"Of course it's important!" He shook his head at me. "Elementary mechanics, that."

"Well, I'm not a mechanic."

"Obviously."

Sorely tempted to brain him with the torch, which by some chance I'd remembered to bring upstairs, I jumped down from my stool. "It's all yours," I told him. "Oh, and by the way – would you mind collecting any dead birds while you're up there?"

"Yeah, okay. But I charge extra for that." He disappeared into the cold, dark void. "Throw the torch up, will you?" he called.

"There's a light switch on your left."

"That hasn't worked since Domesday." Expertly, he fielded the torch. "Thanks very much," he muttered. "Oh, God! What a stink! I expect you got dead rats up here, too."

"Do you intend to have lunch today?" he enquired as he re-emerged, birdless, ratless but very dusty, half an hour later. Quizzically, he grinned. "Or do you actually live on biscuits, toast and tea?"

"Of course I don't." I'd collected up some more dusty china, washed it, and now, very carefully, I dried a piece of Spode. "In fact, I was just thinking of going to have a look in the cupboards."

"I could nip down to the shop."

"It will be closed by now."

"Then we could go out somewhere."

"I'm too busy." The truth was, of course, that I didn't want to be seen out. Or at any rate, not with Nick Singer. "I've too many things to do."

"Oh, come on!" He grinned at me. "You can't spend the whole day cooped up in this place, washing your mum's dirty old crockery."

"Why not?"

"Because even you must need fresh air and exercise. Not to mention a little rest and recreation, once in a while."

"So how would you know?"

"Oh, Lindsay!" He sat down on the kitchen table. "Don't be like this!" he cried.

"Like what, exactly?"

"You know what I mean."

"Do I?"

"Yeah, you do." He looked at me. "Last night," he continued, "you were having a laugh. Letting yourself go a bit. But today, you're all prickly and irritable again. Just like Mrs Tiggywinkle, with toothache and PMT."

I was about to observe that he was a fine one to talk about prickliness and irritability – but then, looking back at him, I noticed his grin had faded. Now, he actually looked concerned. Solicitous, even. I remembered how kind he'd been to Rebekah. How he'd helped *me* out, too . . .

Ashamed of my sharpness, I tried to make amends. "I'd quite like to go out," I admitted. "But don't you think it's a bit cold for a picnic?"

"All right, we'll go to a pub." He snatched up his car keys. "Come on, Lin. Get your coat, eh?"

"All right." Suddenly, the idea seemed attractive. If we went out in his car, moreover, if we went over towards

Malvern or Ledbury way, nobody from Hartley Cross was particularly likely to see us. "Give me two minutes," I told him.

"Make it five." He grinned, and held up his hands. They were black. "I need a wash," he said.

We got into the Escort, which he'd parked round the back of the house. The engine spluttered and coughed, then came to reluctant life. "Where are we going, then?" he demanded.

"To Malvern," I replied.

"Edward Elgar country." He reversed out of the weedy drive. "*Dream of Gerontius. Enigma Variations.* Yeah?"

"That's right," I agreed. "A rather nice cello concerto, too."

"I know. I've got a cassette of that somewhere. Jacqueline du Pré, I think."

One day I'll catch him, I thought. One day, I'll find I actually know something Mr Clever-Dick Singer doesn't. I did realise I might be in for a rather long wait.

We approached Malvern by way of Wynds Point. The hills looked beautiful in that limpid, early afternoon light. Already winter here, an icing-sugar dusting of snow had whitened their summits and settled in their vales.

Soft and rounded except for the places where human beings had defaced them by quarrying for the rather unattractive grey stone with which they faced their houses and built endless miles of dry stone walls, the two Beacons looked like giant porpoises lying fast asleep.

We drove into Great Malvern, parked on an incline of one in three, then had some lunch in a pub in the town. "I see it all now," I remarked, as I watched Nick wolf down chicken pie, double baked beans, peas and chips. "Fresh air and exercise, my foot. You just wanted to top up your cholesterol."

"Well sussed." He grinned at me. "Do you want a chip, then?"

"No, thank you."

"Go on." He speared one on his fork, then offered it to me. "Just the one won't kill you."

"Maybe not." I bit into my cheese and celery baguette. "But I happen to prefer more natural food."

"So do rabbits," said Nick. "You know diet plays a big part in evolution, don't you? Well, you want to watch it. You'll end up growing whiskers and a little furry tail."

We finished our lunch, then had some coffee. But, in spite of downing two cups of almost pure caffeine, I now felt so dozy that I could have fallen asleep. It had been so warm in the saloon bar of the Black Boar that, coming out into the chilly street, I shuddered convulsively.

"A brisk scamper on the hills. That's what you need." Encouragingly, Nick patted my shoulder. "Come on," he continued, "I'll race you. I could do with some exercise, too."

So we huffed and we puffed – well, *I* huffed and puffed, while Nick bounced, like Tigger – up a steep and rocky pathway. At this rate, I thought, I'll be needing oxygen soon . . .

Eventually, however, to my inexpressible relief, we found ourselves following a relatively level track, which snaked south towards the Herefordshire Beacon, and hopefully to a café where we could get a cup of tea.

"Pick your feet up!" urged Nick, who was going great guns now. "Try to look as if you're enjoying it, anyway."

"Bully!" I gasped, hating him. I could manage our little

local hills, no problem. But the Herefordshire Beacon was something else entirely. "I want to go home!"

"Well, you can't. You need to work off all that rabbit food."

I did my best. But then, as we rounded a bluff, we saw that the path had become so narrow and overgrown that we would need either to make a detour, or to climb over the boulder which a previous ice age had dumped right in our way.

We, or rather Nick, chose to go over. Charitably, he offered me his hand. Since the alternative was fighting my way through a bramble tangle, I took it, and let him pull me up on to the rock. "You're not very fit," he observed.

I was too breathless to comment. But I thought, just let him wait.

The hills were alive with the sound of hiking boots, and as we tramped along other walkers grinned and said hello. As, of course, walkers do.

"It's just like exercising a labrador, isn't it?" smiled a lady who was going in the opposite direction and whose male companion – I knew he belonged to her, for they wore matching yellow bobble hats – was, like mine, several hundred yards ahead. You're not kidding, I thought, as I stumbled on. Except that you can keep a labrador on a lead. I was fast deciding I much preferred dogs to men.

I squeezed past a blackberry bush to find Nick sitting and waiting for me, on a bench given to the Malvern District Council by the relatives of somebody who had Loved These Hills. I flopped down beside him. "I'm going to die," I wheezed.

"No, you're not." Nick grinned. "All that exercise has actually done you good."

"Garbage. I'm absolutely shattered. I've gone deaf, as

well. That wind's practically blown my ears off." I pulled some twigs and leaves out of my hair. "I bet I look like the *Wreck of the Hesperus*, too."

"You look wonderful. All bright and glowing." Then, suddenly, Nick Singer darted towards me. He took me by the shoulders. He kissed me on the mouth.

It was only a kiss. Not a snog, none of your tongue sandwich business or deep throat routine – just a friendly kiss, that's all. But, in spite of that, it startled me.

For a long moment I stared at him, speechless, wondering what he was going to say – or do – next. But Nick just sat there. Finally, regretfully, he shrugged. "I'm sorry," he said.

"So you should be," I retorted. I felt my colour rise. "That was assault."

"Good grief!" I'll give him this, he was at least trying not to laugh. "Do you intend to report it?"

"I–well, I suppose not." I shrugged, too. But then, to my horror, I found I was grinning back at him. "You're the most peculiar man I've ever met," I told him. I shook my head. "Weird! That's what you are."

"I can't help it." He looked down at his hands. "Don't mock the afflicted. You should pity me."

"It's time to get back," I said.

We walked on down the track, towards where it joined the road back into the town. We were trudging along when we were hailed by a passing motorist.

"Who's that?" asked Nick.

"I've no idea," I replied.

The truck in front of us slowed right down. It stopped. "I thought it was you!" The window was open, and the driver rested his elbow on the ledge. "Whatever you doin' all the way out 'ere?"

"We went up on the hills, for a walk. Hello, Nathan." Relieved that it was only Nathan Casson, and not one of the village motor-mouths who would spread gossip about nothing all over Hartley Cross, I smiled. I eyed the smart, new – well, newish – van. "When did you get this, then?" I enquired.

"Last week, off a bloke as had lost his licence." Nathan chuckled. "The loan sharks was after him, he had a fine to pay, so he practically give it away to me."

"So you did all right. Do you remember Nick?" I asked. For, after all, he'd been well away last night.

"Sure I remember!" Cheerily, Nathan grinned. "How you doing, mate?"

But Nick only nodded in reply.

"You want to get back," said Nathan. "That's why I stopped, to tell you. There's snow on the way, I heard it on the forecast just now – and if you ain't got four wheel drive, them roads down to Hartley Cross can be tricky."

As if to second this, Nathan's black labrador leaned across and poked his head out of the window, nodding and grinning in agreement with his master's voice.

I glanced up at the sky. Heavy grey clouds lay banked in the east, so it looked as if the forecast was right. It had been kind of Nathan to stop, and warn us. "I can't give you a lift," he was saying now. "I would, but I got all this furniture and stuff in the back. You got far to go?"

"Only into the town," I said.

"Half a mile. You'll make it." He revved the engine. "Well, I better be on my way. See you."

"See you," I repeated.

He drove away.

We did as Nathan had suggested. Driving home to The Larches, however, neither of us said much. I imagine Nick was mulling over his latest set of results. Trying, as always, to fathom the mind of Nature, if not of God. As for me, I was thinking about Nick himself.

I'd never had a friend who also happened to be of the opposite sex. I'd had boyfriends, I'd had lovers, I'd even had a live-in partner for three or four terrible months. That was a couple of years ago, and I'd sworn never to repeat that particular experiment in co-operation ever again. But I would have liked a friend . . .

By the time we arrived home, I'd decided that whatever his shortcomings – which were legion – I liked Nick Singer very much indeed. As much as I liked the best of my friends.

But I also knew that I was still in love with Simon Dyer, and being kissed by Nick had only brought that sad fact home to me.

Chapter Twelve

As soon as we arrived back at The Larches, Nick gathered his bits and pieces together, then took his car keys out of his pocket and said he had to be on his way.

"But don't you want a cup of tea?" I asked, as he shoved a mass of computer print-out into a bulging blue folder. "A digestive biscuit – or six?"

"What?" He frowned at me. "Oh. Sorry. No."

"You don't need a shot of caffeine, then? A carbo-hydrate hit?"

"I need to get back to Oxford," he replied, as he opened the front door.

I followed him down the drive.

"Will you be all right?" he asked, as he dropped a large bundle of scientific periodicals into the boot of the Escort. "What I mean is, will you mind being on your own?"

"I doubt if I *shall* be on my own very much." I handed him a jumper, which he'd left lying on the kitchen floor. "Mrs Denny will be round first thing tomorrow morning, to get on with the sorting out, and to see that I'm eating properly. Mrs Sidderfin will come in with a chocolate cake, then stay for a good snoop around. Mrs Joby from the shop will bring me a pint of milk, and some bread."

"I wasn't exactly thinking about that."

"Oh?"

"No." Steadily, he met my gaze. For a very short moment, I thought I was going to be grabbed again. But he only shrugged. "Take care, then," he said.

"I shall," I promised. "Don't worry about me."

"If you need anything sorted, just give us a ring."

"I'll do that. Nick?"

"What?"

"Thank you for coming over and helping me out, especially this weekend."

"That's okay." He grinned. "I'll be off, then. Give my regards to all the Starkadders. Particularly to the lovely Elfine. Tell her, if she ever gets sick of fields and trees and water voles, I'd be only too happy—"

"Hadn't you better get going?" I interrupted, laughing at him.

"I suppose so. I'll start overheating otherwise." He revved the engine. "See you," he said.

Monday dawned bright and beautiful. One of those clear, crisp autumn mornings which can cause the most sluggish blood to sing and even the heaviest heart to lighten, it was far too lovely a day to spend in the gloom of the loft, getting dusty and fed up. I decided to go out.

But not to visit Simon. For some reason, my courage wasn't quite high enough for that. Instead, I would go and do some drawings from life. I'd take my box of pastels, and try to get some of those late autumnal tints and shades just right.

The snow with which the Met Office had threatened us had fallen on the hills, but completely failed to materialise down here in the valleys. Instead of wading through drifts, I crossed meadows sparkling with hoar frost, and brushed against hedges damp with glistening dew. Sitting on a stile,

I made some pencil sketches of holly leaves and round, red fruit. I drew frosted brambles, and straggling garlands of half-dead bryony.

When my mittened hands had finally become too cold to hold my pencil anything like comfortably, I slid from my seat, pushed my artist's materials into my poacher's pockets, and started for home again. I was hungry, so for lunch I'd have hot chocolate and toasted cheese, a Walnut Whip from the shop, and some of Mrs Denny's lovely orange marmalade on fresh brown bread.

Anticipating this little feast, I skipped over frozen puddles and walked briskly across the cold, wet fields. My chosen path back to The Larches took me past the village pond and then along Ruddle Pit Lane. It seemed a shame to pass Jael's house and not call in.

So I did.

"Hello." She opened the door almost at once. I suppose she'd seen me from the road. "You're ever so muddy," she observed, frowning. "Where've you been?"

"Over the fields, towards Stockley Bridge." I grinned at her. "Don't worry. I'm not stopping. But I was passing, so I thought I ought to knock. To thank you for—"

"You look like you could do with a nice hot drink." Jael turned to go back inside. "Leave them dirty wellies in the porch, and come in for five minutes, eh? I just made a pot of tea."

So I sat at the breakfast bar, watching Jael set out cups, saucers and spoons on a pretty green tray. She was so precise in her movements, so extraordinarily graceful in her every act, that it was pure pleasure to observe her.

But, although her astonishing beauty had scuppered any chances of childhood friendship, these days I wasn't bothered by it at all. I was aware of it, of course – it would have been impossible not be be – but I had long ceased to resent the fact that Jael Taylor had the most fantastic legs, the most beautiful sloping shoulders, a face like the young Audrey Hepburn, and all the rest of it.

For, *I* was an artist. I had a talent, a very little talent certainly, but a talent just the same. Jael, on the other hand, was a housewife in a country village, who would live and die in obscurity, and leave nothing behind her but a name on a grave.

Her kitchen was immaculate again. A gleaming *Homes and Gardens* ideal of varnished pine, reflective chrome and warm red tile, not a single trace of Saturday night's excesses remained. "That was a lovely party," I said, as I accepted my cup of tea. Served, I noticed, in the best china today.

"I'm glad you enjoyed it. Excuse me." Yawning hugely, Jael rubbed her tired eyes. "The babby kept me up nearly the whole of last night," she went on. "It's them first molars. Trying to come through, see."

"I see."

"The nurse at the clinic says to give it a week. Things're bound to improve by then. Meantime, she let me have summat to put on his gums."

"Does it help?"

"I dunno. He just licks it off, seems to me. But he's gone down this morning good as gold. So perhaps we're getting somewhere." Wearily, Jael smiled. "I hope you wasn't bored on Saturday? At the party, I mean?"

"Good heavens, no!" I smiled back at her. "That was why I called in. To thank you. I had a great time. I wasn't bored at all."

"I'm glad to hear it." Jael freshened my cup. "I know it was only a family affair. But when I saw you last week, I thought you looked ever so down. Like you needed a bit of fun, sort of thing."

"A bit of singing and dancing, like?"

"That's right." Then, foxily, Jael grinned. "That young man of yours – he's ever so nice."

"He's not my young man." I looked her straight in the eye. "He's a friend. That's all."

"Oh, yeah?" Still Jael grinned. "Well, whatever he is, I reckon he's all right. He made our Reb's day, and she ain't stopped going on about him since! It's not everyone as can get on with the handicapped, is it? When's he coming back again?"

"I have no idea." I stirred the dregs of my tea, round and round and round. "Perhaps he isn't coming back at all. He sends you his regards, by the way."

"You can give him mine, too. When you see him, that is." But then, Jael frowned. "Look, Lin, I don't mean to pry or anything. But it's not still old Simon, is it?"

"What do you mean?"

"You know." Sighing, she shook her head. "You were so smitten with him! When you two were going around together, you floated about the village two feet off the ground. Or so it seemed to me."

"Oh, Jael! That was ages ago! I was just a child."

"Yeah. I suppose." Jael shook her head. "You don't still love him, then?"

I blushed scarlet. "Well, I'm not *in* love with him," I replied.

"So what were you looking so upset about, on Saturday night? Our Nathan reckons that earlier on, you was almost in tears."

"Did Nathan tell you why?"

"No. But—"

"It was because Simon ignored me. That's why. I went into the kitchen to get some clean plates. I said good evening to Simon and Nathan, who were sitting at the table there. Nathan was all smiles, but Simon cut me dead." I shrugged. "I was hurt, I suppose."

"I'm not surprised." Jael's eyes met mine. "Old Simon – he's a nice chap. But he can be a bit of a misery, just the same. So that's all it was?"

"Yes, of course."

"Right." Jael nodded. "I just wondered. Like I said, I—"

But, before she could finish her sentence, the front door slammed. Heavy footsteps echoed along the hall. "Don't go yet," said Jael, as she rose to welcome her visitor. "Stay for another cup of tea. Have a bit of a natter with Nathan. Yeah? Look, I got some gingerbread in the tin."

"Well, I ought to be going, really . . ."

"Hello, ladies!" The kitchen door opened, and Nathan Casson walked in. Leaning across the breakfast bar, he gave his sister a kiss. "It's all right for some," he observed.

"We was taking a break, that's all." Jael sashayed over to the sink. "You want a cup of tea?"

"Dyin' for one." Nathan took his sister's place. He grinned at me. "You get home all right yesterday?"

"Yes, thank you." I smiled. "What about you?"

"I was okay. Well, it was a bit slippery up Link Top, but they'd gritted down Colwall way, so we coped." He turned to glare at his sister. "Here, you got that kettle on yet?"

"So what's the big rush?" Jael set a plate of gingerbread before him. "Get that down you, eh? It'll give you summat to do with your jaws. Lindsay, do you want a piece?"

"No, thanks. I must be getting home."

"Hang on ten minutes, and Nathan'll give you a lift."

142

Jael poured boiling water over the tea leaves. "So, what you been doin' with yourself today?"

"I went over to see Colonel Harding, up West Bank." Nathan spoke through a mouthful of ginger crumbs. "He says I can cut all that coppice of his for fifty quid, if I'll take the lot away."

"So then you'll sell it, will you?"

"If I can." Nathan shrugged. "There's some new travellers camped down by the ford. I was wonderin' if they're stayin' for the winter. If they makes baskets or anything. I could maybe sell the stuff to them."

"They'd pay you in dud reefers. Not hard cash." Jael pulled a face. "I expect Mr Jackson will move them on, anyway. He won't want his water courses fouled by a load of college drop-outs pretendin' to be earth mothers and stuff. Chuckin' their kids' dirty Pampers and that all over his land." Derisively, she sniffed. Then, "Lindsay enjoyed the party," she added, complacently.

"I should think she did! I never seen her shake a leg like that before. Old Daniel thought it was his lucky night." Slyly, Nathan winked. "We all liked your new bloke," he added. "You thinkin' of getting engaged, or anything?"

"He's just a friend. So she says." Jael milked Nathan's cup. "But he does live with her. In Oxford, like."

"Oh, yeah?" Again, Nathan grinned. "Like that, is it?"

"It's not like anything!" In spite of myself, I found I was blushing furiously. "Nick and I share a house, with several other people. The arrangement is purely financial, and we all have our own—"

"Yeah, course you do." Jael shook her head. Then, she tapped her brother on the shoulder. "Here's another one as can't make up his mind."

"Here, watch it," growled Nathan. "Don't start goin' on. I won't have it!"

"He's got a girl, you know," continued Jael, unabashed. "Gina, isn't it? Lives in Worcester, works in the big Debenhams there. Supposed to be quite a looker, by all accounts. We wouldn't know. He won't bring her home."

"Can you blame me?" Meeting my eye, Nathan grimaced comically. "So I brings her over to Hartley Cross, yeah? What happens then? The Casson family scares the living daylights out of her, that's what! I never sets eyes on her again."

"Oh, come on, Nathan! We never would!"

"Here, Lin. You saw them, Saturday. Carrying on, they was, yelling and shrieking – behaving like Apache Indians, all they wanted was the tomahawks and war paint."

"We wasn't drunk, though! We wasn't incapable of standin' on our own two feet!" Stung, Jael glared at him. "It was you as was pissed out of your head! Slobbering over that old dog of yours, hardly able to walk."

"That was all an act." Reflectively, Nathan shook his head. "Fact is, I was just keeping old Simon company."

"So what *was* the matter with him?" frowned Jael. "I know he gets the miseries now and then, but – well, talk about a wet week and a month of Sundays!"

"He was just a bit low." Nathan shrugged. "I dunno why."

"He's always been moody." Feeling a bit of a traitor, I was nevertheless moved to add my mite. "Even as a boy, he had his off-days, when he wouldn't speak to anyone. Nobody ever knew why. Look, Jael – I must go."

I walked back to The Larches to find Mrs Denny on her hands and knees, scrubbing the tiles in the hallway. When she saw me, she grinned. "Our Alan's coming for the sideboard Friday," she announced. "He's borrowin' Harry Fowler's old lorry, as he takes the pigs to Baines Brothers in."

"Right." Cautiously, I edged past her. "Actually, Nathan Casson's just got a new van. The sideboard would go in easily, so why don't you ask him?"

"I don't want nothing to do with Nathan Casson, thank you very much all the same." Mrs Denny pursed her lips. "Like I said, it's all arranged with Harry Fowler now."

"Okay." If Mrs Denny wanted pig shit all over her new sideboard, that was her affair. "I'm about to get myself some lunch," I told her. "Would you like a sandwich?"

"I only had me dinner half an hour ago! Meat and two veg, nice bit of gravy, that did me. I wouldn't mind a cup of tea, though. If you're making one, that is."

"I'll put the kettle on," I said. I walked into the kitchen.

"There's some teabags in the tin by the stove!" called Mrs Denny. "Lindsay? Don't give me no more of that Earl Grey stuff! It smells of Harpic and tastes like water bewitched, seems to me!"

"How much do I owe you?" I enquired, as Mrs Denny sat at the kitchen table, blowing on her dark brown tea but declining extra milk since, as she frequently pointed out, I didn't keep a cow. I found this business of being an employer so embarrassing. "What I mean is, did my mother remember?"

"We was bang up to date, dear. You don't have to fret about any of that." As cool as I was flushed, Brenda Denny grinned. "So what I reckon is, if you gives me a round thirty quid, that should see us clear up to today. Then, when you goes back to Oxford, I'll pop in now and again, to make sure everything's all right. Shall we say a tenner a week for that?"

"Well, yes. Okay. If you're sure it's enough?"

"It's plenty." But then, her grin faded. "I cleared up all that mess on the lawn," she said.

"Oh, hell!" I clapped my hand to my forehead. "I'd forgotten all about that! Whose were they? Do you know?"

"Well, dear, that's the funny thing." Mrs Denny frowned. "I spoke to Doris Gregson, *and* to Martha Hunt. I even rang that place on the Stockley Road – Williamson, that's the name. But all their birds seem to be present and correct."

"They must have belonged to somebody we haven't thought of, then. Someone who keeps a few bantams in a run. In a back garden, maybe."

"Garden, dear? How do you mean?"

"Well, it must have been the work of foxes."

"No fox done that!" Fiercely, Mrs Denny shook her head. "Where was all the feathers, for a start?"

"That's a point." Puzzled now, I frowned too. "Well, maybe they were pinched from a—"

"They was laid out, too. All the bones, I mean." Brenda Denny looked hard at me. "You do keep your back door bolted, don't you? Especially at night?"

"Yes, of course. But—"

"You mind you do, as well. Close the shutters on the windows, an' all. You can't be too careful. Not these days."

"I'm sorry?" I stared back at her. "Mrs Denny, what are you trying to tell me?"

"Just you make sure you lock up, is all I'm saying. What with all these hippies and what have you about the place. Mrs Cox was sayin' to me only yesterday, there's some more of 'em camped up the common now, been there since Wednesday last. Livin' in them bender things, they are. It's disgustin' if you ask me. Jesus and Mary, my poor old knees today!"

Like a rheumatic hippo, Mrs Denny struggled to her feet. "I reckon we should wash some of that old china this afternoon," she murmured, as she stumped over to the sink. "I got the two big kettles ready. I see you've made a start. So, if we fill the old sink with nice soapy water and add a drop or two of vinegar, we could get the rest of them little cottage things cleaned up nice."

Chapter Thirteen

That Monday evening, after Mrs Denny had gone, I did as she had said. I locked the doors, I closed the heavy, wooden shutters, I drew the curtains, and only then did I sit down to my solitary supper by the kitchen fire. The radio assuaged my loneliness a little. But, all the same, I felt very low.

I was seeing my mother's solicitor the following morning. Perhaps, I thought, I'd ask him to take over completely. To find out if the house was indeed mine and, if it was, to sell it for me and generally wind things up. Then I could go back to Oxford. I'd need never return to Hartley Cross again.

But then, as I stirred my soup, I thought of Simon. I wanted so much to see him, and when I'd finally plucked up enough courage to call at Brougham Gate, see him I would. So, I couldn't leave. Not yet. There was unfinished business between us and, until it was transacted, I knew I'd never rest.

When the telephone rang, I jumped. For a few seconds, I simply stared at it, as it sat there yodelling on top of the fridge.

But you know how it is when the phone rings unexpectedly. How sometimes you think, you just *know*, who is calling? I knew now. It was Simon. Jael or Nathan had

had a quiet word, and he was ringing to apologise, to say sorry for his behaviour on Saturday night. To suggest that we should get together, some time very soon . . .

I hugged myself, aware that a silly grin was spreading itself like butter, right across my face. But then, I pulled myself together. I picked up the handset. "Hello?" I said, as off-hand as you please.

"Good evening!" Nick Singer sounded as if he were on the other side of the world, not just of the Cotswolds. He'd rung, he explained, to tell me my car had been repaired and that he had collected it. "I've parked it at the Clarendon," he told me. "The porters there can keep an eye on it. If that's okay with you?"

I don't honestly know how I managed to reply. But, eventually, I did. "Th-the garage people let you take it away?" I stammered, incredulous. "Just like that?"

"Yes," he replied. There was a theatrical pause. "After I'd paid the bill, of course."

"Oh, Nick, you didn't?"

"I most certainly did." There was another pause. "All right, you don't have to say it. I already know I'm wonderful. But now, I'm afraid, you have to pay *me*."

"I'll post you a cheque, first thing tomorrow morning."

"Please make sure you do."

"I promise, on my honour." I reached for a notepad and pencil. "How much do I owe you, then?"

"Two hundred and fifty-three pounds, seventy-four pence. It does include VAT."

"I can probably get that back." All the same, I thought, it's a lot of cash to find at once, and is the car actually worth two hundred and fifty quid? I rather doubted it . . .

But Flora wasn't just any old car. She was my friend, and I loved her dearly. I was glad she was better again.

"Right," I told her redeemer, "consider yourself repaid, with all best wishes and many thanks. Oh, and Nick?"

"Yes?"

"How's work?"

"Well, I don't know if I dare say this out loud. But I think – I hope and pray – that I'm getting somewhere at last."

"That's good!"

"It is, isn't it?" I thought he'd ring off then. But, to my surprise, it seemed he actually wanted to talk to me. "Tonight," he continued, "it's all systems go. I've got some quite positive results. I've also stopped listening to Maclean."

"Who?"

"My supervisor. Professor Adrian Maclean, CBE." Nick grunted in disgust. "Should be NBG for 'no bloody good' as well, if you ask me."

"Why, what's he done?"

"Only wasted eighteen months of my life, the stupid bastard. He's supposed to be a physicist but – and I didn't know this until recently – last year he went off his head. Became a born-again Christian, if you please. He goes to some Pentecostal church in a scout hut up the Banbury Road, along with blokes who've got dandruff in their beards, and girls in hideous flowery skirts who never shave their legs up past their knees."

"Oh, Nick!" In spite of myself, I giggled. "You shouldn't mock."

"I'll mock all I please," growled Nick. "You don't understand what I'm saying, do you? The fact of the matter is, my supervisor's lost it. If I were a medical student, I'd probably have killed off half a dozen patients by now. There'd be summonses flying about all over the place."

"It's that bad, is it?"

"Worse." Again, Nick grunted. "But, fortunately for me and everyone else concerned, *I* mess about with inanimate matter. Rather than with human beings, who can object and complain."

"Couldn't you change your supervisor?"

"That would be quite difficult, actually. I'm not sure I would want to, anyway. You see, before he went round the twist, Adrian Maclean was an acknowledged world expert in my particular field. At one time, he was even tipped for a Nobel prize."

"What went wrong?"

"It's hard to say. Alzheimer's, perhaps? CJD? I blame his wife, myself."

"Oh? Why's that?"

"She's an awful woman! Built like a tank, ugly as sin, and mad as a March hare. She calls herself a psychic. I believe she holds seances, where she raises the spirits and makes pots and pans fly up in the air."

"Goodness!"

"The very first time I met her, she told me I had the most hostile aura she'd ever seen. My mind was closed, I was a mysogynist, a misanthropist and – oh, I can't remember what else. Mass murderer in the making, I dare say. I'd never be a people person, she said. Oh, and I also have this obstruction around my third eye."

"I bet that's painful," I teased. "Poor Nick. But maybe you *should* open your mind a little? Find your own personal karma. Then you'll stop chasing married women, and take more interest in people as a whole."

"I do take interest in people! I take a very great interest in some." He paused for a moment. "But I do tend to take the long view of world history. On that sort of time scale, human life is a mere blip on the screen."

"Your professor who's found God – perhaps he's taking the long view, too?"

"In a scout hut up the Banbury Road? I doubt it. Adrian's just off his rocker. Or perhaps he's having it away with a gorgeous undergraduate and this is all a cover? Now there's an entertaining thought. Well, I suppose I ought to let you get on."

"Hang on a moment!" The truth was, I didn't want him to leave me. I hated being alone in this great empty house, and if I could keep him talking all night, then I would. "Nick, I . . ."

"What?"

"I want to ask you something." Cast around for a big subject, I thought. Yes, that'll do. I drew a deep breath. "Nick, do you really think all religious belief is delusion?"

"Of course. It's garbage. All of it. Although I'll admit some religions offer their adherents a load of extremely *refined* crap."

"Why are so many people religious, then?"

"Because they don't want to die."

"I'm sorry?"

"Most, in fact, *all* the religions I can think of promise eternal life. In one from or another. So, dear Lindsay, religious faith is a must-have, especially for people who think they're so damned important that no way can the death of the body be the end." Nick sighed. "There are a depressing number of conceited bastards out there."

"What about you, then?" I enquired. "You're important, aren't you?"

"Of course I am. To me, anyway." He laughed. "I don't go in for all that, 'I look at the stars and feel humble and insignificant' stuff, definitely. But in certain moods, I *do* feel comforted by the thought that human life is not here to stay. The planet will outlast us. I like that idea very much indeed."

"We'll never be able to blow it to smithereens, then?"

"No chance. We'll dent the surface a bit, that's all. We'll destroy most present forms of life, perhaps. But viruses and bacteria may well survive intact. Then, after a few million years, higher forms of life will re-emerge from the mess."

"Will they?"

"Certainly. They'll be mutated, of course. Totally buggered up. But I hope and believe that if we do foul things up completely and blow ourselves to kingdom come, everything will start all over again. You never know – purple hedgehogs and green aardvarks might well make a damned good job of civilisation."

"Oh." I shivered. "Talking of viruses, I read an article in the *Independent* recently, which talked about some awful virus they think could take over the planet."

"A virus might," he agreed. "Yeah, a little squirmy thing with no brain might just finish off the lot of us."

"Don't sound so gleeful about it."

"Sorry."

"I'd like to believe in God," I said, almost wistfully.

"I'd like to *be* God." Nick cackled then, and I could just imagine him grinning his mad scientist's grin. "Creating galaxies, hurling solar systems into the big black void. That would be my idea of fun!"

But now, he yawned. He was bored by this conversation. He wanted to get back to his experiment, I could tell. "Anyway, sweetheart," he said, as if on cue, "this phone call must be costing a fortune. I'd actually meant it to be quick. Just to tell you your car's been fixed."

"I'll stick a couple of quid in the jar," I told him. "When I get back to Ferry Road, that is. I kept you talking, after all."

"Right." Nick sighed. "It must be wonderful, to have a proper job. To earn real money, to be able to afford expensive phone calls, and that. I sometimes wish I were you. Instead of an impoverished postgraduate, with the biggest overdraft known to mortal man."

"I must actually *do* some work this week," I said. I had a commission to paint a series of greetings cards, for a gratifyingly up-market graphics company. "So anyway, thanks again. I'll expect I'll see you soon."

"Before you go, just tell me something."

"What?"

"That Simon guy," began Nick. "He—"

"What about him?" Suddenly, my mouth dried. My heart began to thud. "Nick?"

"He means a lot to you, doesn't he?"

"W-why do you ask?"

"Sorry?"

"Who's been talking to you about me?"

"Nobody." Again, Nick sighed. "Nobody, honestly. It's none of my business, anyway. Good night, Lindsay. Sleep tight."

Chapter Fourteen

After I'd spoken to Nick, I felt calmer. It was much too early to go to bed, so I did some work on the commission, which consisted mainly of painting a selection of summer flowers in watercolour from photographs, pencil sketches and memory. I hoped this might lead to a contract to illustrate a gardening manual. Photographs are more generally used, it's true. But line drawings and the occasional painting are also commissioned, as it's thought they give that sort of publication a bit of class.

One day, I thought, as I worked on into the night, I might actually paint a picture to hang on a wall. A picture I wanted people to stand back and look at. Rather than stick on a shelf for a week, then throw away. One day, one day . . .

The following morning I went into Hereford and saw the solicitor, who looked at me over his half-moon spectacles and informed me that these things took time. That he wouldn't be at all keen to take over completely, not at present anyway, and that it would be most convenient for all concerned if I could stay at Hartley Cross, at least for the time being.

"But how long will the time being *be*?" I enquired.

"I'm sorry? Oh – I see." Mr Harrison shrugged. "Until Christmas, at any rate."

"Have you written to my father?"

"I believe there is a letter in the post." The solicitor pursed his lips. "Mr Ellis is being a little unco-operative just at the present time."

"I can imagine." I sighed. "I'd better write to him myself."

"My dear Miss Ellis, please don't do that!"

"Whyever not?"

"I – that is, Harrison, Fenwick and Co – would prefer you left all the official correspondence in connection with the handling of your late mother's estate strictly to us." Mr Harrison spread his hands wide. "But there is, of course, no reason why you should not *speak* to your father, either in person or on the telephone. No reason at all."

"Thank you." I stood up. I was getting nowhere here so, after glancing at my watch, and realising that if I were to catch the two-twenty bus back to Hartley Cross I'd have to run, I collected up my carrier bags. "You'll be in touch, then?" I enquired.

"Of course!" Mr Harrison smiled. He'd put me straight, so now he could afford to be nice. Old-fashioned gentleman that he was, he rose to his feet and moved smartly across the room in order to open the door. "Good day to you, Miss Ellis!" he cried. "My goodness, just look at that sky. Do you think we may have snow?"

I spent the rest of that week holed up in my bedroom, working. I saw nobody, I heard nothing, and I refused even to think about Simon Dyer. This required an enormous effort of will. But finally, by the simple expedient of forcing myself to concentrate on roses and violets and delphiniums, I managed to block him out of my scheme of things.

156

I find that if I eat too much, my mind tends to wander. So that week, I ate enough to survive on, but no more. I squirrelled my way through a bag of peanuts. I spooned up yogurt. In the fridge was a huge piece of mousetrap cheddar, from which I cut great hunks, to munch on as I drew.

On Friday morning, Mrs Denny came stumping up the garden path. Depositing her bag and brolly in the scullery, she fished in the closet for her lime green nylon overall, then shouted up the stairs to me. "Lindsay? You all right up there?" Then, meaning to entice me down, "d'you want a piece of my walnut sandwich?"

I could think of nothing I'd like better. "Yes, please!" I shouted back. "Have you put the kettle on?"

"I'm just going to, now." Mrs Denny waddled back into the kitchen. She opened the door of the fridge and then, as I'd expected, I heard her exclamation of dismay. "You been starving yourself, girl?" she cried as I appeared in the doorway, muffled in at least three jumpers and bearing a dozen or more dirty mugs and plates on a butler's tray. "You ain't gettin' that anex-whatsitsname business, are you?"

"Anorexia nervosa? Of course not!" I ran hot water into the big china sink. "But when I'm working, I never stop to cook. There simply isn't time."

"So, you been living off that there lump of cheese." Mrs Denny clucked her disapproval. "It's a wonder you ain't had bad dreams! Well – I expect you *have*. If I'd realised, I'd have fetched you over a few plates of stew."

The kettle boiled. I made a pot of tea, then we both sat down at the kitchen table, to drink it. "Just a little drop of milk," said Mrs Denny, as I poured. She'd add more later, but surreptitiously, as if having enough milk in one's tea was a wicked indulgence, and pouring it a disgraceful act.

The walnut cake was excellent, so I ate three large slices, which pleased Mrs Denny enormously. "You're just like your mother," she remarked, as she watched me stuff myself. "*She* wasn't interested in food, neither. Never ate anything as wasn't plonked down smack in front of her, with written instructions as to what to do next!"

I grinned, as I knew I must. "This cake is delicious," I told her. Pouring more tea, I gave Mrs Denny what I hoped was my most disarming smile. "How is your rheumatism this week?" I asked her. "Did those new tablets from the doctor help at all?"

"I suppose they mighter done." Mrs Denny sighed her Christian martyr's sigh. "But it ain't been wet since Tuesday, so I wouldn've had that many aches and pains anyway. When it rains'll be the testin' time."

"Did you find out who lost the chickens?"

"Chickens?" Mrs Denny frowned. "Oh, you mean them things on your lawn. No, I never heard nothing about that."

"Somebody must have mentioned it, surely?"

"Maybe. But, like I says, *I* ain't heard nothing." Mrs Denny looked straight at me now, staring directly into my eyes. "If I was you, I'd forget all about it."

"Why?"

"Some things is better left alone. That's why."

"But it was only a few dead chickens."

"You take my advice." Pursing her lips, Mrs Denny nodded sagely. "Do as I do – keep your bowels open, and your mouth closed."

I smiled at this, but Mrs Denny didn't, and it was with

158

some disquietude that I realised she hadn't meant to make a joke. I was just about to ask her to explain herself when I heard the sound of a car's engine.

It was *my* car's engine! I ran to the window and – yes, my own dear little Renault had come home! There it was, all bright and shining, idling in the drive!

"That your fella come back?" enquired Mrs Denny slyly, as she observed my stare of delighted disbelief.

"I don't know." But I did know! I flung open the back door. "Let's go and see."

We appeared on the gravel sweep just as Nick was locking the driver's door. At the sight of him looking all dishevelled, and of Flora looking all bright and new and washed and clean, I grinned like an idiot. "Well!" I exclaimed. "*What* a surprise!"

"A pleasant one, I hope." Nick looked grave. But I could see his lips twitching at the corners, so knew it was only a matter of moments before he would start smirking all over his face. He wouldn't be able to help it. He'd met Mrs Denny at the shop, and she was one of his favourites. She and Mrs Sidderfin occupied a particularly special place in his gallery of rural grotesques.

But I don't suppose Brenda Denny thought much of Nick, either. He was scruffy, he was cheeky and, as her best friend Mrs Sidderfin knew full well, he hadn't two brain cells to rub together. He went out in winter without a coat on, wearing just a grubby old jumper, which let the damp right through. "Well, young man," she muttered, "I expect you'll need a cup of tea next." She stumped off into the darkness of the house.

Nick and I stood on the sweep. "You weren't insured," I observed, as he handed me the bunch of keys.

"Then it's just as well I didn't have a shunt." Yawning,

he rubbed his eyes. "That old dragon said I needed a cup of tea."

"So she did."

"Do I get one?"

"Of course!" I beamed at him. "I'll make you a sandwich, too!"

"Does it have to be cheese?"

"I'm afraid so. But there's walnut cake to follow."

"Then I suppose I'll come in." But now, Nick glanced towards Flora. "There was a bit of a rattle as I drove through the village," he told me. "I'll take a quick look, I think. Whilst the engine's still warm."

"I'll go and make your sandwich," I said.

"So, *is* he your young man?" demanded Mrs Denny, as I spread butter on thick slices of fresh, brown bread. "All official, like?"

"Good heavens, no! He's a friend, that's all." I cut into my still enormous lump of cheese. "He's a fellow tenant, at the house in Oxford where I usually live."

"Nice looking lad." Reflectively, Mrs Denny sucked at her false teeth. "I always like a dark-haired man meself. In *my* opinion, yeller hair looks daft on a boy. Why did you say he come here?"

"My car broke down. He gave me a lift. I'm sure I told you."

"P'raps you mighter said something." Mrs Denny looked round for her bag and umbrella. "Well, I suppose I'd best be getting on my way. I only popped in to find out how you was."

"I'm fine. As you can see." I smiled. "Thank you for the cake. It was lovely."

Mrs Denny went home for her dinner. Nick ate his lunch, then suggested going out for a walk. "I ought to be

160

working, really," I told him. "Especially just now, whilst the light's so good."

"Whilst the creative mood's upon me. Whilst the Muse is whispering sweet nothings into my shell-like ear," Nick mocked. Frowning, he shook his head at me. "God, but you look peaky!"

"Do I?"

"Yeah, you do! So come on, Picasso. You need a bit of fresh air and exercise today."

"Maybe," I admitted. Well, I supposed he was right. I *had* been shut up for the best part of a week, after all. So I fetched my coat and boots.

"How much of the land around the house actually belongs to you?" enquired Nick, as we set off down the drive.

"All of it," I replied. "Why?"

"I just wondered." He shrugged. "It's a bit of a mess, isn't it? But I suppose you'd need a full time gardener and half a dozen people under *him*, to keep all this looking good. So tell me, do you actually have some fellows in your employ?"

He was off again, the sarcastic bastard. "Mr Cox used to come over now and again," I muttered. "Nick, please don't go on—"

"If you've got a scythe or something," he interrupted, "I'll have a go at all that long grass some time." He grinned. "Come on, then! Pick your feet up, otherwise we won't get there until it's time to come home again."

We crossed the paddocks behind the house, then began to make for a stand of poplars half a mile or so away. "That's better," said Nick, as he stood aside to let me go through a five-bar gate. "You've got a bit more colour now."

161

"You mean, I'm bright red in the face?"

"No, you look less washed-out. That's all." Again, he shook his head. "When you came round the side of the house this morning – as I was locking up the car, I mean – I thought you looked like one of the living dead. All pale and bloodless, you were. Just like a ghost."

"I'm always pale."

"Yeah, I've noticed." He followed me through the gate. "I reckon you might be anaemic," he continued. "Well, you're always cold, aren't you? Always shivering. I suppose that's because you're too thin."

"Hasn't anyone ever told you it's rude to make personal remarks?" I could feel my colour now! Two spots of red embarrassment were blotching my pale cheeks. "Look, I might think *your* appearance leaves a lot to be desired. All the same, I'd never dream of saying so."

"But I didn't mean it like that!" Nick stared at me. "I never meant to suggest you were . . . well, the fact is, you're a very attractive girl. It's just that you—"

"Please don't say any more." I glared at him. "Okay, you're right. I need to eat more, I need to put on *huge* amounts of weight. We're agreed. Happy now?"

I didn't wait for his answer. My hands in my pockets, my face still crimson, I strode on ahead, leaving Nick to catch up as best he could.

If he wanted to.

The stile into the next field was narrow. The lower bars were very muddy, and instead of my usual jeans or leggings, that day I was wearing a fullish, longish skirt. Bunching it round my knees, I began to clamber over. Then, however, my left foot slipped, and I fell.

But, instead of tumbling head first into a muddy puddle, I was suddenly pulled upright again. Steadying me by the elbow, my rescuer held me until I'd regained a precarious balance. As the alternative was falling flat on my face, I was more or less obliged to let Nick help me down.

"I'm sorry," he said, as we stood on level ground once more. "I didn't mean to annoy you back there."

"I know you didn't." Somewhat less annoyed now, I met his gaze. I shrugged. "It was my fault," I told him. "I'm a bit touchy today."

"No, you're not. Your anger was perfectly justified. *I* was very rude." He tried to look contrite, I'll give him that. I didn't know whether to kick him or laugh at him, lousy actor that he was, thinking he could get round me. Just like that . . .

I chose to laugh. Nick grinned. "Can we be friends again?" he asked, in the smallest, meekest voice imaginable.

"Only if you'll share your crisps at break-time, and let me borrow your new ruler," I replied.

We reached the stand of poplars and sat down on a bed of crisp, dry leaves. The afternoon was clear and blue, and the horizon sharp, even though it was six or seven miles away.

I picked up fallen leaves, examined them, tore them along their veins to aid decomposition, then put them down again. But Nick sat staring into the middle distance, his arms wrapped round his knees. "Doing another sum?" I enquired.

"No." He turned to glance at me. "I don't mean to upset you," he began. He looked away again. "You'll find this hard to believe, I know. But most of the time, I'm trying to be kind."

"I do know that." I shrugged. "Don't take any notice of me. I'm always—"

"I upset you on Monday, too," he continued. "When I rang you about the car."

"No, you didn't. I was very pleased."

"About the car, yes. But when I asked about that Simon bloke, you were very annoyed."

"You took me by surprise. That's all." Again, I shrugged. "Honestly."

"Good." He looked at me. "I'm not being nosy, but . . ."

"But what?"

"You and Simon. I don't want to pry . . ."

He was trying so hard to be tactful that it was almost funny. "Simon and I were lovers," I said.

"Ah." He held my gaze. "But you're not any more?"

"No." I picked up a fallen twig. I examined it minutely, then let it fall again. "In fact, until this month, we hadn't seen each other for ages. Years, actually. There've been no letters, phone calls – nothing. The break was complete."

"I see," said Nick.

"I expect you guessed, anyway."

"No." He shook his head. "You've taken *me* by surprise this time."

The field we sat in was dairy pasture. Black and white Friesians stood under the trees and out in the open meadow, pulling straw from scattered bales, investigating salt-licks, or patiently cropping the damp, winter grass.

I was surprised to find Nick was unfazed by this. After all, city-bred people are often afraid of cows. Now, one came right up to him, staring gormlessly into his eyes. "Bugger off, Buttercup," he muttered. He gave it a shove. It buggered off. "What happened here?" he asked, softly.

"Nothing much." I tore another leaf into two jagged bits. "Well, somebody died."

"Do you want to talk about it?"

"To you?"

"If you like." Nick shrugged. "But only if you want, of course."

"It's Saturday tomorrow." I tugged at a piece of dry, brown grass. "I expect you're looking forward to a game."

"No. I shan't be playing for weeks yet. It's all that time spent in the lab, you see – I'm seriously unfit these days." He grinned. "Those bastards from Corpus would make mincemeat of me."

"Oh." I tore up more grass. "I'm surprised you play rugby," I observed. "I would have thought your game would be soccer. Since you come from down south."

"I went to a school where the headmaster was a Welsh-man. So we could choose one or the other." Again, Nick shrugged. "I decided I preferred rugby."

"Why?"

"It's far more civilised."

"*Is* it?" Incredulously, I laughed. "So tearing other people's ears off and knocking out their teeth is civi-lised, is it?"

"You've changed the subject," he said.

"Yes," I agreed.

"Does that mean I'm to mind my own business?"

"Not at all," I replied.

So then I told him. How Simon and I had been so crazy about one another, so passionately, insanely in love that nothing else mattered. How, one sunny afternoon in high summer, I had found his father lying lifeless in the cool half-light of the kitchen at Brougham Gate. How, after his father's death, Simon had become so distraught that he had a breakdown.

I had wanted to comfort him – yearned to help, even if helping him amounted to nothing more than standing by his side – but I'd been unable to do anything at all. Simon had wanted nothing to do with me.

In spite of leaving out the details of Simon's arrest, his trial, and all the particularly horrible parts of the tale, I found I was almost in tears by now. But Nick made no attempt to comfort me. Instead, realising there was a great deal of the story missing, he prompted me to go on. "What happened to Louis?" he enquired.

"I told you. He died."

"How?"

"It's shocking. Disgusting."

"Yes?" He didn't press me, but I felt his interest – I won't say curiosity, for there were no undertones of prurience, or ghoulishness, or anything like that – and, to my surprise, I realised it would be an enormous relief to tell. "If you must know," I muttered, "somebody broke into the house and murdered him."

"I see."

"Do you want to know how?"

"Only if you want to tell me."

"They beat him unconscious, then nailed him to the floor with a marlin spike. Or a piton. Something like that, anyway. You know, the sort of thing rock climbers use."

"I know." Nick didn't look shocked. Or disgusted. Just interested. "Did they – um – was he pierced through the head?" he enquired.

"How did you know that?"

"I didn't know. I guessed." He shrugged. "It's just like that Bible story, isn't it?"

"Which Bible story is this?"

"Oh, come on! You must know it. The story of Jael and Sisera. It's in *Judges*, I believe. Or perhaps it's *Chronicles*. Round about there, anyway." As I continued to shake

166

my head, he frowned at me. "God, you're ignorant," he muttered.

"There you go again!" I glared at him. "I'm sorry, but we can't all be as well-informed as you!"

"Apparently not." Glancing down at his knees, he brushed some dead leaves off his jeans. "I couldn't half do with a cup of coffee," he observed.

"Oh, really?"

"I'm frozen." Once more, he turned to look at me. "You don't look too warm and cosy yourself. Shall we go home?"

I scrambled to my feet.

"Didn't they offer you counselling or anything?" asked Nick, as we strode briskly across the open fields, making our way back to Hartley Cross.

"I had a long chat with a policewoman, if that's what you mean." Remembering, I shrugged. "She was trained to comfort traumatised females, apparently. Rape victims. Battered wives. Assaulted old-age pensioners, and that. I suppose they felt she was the ideal person to talk to me."

"But they didn't suggest you should see a specially trained counsellor? Or a psychiatrist, or have any other sort of therapy?"

"No. Do you think that would have been a good idea?"

"Possibly." Momentarily, Nick glanced at me. "It might have helped, to talk things through."

"I don't think my mother approved of talking things through. Not with psychiatrists, anyway. She'd have said that sort of thing was self-indulgent and unnecessary."

"Did she discuss it all with you?"

"Good heavens, no!" I laughed. "My mother was a hoarder," I told him. "She kept all her thoughts and fancies in neat little parcels, and stored anything unpleasant away, at the back of her mind. There it stayed."

Back home at The Larches, I made a pot of coffee, then took it through to the drawing room, where Nick was trying to coax some action from the invariably sullen fire. He soon had it drawing nicely, and I was impressed. The wretched thing would only ever smoke for me. "You're a genius," I told him, as the bright scarlet flames blazed.

"Shall I tell you the secret?" He sat back on his heels. "You screw up some old newspaper, lay—"

"I know all that," I interrupted. "But I think getting a decent fire going is like making a good sponge cake. You just have to have the knack." I covered the coffee pot with an old tea cosy. "Tell me that story," I said.

"What? Oh – yeah, okay." He rubbed his eyes. "Once upon a time," he yawned, "there was this king of Hebron. Or Jericho, or somewhere. The Israelites were giving him a bit of aggravation. Pinching his goats and sheep, I suppose. Raping his virgins, and that.

"So, he sent his army over to sort them out. Sisera was the king's general, or something – at any rate, he was the bloke in charge. May I have some coffee?"

"In a minute. Go on."

"If you go and get your Bible, you can look this up for yourself."

"I said, go on!"

"So Sisera gets his act together, the Israelites form up, and there's a battle. The Israelites win, and soon Sisera and his army are on the run."

"What's this got to do with Louis Dyer?"

"Hang about. On the way back to wherever it is, Sisera comes across this camp belonging to some tribe or other which has a treaty or something with the Israelites, but

168

Sisera doesn't know that. Their guy in charge is somebody whose name I've forgotten. Jael is his wife.

"Jael decides to deal with Sisera once and for all. She sees he's dead beat, so she invites him to take a nap on her goatskin rug. Then, whilst he's asleep, she gets a tent peg and hammers it through his skull, nailing him to the landscape."

"Oh." I swallowed hard. "Charming."

"Isn't it just?" agreed Nick.

"Yes." I narrowed my eyes at him. "But now I'm wondering if you just made all that up."

"Of course I didn't!" Innocence personified, Nick stared back at me. "Tell me, Lindsay – where *did* you go to school? The Bash Street Comprehensive, was it?"

"No. I went to Bishop Latimer's Church of England Grammar. It was direct grant, as a matter of fact."

"Yet you don't know the story of Jael and Sisera. That's absolutely terrible." Gloomily, Nick sighed. "The country's going to the dogs. Could I have that coffee now?"

"Certainly." I make excellent coffee, anyway. I know the trick of it. You must catch the water just off the boil, then pour it very slowly over the grounds. Not slosh it in, any old how.

"What do you want to do about supper tonight?" asked Nick, as he stirred in sugar and cream.

"I'll make us some scrambled eggs on toast," I replied, daring him to demand chips. "Then we'll have some more of the walnut sandwich."

"Okay." He sipped his coffee. "I was afraid it would be something healthy, like salad. But scrambled eggs will be fine by me."

To my surprise, Nick and I went on to spend a most

169

pleasantly companionable evening. Relaxing in the wing chairs which were planted on either side of the fireplace, Nick studied his yards and yards of computer print-out, occasionally stabbing at it with a felt tip pen, whilst I did some sketches for a new series of birthday cards. They weren't half bad.

At half-past nine, we both had hot chocolate and cinnamon biscuits, the latter courtesy of Mrs Sidderfin, who had – as she put it – just dropped them in. She wanted to size up the situation between me and Nick, I supposed. She must have been very upset when she did not find us *in flagrante* on the kitchen floor.

At ten, I went to bed.

As I lay snuggled under my duvet, dozing off, I heard Nick go into the kitchen. He drew the big bolts across the back door, then put the covers down on the range. He locked the front door, too. Then he went back into the drawing room, closed the shutters, and presumably settled down to more sums.

He did lead an exciting life.

Saturday was spent clearing out the last of the lumber from the biggest of the attics. It was growing dark, and I was just about to suggest driving into Worcester to have an Indian meal, or go to the cinema – my treat – when Nick said he had to get back.

No, he couldn't stay the night. There was something he had to do, and Sunday was a good time to be in the labs, for the undergraduates were all lying in bed with hangovers, and Professor Maclean was busy praising the Lord.

"Can you give me a lift to Worcester?" he asked. "In about ten minutes time? I could catch the fast train back to Oxford then."

So I took Nick to Shrub Hill station, then drove home again for another early night. I went to bed with a mug of hot milk and the last slice of walnut sandwich. I'd found my mother's Coronation Bible, too.

"*The Book of Judges*, I would guess," Nick had muttered, when I'd pressed him. "Oh, I dunno where! Near the beginning, probably. Round about Chapter 4, I think."

He was spot on. What a well-informed little physicist he was, I thought, as I read the story through.

Putting the Bible to one side again, I shuddered. Nick hadn't got it quite right, but it was a perfectly horrible story all the same. As for the tent peg business – it seemed that whoever killed Louis had certainly wanted to implicate Jael.

Very clever. Except that nobody in Hartley Cross had picked up the reference! So all that work with the marlin spike had been for nothing.

What a shame.

So was Simon guilty after all? Had he tried to point the finger at Jael? Or – since he was the one who'd been arrested, and he it was who had stood trial – had he in fact been protecting Jael?

Could Simon and Jael have been in it together? Had they conspired to kill Louis, and divide the spoils of murder between them? Frowning, I bit my lip. It had never occurred to me before.

Simon and Jael. She always spoke of him with concern. She always looked out for old Simon. So, were they lovers? Quite possibly. I shuddered again. Oh God, I thought, how could I have been so blind?

I wanted to talk to Nick. He had promised to come back the following weekend. I wished he were here now! I needed him.

Chapter Fifteen

The week dragged by. I stayed indoors and worked on my commission, spending hour after painstaking hour over the execution of one small rosebud, one individual flower head. I suppose I was quite pleased with the results.

But, all the time, my internal radar was trained on Brougham Gate. My thoughts and yearnings turned towards Simon Dyer, whom I longed to see – but was now too afraid to go and call on. For, if I saw him, would I be able to tell? Might it be perfectly obvious that he and Jael shared a terrible secret? If so, what would I do then?

I had been a pawn in the game. That much at least was clear. I had been meant to find Louis Dyer's body, for the murderer had known I would return to the house. He had also intended that the person to raise the alarm should be me.

But who *was* the murderer? Simon? Jael? Simon and Jael together? Or a jealous and furious Saul Casson, perhaps, already outraged by Louis Dyer's seduction – actual or metaphorical, it wouldn't have really mattered to Saul – of his daughter, and fearful for the safety of his other children? Particularly for that of the helpless, damaged one?

Ten times in the course of that week, I put on my coat and boots and set off in the direction of Brougham Gate.

Ten times I reached the village shop, went in and bought a newspaper, then went back home again.

"You don't still love him, then?" Jael's simple question, which had seemed so innocent and sympathetic at the time, echoed round and round my head until it became a sneer of triumph. A confident assumption of her own superiority. "That's just as well, really," she was implying, "because Simon Dyer loves *me*. He always has, and he always will."

Did the whole of the Casson clan know about their affair? Daniel and Nathan, Samuel and Naomi – did they all know what their sister got up to, behind her husband's back? As for poor, deluded Lindsay – were they so kind and considerate nowadays simply because they pitied me?

I longed for Nick to come to Hartley Cross. He'd promised to return that weekend. But I knew how important his work was, and I'd already steeled myself for a hurried phone call to tell me that this was it, he was at last turning base metal into gold. So he couldn't get away. Sorry, and all that. Some other time, perhaps.

All the same, on Saturday morning I was up early. I made up a bed for my guest, then I dashed down to the shop for a loaf of white, steam-baked sliced, some of Mrs Joby's Rhode Island Reds' delicious brown eggs, and a few cans of Heinz baked beans for Nick to have on toast.

But Nick did not turn up. Ten o'clock, eleven o'clock, twelve o'clock came and went. Finally, I made myself some very late elevenses, then plonked myself down at the kitchen table, where I dunked a ginger biscuit sulkily. He might have rung, I thought. He might have written a postcard, dropped me a line.

One o'clock struck. Two o'clock. Three. By half-past

three, I'd given him up. Then, just as I was about to go and fetch another tray load of antique china to wash and put away, I heard the car wheels crunch on the gravel drive.

My expression set like concrete in a where do you think *you've* been until this time sort of scowl, I went to open the kitchen door. But, as I flung it wide, Nick came sauntering up the garden path, and the grin on his face was so delightful – and delighted, I might add – that I found I was grinning back.

"Hello, Lin." He stood on the threshold, evidently not daring to presume right of entry, but looking so jaunty and self-confident that he clearly had no fear whatsoever of being turned away. "So how are you?"

"I'm fine," I replied. "Just fine!"

"That's good. I must say, you look very well." His eyes searched my face. "You've been taking a few breaks, then? Getting out into the fresh air now and again?"

"Now and again," I agreed. Well, I had been down to the minimart.

"Coffee?" he prompted.

"Of course." I stood aside. "Come in."

We drank coffee, ate some sandwiches, then Nick decided he wanted a newspaper. Even the *Telegraph* would do. So we walked down to the shop.

In the chilly twilight, with the shadows lengthening and the creatures of the night rustling and chittering, getting ready for their own Saturday night out of killing or being killed, I was glad of Nick's solid, reassuring company. For I have never liked that part of the day, the hour when time hovers spookily between darkness and light.

We went into the shop. A trio of teenagers, their hair spiked and gelled, were negotiating with Mrs Joby, who was wearily trying to insist that she wasn't legally allowed to sell cans of Hooper's Hooch to anyone under eighteen.

"Sell it to us *il*legally then," suggested Matthew Pryor, the son of the local vet. Slapping a five pound note down on the counter, he grinned encouragingly. "They're for my sister's party, anyway. Not for me."

"Gissa packet of B & H?" added Gillian Hardwick, whom I'd last seen sitting in her pram, with melted chocolate biscuit smeared all over her pudgy face. "They're for me mum. Really they are!" Inspired, she grinned. "She says to put 'em on the slate, an' she'll be round to pay you when she gets her giro, oughter be first thing Monday morning."

"What can you say to them?" sighed Mrs Joby, as the children trooped out again, booze and fags in an anonymous carrier bag, triumphant grins on their round, babyish faces. "If *I* don't sell 'em the stuff, they'll only go and pinch Mr Pryor's animal drugs or summat, and prob'ly kill theirselves then, into the bargain. Trouble is, they got nothing else to do."

"Don't they belong to the Young Farmers' Club?" I enquired.

"There isn't one in Hartley Cross." Again, Mrs Joby sighed. "Not any more. There's only about half a dozen teenagers lives in the village nowadays. Yes, me dear? You want that last *Telegraph*, do you?"

"Yes, please." Nick handed over a fistful of change. He regarded the postmistress gravely. "I'm almost old enough to buy it, honestly."

Mrs Joby gave him a very old-fashioned look.

As we came out into the cold twilight again, we almost fell over Jael. Her hair swept up into a luxuriant chignon, her lovely eyes sparkling, her complexion glowing golden in the early evening light, she looked so beautiful that I felt all the resentment, jealousy and dislike of childhood wash over me like a bitter tide, swamping me anew. It was all I could do even to mouth hello.

Then, out of the shadows, loomed other Cassons and I realised this was a family outing. Jael, Nathan and Rebekah had, I supposed, been to visit Naomi. They were coming from the general direction of her house, anyway. Now, they were going back to Ruddle Pit Lane, where they'd have a nice meat tea, courtesy of Baines Brothers, Slaughtermen.

But this particular outing was also a show of opulence, for Jael's baby was taking what was evidently his first airing in a magnificent new pushchair. Padded and chromium-plated, mud-guarded and accessorised, it was top of the range at Mothercare, most definitely. Grinning from ear to ear, Rebekah was proudly steering, while Nathan ambled along the kerbside, presumably to avert any blunder or mistake on Rebekah's part.

It was just as well Nathan *was* sauntering along by his sister's side, for when she saw who was with me, Rebekah let go of the buggy at once. Throwing her arms around his neck, she planted a great, wet kiss on each of Nick's cheeks. "Nick!" Beaming like a lighthouse, she hugged and kissed him like a brother, then kissed him again. "Oh, Nick!" she breathed, grinning in ecstasy.

"Hello, Reb." Equanimity itself, Nick submitted to these damp embraces with a fortitude which almost made me love him. "How you doing, then?" he enquired.

"How you doing?" Rebekah frowned. But then, understanding, she laughed out loud. "How you doing, how you doing," she cried, while Jael grimaced, Nathan looked well entertained, and poor Nick was almost asphyxiated in a bear hug which pinioned his arms to his sides and left him defenceless against Rebekah's enthusiastic delight.

"Well now, young Lindsay," observed Nathan, shaking his head and grinning in sympathy, "I reckon you got a serious rival there!" He tapped Rebekah on the shoulder. "Let the poor bloke breathe," he advised. Gently, he unfurled his sister's arms. "Show him the babby, eh? He ain't seen the babby before."

"We're all going up to see Dad," explained Jael, as Nick was shown the child and told all about the troubles he was having with his teeth. "We went round Naomi's specially, as it happens, thinking he'd be there. But *she* ain't seen him since Tuesday week."

"I hope he hasn't been taken ill," I said politely. I had to say something, after all. "But surely Daniel or Rachel would have called at his cottage since then?"

"Yeah, they did." Unconcerned, Jael shrugged. "Daniel saw him up the breaker's yard, in fact, only yesterday. But Naomi had his favourite dinner cooked, see, and he never turned up to eat it."

"Oh, dear."

"Dried out, it did." Jael pursed her lips. "Went all crusty round the edges, so she 'ad to give it the dog in the end. She was that annoyed! Eh, Nathe?"

"What? Oh – yeah. She was tampin' mad," agreed Nathan, complacently.

"So, we're going over to sort him out." Jael grasped the buggy's handles. "Come on, Reb," she added. "You know you'll get all chesty if you stay out in this damp, an' *I* don't want to 'ave to nurse you. I got enough to do these days. Nathan? Grab hold of her hand, will you?"

Nathan did as he was told. Then, they all said their goodnights, and strolled off into the dusk.

177

I stared after them, puzzled. They were taking a round-about route to old man Casson's house, there was no doubt at all about that.

For a moment, I was actually frightened. Had they been spying, I wondered, had they been keeping an eye on *me*? But then, I realised what it was all in aid of. As I'd first surmised, this was a triumphal progress. Jael had walked through the village to show off her baby and his splendid new pushchair. She had wanted to put her wealth and consequence on display, for all to see.

It was, as it happens, one of the great mysteries of Hartley Cross life, the fact that the Cassons always seemed to have plenty of cash. Despite her husband being on almost permanent short time, Jael frequently had nice new clothes. These were from chain stores and catalogues certainly. But, all the same, they weren't exactly cheap.

As for Nathan, he might be unemployed, but *he* literally threw his money away, both at the local races, and in the Lamb and Flag.

In country districts, however, there is always casual work available, and practically all journeymen labourers are paid in cash or kind. I decided that, God-fearing and church-going though they might be, most members of the Casson family were probably on the fiddle these days.

It was not until the little procession had gone on its way and been swallowed up by the darkness of Home Farm Row that Nick rummaged in his pockets for a tissue, with which to wipe the great gobbets of Rebekah's snot and saliva from off his face. "She's a nice kid," he observed, as he cleaned himself up. "But I ain't been slobbered over like that since my Aunty Maureen's Alsatian decided it was in love with me."

"She can't help it." Reproachfully, I met his gaze.

"Poor Rebekah. It's not her fault she's handicapped. You shouldn't compare her to a dog!"

"But I loved that dog!" Remembering, Nick shook his head. "It damned near broke my heart, when poor old Sheba died. Here – I thought we might go and see a film tonight. Do you fancy that?"

"Which film do you want to see?"

"Something stupid, violent and filthy, I think. Starring Sharon Stone, preferably." He grinned. "I'm not bothered about anything artistic or worthwhile, anyway."

So we went into Worcester and sat in the warmth and comfort of the new Multiplex Super-Screen, shoving popcorn into our faces and watching a blood-spattered celluloid epic of absolutely stupendous mediocrity, along with a few hundred other morons who had nothing better to do on a Saturday night.

We got back to Hartley Cross about midnight, parked Flora in the driveway, then went into the house. As we walked into the kitchen, Nick sniffed the air. "You've had a visitor," he observed.

"What?" I frowned at him. "How do you mean?"

"I can smell scent. But it isn't yours." He frowned, too. "Who else has a key to this house?" he enquired.

"Only Mrs Denny." I shrugged. "She might have popped in. But she'd have left a note. Nick, *I* can't smell anything."

"Perhaps I'm imagining things." He tried the kitchen door. It opened. "You didn't lock up!" he scolded, as I filled the kettle and put it on to boil. "For God's sake, Lindsay! Don't you ever check to see if—"

"The burglar alarm is working, and the mantraps are all primed or sprung? This isn't some crime-ridden district of an inner city, you know!" I reached for some mugs. "Calm down," I soothed. "Do you want tea, chocolate or coffee tonight?"

"Coffee, please," he muttered, absently.

"I bought some new shears and secateurs last week," I began hopefully, as we sat at the kitchen table, drinking filter decaffeinated. "I was wondering . . ."

"*I* brought some proper tools with me this time," he interrupted. He dunked a digestive biscuit. "Those window frames of yours are rotten. None of the buggers will open properly. So tomorrow, we'll mend some of the sashes, stick a bit of filler into the biggest cracks, and—"

"But I thought we were doing the garden!" I cried. I stared at him. Startled, he stared back. Embarrassed now, I rephrased that. "I was going to tidy up a few of the borders," I murmured, meekly. "I'd wondered if you might like to help."

"I don't know a hollyhock from a turnip. So I'd be slashing my way through your rambler roses, and leaving the thistles to seed themselves all over the place."

Nick shook his head. "You'll have to get Tessa down here for anything like that. Like I said before, I *will* cut some of that long grass for you. But these window frames are in a terrible state. So if I patch some of them up – replace the cords, fill up the holes and that – you could give them a coat of paint, and you'll have at least a few looking okay."

"But can you do that sort of work all by yourself?"

"Of course I can." He grinned. "I'll nip over to Homebase or somewhere first thing tomorrow morning. Collect the stuff I need, then get stuck in. If I don't finish Sunday, I'll stay over until Monday and see the job done."

"Well, that's very good of you. But can you spare the time?"

"The experiment's looking after itself at present. I need to do some thinking."

"I see. Actually," I said, "*I* need to go into town on Monday morning, to see about the will. But I'd feel very guilty if I left you here alone, working for me."

"Don't worry about that. I can amuse myself." Nick grinned. "Anyway – I might not *be* alone! One of my girlfriends might drop by. So, I don't want *you* in the way. Queering my pitch, and—"

"I see it all now." I laughed. "Mrs Denny always calls on a Monday morning."

"I can't wait," Nick said.

Nick seemed to have decided it was his job to check over the house in the evening, putting out lights and damping down fires and locking up for the night. So, after I'd finished my coffee, I said goodnight and went up to bed.

As soon as I walked into my bedroom, I smelled it. A woman's perfume, it was a sweet, light fragrance, with identifiable top notes of jasmine, lavender and roses.

I frowned. Could I have knocked something over, perhaps? I glanced towards my dressing table. But everything seemed to be in order there. In any case, I didn't own any perfumes or cosmetics which smelled like that, since I prefer spice or citrus to flower scents. The drowsy perfume of summer roses has bad associations for me.

I almost called Nick then, to see what he thought, to ask did he think it was the same scent as he'd noticed downstairs? But then, I checked myself. To invite him into my bedroom would have been asking for trouble. Or at any rate, asking for embarrassment and misunderstanding, and I didn't want to risk spoiling my relationship with the only member of the male sex I'd ever thought of as a friend.

In any case, as I sniffed again, I realised – I assured

myself, anyway – that I'd been imagining things. So, having told myself again not to worry, I went to bed.

We spent Sunday working on the house and garden. The following Monday morning, leaving Nick deep in scientific thought and aromatic wood shavings, I drove into Hereford.

I found a parking space near the Castle Pool, then called on Mr Harrison, only to be told that although he would normally have been in the office, earlier today some hooligan in a stolen Fiesta had smashed into a bollard in Widemarsh Street and knocked an old-age pensioner flying. So the solicitor had been called to the police station, where his unhappy client now languished in a prison cell. I could make an appointment for Wednesday morning, if I pleased.

"I'll ring you," I said. So with that, I left the offices of Harrison, Fenwick and Co, and walked into the city centre, threading my way through narrow medieval lanes towards the cathedral, the tower of which pierced the bright blue sky.

All around me I heard the lilting speech of the Welsh marches, of Herefordshire people born and bred. The soft accents of the countryside mixed and mingled with the flatter, less musical speech of the city dwellers and, listening to this vocal symphony, I felt happy, relaxed, at home again.

I saw no one I knew. But I supposed then that the people I'd been to school with had probably all moved away, for there was little opportunity for the younger generation here. I went into Marks & Spencer, where I bought some food – a wicked extravagance, I know – and on my way out stopped again by a display of glittery jumpers, which were absolutely horrid, then by some white linen shirts, which were so lovely that I bought two.

"Be nice for the summer, these," remarked the assistant, as the machine printed my cheque for me.

"Yes," I agreed, thinking, they'd be nice for the winter, too.

"It gets earlier and earlier, don't it?" she continued, offering me her biro. "Comes far too early, if you ask me!"

"Summer?" I enquired, puzzled.

"No, my dear. We gets the summer *stuff* in earlier and earlier! At this rate, we'll be out of cottons and into wool again, come the first of July!" The woman folded my shirts. "You looking forward to summer, then?"

"I suppose I must be," I replied.

"I expect you tan easy, as well. Being dark, like you are." Dropping my purchases into a green carrier bag, the woman smiled at me. "Mind how you go, now."

How nice country people can be, I thought, as I walked out of the shop. How pleasant, how relaxed, how easy to get on with, to pass the time of day! You'd never have had a conversation like that in the Marble Arch store.

I walked up Church Street, hurried past the cathedral again, then cut across a bit of green. Flora was waiting for me. Glancing at my watch, I saw I was half an hour late, but no parking ticket adorned the windscreen, no meter maid was anywhere to be seen, and I congratulated myself on my good fortune. The sun was shining, I'd bought some nice new clothes, there was a delicious vegetarian curry for lunch, which even Nick Singer would enjoy – life wasn't so bad after all.

As I searched for my keys, I noticed a few dark red spots spattering the white lines which marked out the parking spaces on the road. I thought nothing much of it until, jerking open the boot, I was about to chuck in my shopping when I saw it.

It was horrible! Absolutely horrible – I've never seen anything so vile. A sheep's head, slashed and hacked and gored, its stupid glazed eyes staring, its nose bleeding and its muzzle torn, the dark blood from its severed arteries staining the piece of pale carpet on which it lay.

As I stared, it seemed to blink at me. I half expected it to open its poor battered mouth, and bleat in indignation.

The message, scrawled in purple felt tip, was written on a piece of computer print-out. "Don't Meddle No More," it said. Each word was underlined three times. *Don't Meddle No More.*

I gaped at it. But, despite my shock and disgust, and not-withstanding my pity for the poor dead sheep, some of my critical faculties were still operational, and I thought, what a strange word to use. How old-fashioned it sounded, how almost Biblical. Meddle. Meddle in what, *with* what, for God's sake? I shook my head. It didn't make sense to me.

It was the shock, I suppose, which made my stomach muscles contract. So now, to my embarrassment and dismay, I was violently sick, spewing my entire breakfast out on to the road, like a yob on a Saturday night.

I don't know how long I stood there. I think I almost blacked out, in fact, and it was only by leaning heavily against the body of the car that I prevented myself from collapsing in a heap on the tarmac.

"Is something the matter?" The voice, strange yet so very familiar, made me start. Still somewhat bemused, I shook my head. Turning to see who had spoken, I wondered if I were imagining things. For Simon Dyer stood by my side, looking anxiously into my eyes.

He was wearing a suit. I'd never seen him in a suit before, for even at the trial he'd worn a crumpled linen jacket and chinos, for all the world as if he were planning to take an afternoon's stroll or go for a pleasant country walk. The newspapers had made quite a thing of his scruffiness, as if this made him guilty by default. But today, he looked exactly like an estate agent, all trim and neat and smart.

Dopily, I stared at him.

He smiled back at me. "I thought it was you," he continued, pleasantly, "so I came across to say hello. I called out, in fact. But you seemed to be in some sort of daze."

"I felt a bit odd for a moment. That's all. I'm quite all right now." Slamming down the boot of the car, I forced a polite smile. "W-what are you doing in town?"

"I needed to see Charles Lawley. He's my accountant." He shrugged. "It's not something I look forward to, this interrogation once or twice a year! But today, I was told things are looking a bit better than they did this time last year. So I didn't get the third degree after all. I was afraid I'd have to sell Brougham Gate, you see."

"I see."

A moment ago, I'd felt terrible. Perplexed, upset, and frightened almost out of my wits. But now, my heart was turning cartwheels. I was almost singing!

For now, I understood. That was why Simon had been so unhappy. That was why he had not made contact, why he'd never phoned or called! The poor man had been worried sick, terrified lest he'd have to sell his beloved Brougham Gate.

But now he felt better. I seized the moment. "It's ages since I've seen you," I began. "Seen you to speak to, properly I mean. Why don't you come over to my place, one day this week? We could have coffee, then—"

"I don't actually go out very much." Again, he shrugged. "Things are – well – things in the village are still a bit difficult for me. But I tell you what. Why don't you come to Brougham Gate?" Lightly, he touched my wrist. "Yes, do that. Come any time you please."

"Any time?" I quavered, the spot where his flesh had touched mine on fire.

"Any time at all." He glanced at his watch. "I must go now," he murmured. "I have an appointment at half twelve."

"Then you'd better get moving."

"Yes." He nodded, then smiled again, then crossed the road. I stared after him.

How I managed to drive back to Hartley Cross without hitting anything, I just don't know. For I was in a daze of complete and utter happiness.

Chapter Sixteen

When I did at last arrive home, still jittery and jumpy, trembling and shaking but happy as Larry, whoever Larry might have been, I found Nick throwing things into the boot of his Escort. His scowl was so ferocious that he looked like the villain in a pantomime, who was coincidentally suffering from the worst sort of migraine imaginable.

"Whatever's the matter?" I demanded. "Nick?"

"Trouble at t'mill." Nick tossed some files on to the back seat. Then, he glanced at me. "I left your phone number at the Clarendon," he muttered. "I hope you don't mind."

"No, of course not. But—"

"One of the technicians just called me here. Apparently, Maclean came into the lab first thing this morning. He's been reading my notes. Prowling around my apparatus, unscrewing things, prising bits apart. I have to get back."

"Yes. I do see that." But now, like an idiot, I just gaped at him. For I, of course, was still on cloud nine.

"I've finished the downstairs windows," he continued. Three more folders were hurled into the boot. "You can lock the buggers now."

"Oh. Good."

"So you just mind you do." He touched my shoulder,

turning me round to face him. "Is something the matter?" he enquired, his eyes narrowed in suspicion.

"No, of course not." Reassuringly, I beamed at him. "I'm fine!"

"You don't look it. You're all flushed."

"I'm okay. Honestly." I shrugged. "I was just a bit surprised, that's all. To find you dashing off like this," I added, unconvincingly.

"Yeah, well – can't be helped." He let me go. "I'll give you a ring," he promised. "If you need to speak to *me*, leave a message on the machine at Ferry Road, and I'll get back to you. Or better still . . ."

He rummaged in his pockets for some paper. He wrote down a number. "Better still, call the lab. That's where I'll probably be."

"Right." I took the scrap of paper. It was a piece of computer print-out. Later, I'd stick it under one corner of the telephone.

"Are you sure you're okay?" asked Nick.

"I told you, I'm fine." Looking up at him, I smiled. "I hope the mad professor hasn't done any real damage. I hope you get the results you wanted, too."

"So do I." He grinned. "Take care, won't you?"

"I shall."

"I'll be seeing you, then."

"Yes. Goodbye."

I went into the house. I wanted to put on loud music! To throw off all my clothes, to dance like a dervish, naked in the rain. To cry with happiness. To shout, to sing. For Simon had invited me to visit him, any time I pleased!

Should I go this very afternoon, I wondered? Or should I savour the delightful prospect as a treat to come? Should I gobble this emotional equivalent of the most expensive sort of chocolate truffle right away – or keep it for later? A bit of a poser, that! I decided to have my lunch, mull it all over, then make up my mind.

In the end, I decided to spend the evening gloating, then to call at Brougham Gate the following morning. For coffee, that's all. I'd be casually passing, and happen to drop in.

I was so happy that I was still singing to myself as I cleaned up the mess in my car. It was probably kids who were responsible, I decided. Children, a farmer's children probably, who watched too many top shelf videos, had been indulging in some silly pseudo black magic rite. I hadn't locked Flora's boot the previous evening and, as Mrs Joby had remarked, the teenagers in Hartley Cross had nothing much to do.

Tuesday morning dawned dull, heavy and overcast. This was the kind of weather Mrs Denny hated, for it made her rheumatism particularly bad. She for one wouldn't be scurrying and gossiping about the village today. For myself, I didn't care if we had hail, rain or sunshine, for in my heart it was high summer once more.

For Simon had forgiven me. He'd turned back to me, decided we could be friends – even lovers, perhaps – again.

Savouring every delicious moment of this glorious epiphany, I strolled through the village, then turned up the lane which led towards Brougham Gate. I walked up the drive towards the house.

Once so neatly raked and immaculately tidy, these days the gravel was scattered everywhere. The weeds grew so profusely, and the shrubs and rhododendrons on either side were so straggling and overgrown, that the overall effect was of a yellowish-greenish forest track. The grandly magnificent driveway leading to an equally grand house had disappeared, perhaps for ever. "But perhaps not," whispered a voice, deep inside my head. "Perhaps, one day . . ."

I rang the bell. Somebody had mended it since I'd last called, for instead of croaking like a dyspeptic frog, it pealed loudly through the house.

I waited. At last, at long last, I heard footsteps on the flags. I tried to relax. To be ready for whatever reception I might receive, be it a curt nod, a welcoming smile, or, hope against hope, a kiss. So I was more than a little nonplussed when the door was jerked open to reveal, not Simon Dyer, but Rebekah Casson standing there.

"Rebekah?" I stared at her. "What are you doing at Brougham Gate?"

"Broom Gate?" repeated Rebekah, peering past me with eyes screwed up against the light. I supposed she was looking for Nick.

But then, to my enormous relief and delight, Simon came shuffling down the hallway. I saw that he was in Yellow Pages Grandfatherly Old Buffer mode today, at least as far as his clothes went, for he was dressed in what looked like a pair of Louis Dyer's ancient Daks, a checked cotton shirt buttoned up to the neckband, and a cardigan with burn holes in the pockets, where somebody had presumably been in the habit of stowing a lighted pipe. He had nothing at all on his feet, which were blue with cold.

I've stroked those feet, I thought. I'd have kissed them, if I'd been allowed. Like Mary Magdalen, I'd have—

"Hello, Lin," said Simon. He smiled at me, and all at once the years peeled away, and I saw him as he'd been at eighteen. Once again he was the young David, the beautiful, slender boy with whom I had fallen so desperately in love.

It was Rebekah who brought me back to reality. "I want a biscuit," she announced. She tugged at the hem of Simon's horrid cardigan. "I want a *biscuit!*" she repeated, grizzling, insistent. "Jael says I'm allowed!"

"Well, there are plenty in the tin." Simon shrugged. "I'm babysitting," he explained, as Rebekah stumped off down the passage. "Naomi's gone shopping, and Jael had to take her little boy to the clinic today."

"Because of his teeth?"

"I believe so." Simon stood aside. "Come in," he invited. "Polly can put the kettle on. We'll all have tea."

When Simon and I entered the kitchen, we found Rebekah had emptied the entire contents of the biscuit tin on to the rather dirty wooden table. Now, she was rooting through them, picking out the jam ones, which were the only sort she liked. "Put the kettle on, Reb," said Simon. "I want a cup of tea."

Rebekah did as she was told. Her mouth full of jammy dodger, she filled one of the great iron kettles from the range. She plonked it on the filthy hob, then lit the gas.

Eventually.

I do hate calor gas. I'm always afraid that anything powered by gas is about to explode, and as Rebekah waved the matches in the air and fumbled for the right dial on the cooker, a horrible cess-pit stink filled the air. "Is she safe, doing that?" I murmured, as Rebekah tipped tea leaves into a big black pot and stood drumming her fingers on the draining board, waiting for the kettle to sing.

"She burns herself now and then, certainly." Again, Simon shrugged. "But she's always anxious to help, and

191

I don't see what harm it can do. Provided she's supervised and we keep any babies or small animals out of her way."

So Rebekah made tea, and the three of us sat round the table, upon which the cutlery and crockery from at least three previous meals mouldered in sticky heaps, drinking diligently.

I wondered how long much longer Jael would be. Half an hour? Two hours? Three? Rebekah would be wanting her lunch soon. She wouldn't get it here. I considered offering to take her back to Naomi's house, handing her over to a cousin or something, then coming back to Brougham Gate to do some tidying up.

But then, as he finally drained his cup, Simon stood up. "Look, Lin," he began, "You'll think this is an awful cheek, but the fact is, I need to get over to see Harry Cox some time this morning. It's the rabbits here in the south paddock, you see. They're getting into his garden, and I promised I'd let him have the money to buy some netting, without fail by twelve o'clock today. Could you . . . would you mind staying with Reb for an hour?"

He looked straight at me. His eyes met mine, pleading, hoping, beseechingly. As if I could refuse him! "No problem," I replied. "We'll get you some lunch, shall we? Reb and I, we'll make an onion tart. Or a cheese flan."

"Bless you, Lindsay." Simon beamed at me. "I'll be an hour. No more." He pulled on a pair of wellingtons, then shrugged on his jacket. Then, he was gone.

Rebekah helped me clear the table. A sweet-natured, obliging girl, she was always interested in what people were doing, and invariably anxious to assist in any way.

She was so clumsy, however, that being helped by Rebekah was more like being hindered by an enormous two year old, who would be quite capable dropping every-thing and bursting into noisy, persistent tears if she felt her efforts were not as fully appreciated as they deserved to be. One had to remember to keep saying, well done and, goodness, that's nice, as one went on one's way.

"Shall we tidy up a bit in here?" I suggested, as we swept the crumbs from the table's rather crusty surface and I wondered where the bleach was kept. If it were kept at all. "Or shall we do some washing up?"

"Washing up!" Grinning, Rebekah nodded. "Do lots of washing up today!"

So we piled up the dirty china and carried it through to the scullery, where there was a big stone sink and cold water tap. I put two large kettles on to boil, then went back to supervise my assistant, who was sluicing the worst of the grot from the plates under a stream of icy water.

The kettles boiled, I filled the sink with warm water and detergent, then stood aside for Rebekah to take over. She picked up a grubby little mop and then, slowly and extremely carefully, she began to wash up.

"Shall I dry?" I asked, as she piled clean dishes on to the cracked draining board, creating a huge, unstable heap of crockery.

"You need a cloth." Frowning, she stared all around. Then, flummoxed, she bit her lip. "Jael has lots," she continued. "In a drawer. But I don't know where Simon's are."

"Don't worry, I'll find one," I said.

Taking up one whole wall of the scullery was a huge Welsh dresser. So now, cautiously, I opened a cupboard door. The cavity behind was full of books and papers, all crammed in higgledy-piggledy, which couldn't have been touched for years. I tried another cupboard next, but

193

found only more books and a lot of spiders. So then I tried a drawer.

Paydirt! "Here they are!" I cried, smiling brightly. All untouched by human hand for the past five years I should reckon, I thought. "Which colour shall we try first, eh?"

But Rebekah was not impressed. Instead, she looked dubious. "Jael doesn't like that sort of cloth," she muttered. "She says they leave fluff on the china."

"That won't matter today. Come on, Reb!" I beamed at her. "Let's get on with it! We'll have this washing up finished long before Simon comes back. Then we'll make him something nice for lunch. He'll be ever so pleased!"

Rebekah nodded. She took up her mop again. But now she'd lost all interest in the dishes, and worked even more maddeningly slowly, sniffing discontentedly all the while.

I was in no hurry, however, so I let her get on with it, complimenting her on her efforts and repeating how pleased Simon would be.

She finished the dishes and started on the cutlery. As she ran more cold water into the chipped enamel bowl, she turned to glance at me. "Lin, are you Simon's girlfriend?" she enquired.

"Simon's girlfriend?" Taken by surprise, I felt myself blush. "No," I replied carefully, "I'm not."

"Oh?" Rebekah inspected an apostle spoon. "I saw him kiss you, though."

"I don't think so." I was still scarlet, in fact my face was on fire. "I used to go out with Simon," I admitted. "But I don't think you would remember."

"Yes, I do!" cried Rebekah, affronted. "I always remember! I remember from a *long* time ago!"

"Oh. I see." I didn't want to make her cry. But if I

confused her now, the tears were sure to flow. "I *was* Simon's girlfriend once," I agreed. "But, as you said, it was a long time ago." The temptation to add, *and I expect he has another girlfriend now*, was almost more than I could resist.

But, to my astonishment, Rebekah answered my unspoken question for me. "Simon hasn't got a girlfriend any more," she said.

"Oh, I'm sure there must be somebody," I hazarded.

"No." Rebekah shook her head. Confidentially, she lowered her voice. "He hasn't got any girlfriends now. Jael says he doesn't want a girlfriend. See?"

"I see," I said.

If Rebekah had just informed me that I'd won the jackpot in the National Lottery and also the Turner Prize, she couldn't have pleased or delighted me more. Soon, my heart was turning somersaults. Doing back flips and half twists! For, I had thought I was alone. I had assumed that, after our affair had been broken off so cruelly, abruptly and unnaturally, *I* was the one who'd suffered. The one doomed to flounder into new relationship after new relationship, only to have each and every one fail miserably.

But, if I was interpreting Rebekah's innocent remarks correctly, Simon had suffered, too. If my own private life had been a wasteland for six years or more, so had his. I had not been replaced. Therefore, there was a hope, there was a more than sporting chance, that he might still love me!

I wanted to kiss Rebekah. But that would have puzzled her, or perhaps even made her cry. So instead I hugged my secret rapture, gloatingly.

I stacked the plates, saucers and dishes, then began to replace them in the dusty racks. My imagination, always

195

vivid, was now in overdrive, running full steam ahead. I would invite Simon to dinner, I decided. We'd have a delicious meal, far too much to drink, we'd talk far into the night. Then, some time during the small hours of the morning, he'd touch my face. We'd kiss, and . . .

I was so wrapped up in my own daydreams and plans for future happiness that I didn't notice Rebekah was sniffing harder than ever now. A sudden gulp brought me back to reality, however, and as I stared at her she turned on the waterworks in earnest. Big, round tears welled up in her narrow, grey eyes. They rolled down her pudgy cheeks and dripped into the washing up water below. "L-Lindsay?" she quavered. "Oh, Lindsay! You mustn't ever tell!"

"Mustn't tell what?" Astonished though I was, I kept my own voice even, neutral, calm. "Reb? Whatever's the matter? What mustn't I tell?"

But Rebekah's sobs only grew harder. "They'll put him in prison!" she wailed. Her anguish almost palpable, she stared back at me, her little face sodden with tears. "Simon never hurt his dad!" she wept. "He never done anything like that!"

"Please, Rebekah! Please stop crying." I tried to take her in my arms, to hug her better. "Look," I soothed, "there's no need to get so upset. Whatever you—"

"But our Dan and our Samuel said!" Poor Rebekah, she was hysterical now. "They said, if you tell, Simon will go to prison! I don't want Simon to go to prison!"

"Well, he won't. Don't worry, Rebekah. There's no chance of that." I hugged her now. I stroked her hair, and murmured soft, cooing, hopefully reassuring nonsense in her ear.

For it was obvious what had happened. Poor thing, she'd overheard some conversation between her siblings, got

196

hold of the wrong end of the stick and had been tormenting herself ever since. "I only fetched the flowers in," she sobbed, as I held her. "I only took the roses and that, for Mrs Wheeler to do the church, on Friday night!"

"The church?" Puzzled, I frowned. Then, I remembered. Mrs Wheeler was a local busybody, a great pal of Mesdames Denny and Sidderfin, but also the churchwarden's wife. She always did the flowers for the altar at St John's, and was so jealous of this privilege that no other member of the WI was allowed near it. They had to content themselves with adorning the lectern and the font.

Mrs Wheeler was getting on in years now, but when I lived at home she could have parked her nose for England, her favourite leisure activity being to drive hither and thither in her ancient Morris Oxford full of dogs, in search of gossip, scandal and news.

In spite of hating her guts and despising her – so he said – for a sex-starved old bag, Louis Dyer was a boozing crony of the churchwarden and always let George Wheeler's wife have her pick of the roses from Brougham Gate. Mr Sidderfin donated his wonderful blue delphiniums, and Harry Cox gave her his lupins, oriental poppies and prize-winning phlox.

As she drove around the village collecting floral tributes it would, I realised, have been convenient for Mrs Wheeler to pick up the roses last of all. For where better could she scrounge a drop of Harvey's Bristol Cream, and hear all the latest chit-chat from Louis Dyer's garrulous housekeeper, than here at Brougham Gate?

I was beginning to feel a bit upset myself now. Suspicion and dread were scratching me with their sharp little nails, and a prickle of anxiety was raising the hairs on the back of my neck. But I continued to hug and coo to Rebekah, and did my best to make sense of all this.

The facts were, Rebekah was always at a loose end. Her father worked for Louis Dyer. So, on that dreadful day, she could easily have been told to go and cut the roses for Mrs Wheeler, to tie them in bunches, then to bring them into the house. Where she must have stumbled over . . . what?

I looked into Rebekah's soft, grey eyes, now so puffy with tears that they were hardly more than impressionist smudges, dark on the pale canvas of her sweet little face. "Rebekah?" I didn't want to alarm her, but I had to know. "You saw everything, didn't you?"

"Never saw nothing!" wailed Rebekah. She pulled away, jerking herself out of my embrace. "Never saw anything at all!"

"No? But, Rebekah—"

"I don't like you!" Rebekah glared at me. A thread of mucus snaked from her nose and quivered on her top lip. She licked it away. "I never saw nothing," she repeated. "Nothing, nothing!"

"But you were here." I felt so cruel. So wicked, to be distressing her. "You brought the roses into the house. You came into the kitchen, and you saw—"

"No!"

"I think you did."

"He hit me!" Rebekah was shaking like a leaf. "Our Dad, he hit me, on the face! He said, if I told – if I said he was in the kitchen, layin' there—"

"He'd do what?"

"He said, he'd take a stick to me! Like he done to our Daniel and our Nathan, when they was bad! He said – oh!" Rebekah almost jumped out of her skin. Blinking rapidly, she stared in terror towards the scullery door.

It swung open, and Nathan's big black labrador bounced in, closely followed by Nathan himself. I don't think I've ever been so pleased to see anybody in the course of my whole life.

"So what's all this, then?" As his dog fussed around her, as it jumped up to lick Rebekah's hands and tear-stained cheeks, Nathan draped an arm around her shoulders. Evidently, he was so used to his sister's sudden breakdowns, her mood swings and her funny turns that he hardly seemed bothered at all. "Whatever's the matter, honeybun?"

It always touched my heart, to see how gently and kindly all the Cassons behaved towards this youngest, damaged one. As for Rebekah herself, as far I could tell, Nathan seemed to be her own particular favourite. So now he was here, she would feel better. Wouldn't she?

But Rebekah didn't even want Nathan today. If anything, she cried even more bitterly now. When he tried to embrace her, she squirmed away, and cowered in a corner of the kitchen, sniffing miserably.

"I'm sorry." I was so ashamed! Interrogating poor Rebekah like that, how could I have even thought of it? So, quickly, I explained. "I didn't mean to upset her," I concluded, lamely. "I only wanted to know . . ."

"Don't you worry about a thing." Sagely, Nathan shook his head. "Poor little bugger, she gets so confused! The fact is, she don't understand nothing these days. I was sayin' to our Naomi only last night, I don't care what they reckons down that assessment centre, seems to me she'll never get no better. She'll only get worse."

"She's lucky to have all of you, then." I felt properly humbled now. "To look after her, I mean."

"Well, she's family, ain't she?" Nathan shrugged. "Our

199

own flesh an' blood, like. We'd never send our own flesh an' blood away!"

"No. Of course not."

In her corner, Rebekah sniffed.

Nathan sighed.

I could think of nothing more to say.

But, just then, the kitchen door opened. Simon came in. For a moment, Rebekah's sniffing intensified. But then, when Simon did not speak to her, she sidled across the room and hugged him. She buried her face against his chest.

Simon and Nathan exchanged glances. "She's a bit upset," explained Nathan.

"Why?" asked Simon.

"Search me." Nathan shrugged. "She has her ups and downs. You know that. She—"

"I thought you were working at Arrowsmith's Yard today," interrupted Simon, coolly. Or so it seemed to me.

"I was, earlier," agreed Nathan. "But he didn't have much for me, an' I'd finished by eleven. So I thought I'd come over here, an' see if I could do anything for you. You still want them old wardrobes taken over to the Collis place?"

"Yes, I think so. Nobody has the space for them as wardrobes, and Jack Collis always does a good job." What Simon meant was, Jack Collis, in his capacity as the local cannibal, would make several desks and occasional tables from two or three old walnut or mahogany robes, and sell them for a very good price. "I've stuck them on the van," added Simon, meaningfully.

"Right you are." Nathan picked up a set of keys. "Come on then, Reb," he muttered. "I'll take you along for the ride. Caesar – heel!" He went out through the scullery, whistling. Obediently, Rebekah and the black labrador followed him.

Simon looked at me. I looked at Simon. "What was all that about?" he enquired.

I could have shrugged it off. In fact, I was going to do just that – but then, I decided not to beat about the bush after all. "Rebekah knows," I told him.

"What?"

"I mean, she knows about your father." I met Simon's startled gaze. "She was a witness to his murder. She may even have watched him die."

"Don't be ridiculous!" Now, Simon stared at me. "How could she? She doesn't even know what day it is, she—"

"She knows everything!" I wanted to grab him, shake him, *make* him see sense. "Simon, don't you realise what this means? Rebekah can tell us who killed him! She could clear your name, she could prove – look, I'm going to find out what happened here!"

"Leave it, Lin," said Simon.

"What?" I gaped at him. "But don't you understand, don't you see . . ."

"I said, leave it!"

"But I want to know!" I cried. "I *need* to know! Listen, you're not at risk – you were tried and found not guilty, no one can do anything to you! But people still suspect. Simon – dear Simon – don't you care about your good name?"

"My *what*?" He shook his head. "That's almost funny, that is."

"Oh, Simon!" My heart went out to him. The rest of me followed. Taking two rapid steps towards him, I took him in my arms.

He sighed. Then, he rested his head upon my shoulder, where it was always meant to be.

201

Chapter Seventeen

Simon stood slumped, dejected, motionless. But he did not seem to mind being hugged. So, I hugged him. Then, lightly, I stroked his hair, smoothing it back from his forehead. "Don't worry," I crooned. "Don't fret."

"Mummy's here." He lifted his head. He looked at me. "Poor Lindsay," he whispered. "Poor old Lindsay, always in the wrong place, at the wrong time."

"What's that supposed to mean?"

"Oh – nothing, really." He shrugged. "Well, take today, for instance. You make a polite social call, and you end up smack in the middle of a row."

"It was hardly a row," I observed. "Poor Rebekah! I never meant to upset her like that. Or indeed at all."

"She's very easily unsettled. But she soon gets over things. By now, she'll have forgotten every word that was said."

"I do hope so."

"Depend upon it." Simon took my arms from around his neck. He crossed my hands neatly, then laid them against my chest. "Lindsay?" he murmured.

"What?"

"I don't think we'll ever get to the bottom of that business. The murder of my father, I mean." Sighing, he shook his head. "I've thought about it so much, over the course of the past few years. I've gone over and over it, trying to work out if there was anything we or the police might have missed. But, in my heart, I know I'm wasting my time."

"Why do you say that? Simon, I'm sure there's something we've overlooked! There's bound to be! *Somebody* must have had a reason, a motive, and if Rebekah—"

"The evidence – if we can call it that – of someone with Rebekah's condition would be worthless in a court of law. What Rebekah saw, or thinks she saw – or more than likely imagined – is irrelevant in this case."

"But—"

"I reckon there was a fight, between Dad and somebody he'd swindled or done down. Or it was a robbery, which went disastrously wrong." Grey eyes steady, Simon looked at me. "Dad had lots of enemies – well, *you* don't need to be told that! But it could also have been somebody we don't even know. A casual prowler, who broke in. Dad surprised him, there was a struggle—"

"But think about the way it was done!" I cried. Shuddering, I remembered that story Nick had told me. How the murderer had seemed determined to implicate Jael. "The piton, or whatever it was, how did—"

"He was beaten unconscious long before that was hammered into his head." Simon spoke with admirable calmness. But I suppose that had come with familiarity and resignation, over the intervening years. "That business with the marlin spike was just the *coup de grâce*."

"You honestly think so?"

"I do." Again, Simon shrugged. "There are dozens of unsolved murders on police files," he continued, reasonably. "Hundreds, even, in this part of the world alone. Oh, Lindsay, real life isn't like on television, where the police always get their man! Often, they don't come anywhere near him! If I can live with that idea, then you must, too."

"Maybe," I agreed.

"Think about it eh? You'll see I'm right." Reaching for an old tartan scarf, which lay like a limp rag across the back of a chair, Simon wound it round his neck. "I ought to go over to Jack Collis's place now," he continued. "I'm sure Nathan doesn't really understand what I want done with those wardrobes. So if Jack starts breaking them up, he—"

"I can give you a lift, if you like," I interrupted, eagerly. "If we walk back to The Larches, we can get my car."

"Oh, don't worry about that." Pushing his hands deep into his pockets, Simon smiled. "I'll go and hitch a ride with Neil Taylor. He's bound to be driving over to Baines Brothers later today, he won't mind dropping me off – and I'm sure you've got lots of other things to do."

"Yes." I know when I'm being fobbed off, and this was definitely one of those times. "Okay, then," I said brightly. "I'll let you get on."

I was not downhearted. Not at all. For, against all the odds, progress had at last been made. A bridge had been built, a road opened. I would reach Simon Dyer! I would heal him, I would make him whole again.

As I put on my jacket, we heard the sound of car tyres scraping across the gravel sweep. Puzzled, Simon frowned at me.

I shrugged my ignorance. So we both went outside.

The visitor was Jael, resplendent in a new, jade green jacket, reclining like the Queen of Sheba in the driving seat of the Taylors' brand new Vauxhall Cavalier.

"Hello, Lin!" she cried, apparently not in the least

surprised to find me at Brougham Gate. Gaily, she waved. "Simon? Neil was saying as how you might want a ride up Jack Collis's place later today. But I passed our Nathan going in that direction not half an hour ago, and—"

"You put two and two together, eh?"

"I did." Beaming, Jael raised her eyebrows, in arch enquiry. "Well, then? Do you want a lift?"

"I suppose I do. Just hang on a minute, while I get some cash." Turning to me, Simon grinned. "She must be psychic," he murmured.

"Must be," I agreed. I arranged a smile upon my face. I met Jael's bland, unblinking gaze. "How's the baby today?" I enquired.

"He's much better, thank you." Jael's grin never faltered. "That big molar's come through at last, an' his little face isn't half so red as it was. He's settled down nicely just now. Gone fast asleep, in fact. Neil's minding him."

"That's convenient." Good old Neil, I thought. Always at the wife's beck and call.

"So I'll take him up the playing fields later this afternoon." Jael was rummaging around in the glove compartment now. "I'd meant to ask you actually," she continued, "but I forgot. Anyway, is this yours?"

"I'm sorry?" I took a step nearer the car. "What is it?"

"Some sort of hair clip." She held it out in the palm of her hand, a little silver slide in the shape of a flower. "I found it in the kitchen," she explained. "After the party. I been asking everywhere."

I shook my head. "It's not mine," I told her.

But now, as she smiled at me, I caught a hint of it. That perfume, that scent of jasmine and roses which I'd noticed in my bedroom, it was in the car! I felt sick then. Sick, confused – and afraid. "Jael," I began, my voice unsteady, "this may seem like a silly question, but have you always worn—"

But then Simon came out again, and Jael switched on the ignition, noisily obliterating anything else I might have been about to say.

Simon climbed into the passenger seat. Jael put the car into gear. "See you, Lin!" she warbled, reversing smartly, then driving away.

I stood on the driveway, watching until the car disappeared round the curve which led to the road.

I walked home slowly, kicking stones across the pathways and scuffing up tussocks of pale, winter grass. I couldn't remember when I'd last felt so ill at ease. So nervous, so upset. I was annoyed with myself for distressing Rebekah, certainly, and remorse always makes me feel somewhat nauseous. But today, more than ever before, I also had the feeling that somebody was keeping a malevolent eye on me.

I already knew someone didn't like me, and was wishing me away. At any rate, those pathetic little corpses and other bits and pieces of animal tended to *suggest* something like that. But why? What had I done to anyone? Whom had I hurt? Whom had *I* upset?

As far as I knew, nobody. But then, a voice began murmuring a name – two names – deep inside my head. "Simon and Jael," it whispered. "Jael and Simon." I'd suspected – and now I was sure. I'd seen the way she looked at him! Those two were lovers. They had to be.

"Jael says he doesn't want a girlfriend." Rebekah's confident assertion echoed and reverberated, its mockery sneeringly triumphant, down the corridors of my consciousness.

So, had the murder of Louis Dyer been a joint effort?

Had its cruel embellishment been the assassins' private joke?

Possibly.

Probably, even!

For, the more I thought about it, the more I realised that there *had* been time. Not very much time, it's true. But time enough. Especially if, as Simon and I had been rolling around in the ancient tithe barn, Jael had been with Louis Dyer.

Also making love? Well, perhaps.

I pictured the scene. There was the old man, exhausted after sex with his demanding young mistress, walking into the kitchen at Brougham Gate. To fetch a beer, perhaps? To find some lemonade, or other cooling drink? Then, whilst his back was turned, an unseen assailant had struck him down.

Later – or perhaps while the murderers were actually at their horrible work – Rebekah had come blundering into the scullery. Her arms full of flowers, she'd stumbled. Over the corpse? At any rate, she'd dropped her roses everywhere. Hastily gathering some up again, dumping them on the draining board, she'd fled.

How long had she kept her secret? One year, two, three? In the end, however, it had all become too much for her, and she had told a brother or sister all about it. Then, of course, the entire Casson clan had brought its considerable weight to bear. But it must have been easy enough to control poor Rebekah, whom nobody credited with any common sense or reasoning power.

"So there it is," I thought. "That explains everything." It accounted for Jael's new clothes, her ghastly modern kitchen, the baby's state-of-the-art buggy – the fact that the entire family seemed to be in financial clover, in spite of the certainty that most of them worked only part time. If at all. It also accounted for the decrepit condition of Brougham Gate. Simon could hardly be expected to find any spare cash for house repairs, if he was being blackmailed by the whole of the Casson family.

So, were he and Jael lovers still? If so, could she really be jealous of me? Murderously jealous, even? Had she been in my room that evening, lying in wait for me?

Jael. Gorgeous but completely cuckoo, Jael with her herbal enchantments and her slinky hips, could she really have stolen out in the middle of the night to decorate my front lawn with the carcases of broiler chickens? When she had her post-party kitchen to clean up, and all her precious glass and china to put away?

The sullen afternoon gave way to an early evening twilight. I tried to work, but ended up throwing most of my efforts away. As night closed in, my heart sank with the setting sun. By the time it was pitch dark, I was very jumpy. No, that's not true. I was very, very scared.

I'd locked all the windows as soon as I got in. Those few without locks I jammed shut tight, using a selection of the wedge-shaped bits of wood which Nick Singer had left lying about. I even jammed those upstairs, although I suppose I didn't *seriously* entertain visions of intruders shinning up the drainpipes or climbing the wisteria, then dropping through the bathroom window.

By the time I'd done all this, I was sweating hard. Perspiration lay between my breasts and trickled down my back between my shoulder blades. My hands were grimed, and my fingernails filthy. Glancing at these, I grimaced in disgust. I needed to wash, I decided, to get myself clean again.

In the bathroom, I locked the door, then pushed an old blanket box hard against it. I undressed and had an all-over wash, shivering all the time, despite the fact that the room was warm and the water boiling. After towelling myself dry, I put on my thickest flannel nightdress, and on top of this one of my father's old dressing gowns, which I belted tightly at the waist.

I opened the bathroom door, but so gingerly that anyone watching me would have thought I was expecting a bag of flour to fall on my head. Noiselessly, I crept downstairs.

The act of washing should have calmed me, but as I tiptoed down the staircase, I realised I was agitated still. Still very scared, in fact. By the time I reached the hallway, I felt sick and dizzy, as if I'd had nothing to eat all day.

I pushed open the door of the kitchen, then went in. Breathless and terrified, I leaned against the ancient Welsh dresser. All I needed now was an asthma attack. Oh God, where was my inhaler? There, on the fridge. Thank goodness, I thought. I'd never have made it back upstairs again.

As I gulped down the cocktail of chemical vapours – one puff, two, make it three, for good luck – I tried to calm down. To make a plan. "I must tell the police," I said, out loud. But then, I thought, tell them what exactly? Simon had been tried once already, and been cleared. He at least could not be tried again.

What about Jael, then? But the very idea of Jael in the witness box, making cow eyes at the jury and playing the simple country girl card for all it was worth, made me shake my head in despair.

The doors! Suddenly, I was shivering again. I'd made all the windows secure, true enough – but had I locked the doors?

The front door had an ordinary Yale lock. This would have secured itself behind me, as I came in. As for the kitchen door – well, I hadn't opened it at all today. There was the key, hanging from the hook on the door frame. I was safe.

I needed caffeine, I decided. A cup of strong, black coffee, that would calm me down. I filled the kettle, but my hands trembled so much that I splashed water all over the quarry-tiled floor. Tearing off a couple of sheets of kitchen paper, I crouched down to mop up the mess.

As I did so, a creaking, squeaking noise came from my right, making me start. Instinctively, I stared towards the window. But all I could see was blackness, the unrelieved pitch darkness of the winter night. Then, however, as I watched the window, the kitchen door shook. The hinges squeaked again. The handle began to turn.

Slowly, agonisingly slowly, the handle moved from horizontal to the vertical. The door began to open. I should have run towards it – yes, I know that now! I should have slammed it shut, bolted it tight. But I stood immobile, for I was turned to stone. Quite literally petrified. As I stared, a rabbit mesmerised by the headlamps of the vehicle which will prove its destruction, Nathan Casson walked into the room.

I could have wept with relief! For it was not, after all, some mad axe-man come to visit, but big, solid, dependable Nathan who'd decided to call in on his way home. He smiled at me now. "I did knock," he explained. "But perhaps you had the water running, and didn't hear me?"

"I – maybe not," I agreed. "How did you . . . why . . . I mean, I thought the door was locked—"

"No." Nathan shrugged, as if to ask, should it be? At this early hour? Then he glanced towards the stove.

"Coffee, is it?" he demanded. "Or something a bit stronger, perhaps?"

"Coffee. Just coffee." I stared at him. "What – why have you come?" I enquired.

"I thought you looked a bit peaky, earlier on. I knew you was on your own – I saw the boyfriend driving off, yesterday. So I reckoned I'd check up on you, like."

"Oh." I sat down. I pulled my dressing gown close to my body, and tied the belt again, very tight.

Nathan stood at the stove, ostensibly watching the kettle. But then, he turned to look at me. Feeling at a disadvantage sitting down, I tried to stand up, but failed. "You seem a bit wobbly," observed my visitor. "Gettin' the "flu or summat, are you?"

"There's nothing wrong with me," I replied.

The kettle boiled. Nathan made instant coffee, two mugs of it. "Here," he murmured, "this'll see you right." He handed me mine.

I accepted it. Although it was still boiling hot, I sipped it.

"That's better," said Nathan. He sat down at the kitchen table. "You got any biscuits?" he enquired.

"Yes, in the tin on the dresser," I replied.

He went to fetch it.

I drank more coffee.

Gradually, I relaxed again.

Chapter Eighteen

Nathan sat opposite me, dunking ginger biscuits in his coffee and sucking off the resultant wet mush. I wished he'd hurry up and finish. Then leave. For, although it was still early, I was tired, and wanted to go to bed. "Nathan," I began, "don't think I'm being unfriendly. But . . ."

He reached for another biscuit. "You went into town yest'day," he observed at last, through a mouthful of gingernut sog. "Yest'day morning early, it was."

"Yes, that's right." So we were going to have an inquest into my recent movements, were we? I took a biscuit myself. "I went to see my solicitor, about Mum's will."

"I saw you walkin' out the office." Nathan dunked another biscuit. "Everythin' coming along all right there, is it?"

"Yes." I shrugged. "Well, no," I admitted. "Not really. There shouldn't be any terrible problems, but solicitors always seem to take their time. I still don't know if I own this house, and—"

"So it might be your dad's after all, eh?"

"It might. But I doubt it." Again, I shrugged. "I can't see my mother leaving it to anybody but me."

"Provided it was hers to leave, of course."

"Exactly."

"If you *do* inherit property here, will you come back to live in Hartley Cross? Permanent, like?"

"I've been thinking about that." Much more relaxed now, I smiled. "Some days, I think I'd really love to live here again. It's so beautiful, especially in the summer time. I work from home anyway, so it doesn't matter that I'd be rather remote."

"There's a fast train service to Paddington, anyway."

"Quite." I looked at Nathan. Did *he* know about Jael and Simon, I wondered. Might Nathan Casson be able to answer my questions, to resolve a few conundrums for me? "It was lovely to see Simon again," I observed, thinking to open the way.

But Nathan only grunted.

"I have missed him, you know." I shook my head. "He meant such a lot to me! Sometimes, I wonder if we could pick up again. Where we left off, I mean."

"You reckon you might?" enquired Nathan.

"I honestly don't know." *Tell* me, I thought! Tell me if I've been imagining things, because if Jael and Simon really are an item, I know for a fact that it's all up for me! "There doesn't seem to be anyone else in his life," I went on, crossing my fingers under the table, hoping against hope that my visitor would agree.

But Nathan merely shrugged. "You don't give up, do you?" he whispered, softly.

"Well, I like to exhaust all the possibilities, certainly."

"I've realised that." Nathan's gaze met mine. He placed his mug on the table, then slid his hands into his trouser pockets. "Like I said, I saw you come out of that office, yesterday. I followed you all round the town, in fact. Then back to the car. I saw you open the boot, an' all."

"Did you? But what—"

213

"Don't interrupt!" He glared at me. "That's the trouble with girls like you! Always interfering, interrupting, askin' stupid questions! As for you, Lindsay Ellis – you've always known better'n anybody else, haven't you? You always got somethin' clever to suggest. Summat smart to say!"

"I beg your pardon?" I stared at him. Whatever was the matter with the man? But then, I twigged. "Nathan," I soothed, "I've told you, I didn't *mean* to upset Rebekah today, and—"

"Godsake, will you shut up about Rebekah?" Nathan's eyes narrowed, becoming thin, grey slits. "I was up Brougham Gate," he muttered. "Earlier'n you thought, I was there! I heard you talking to our Reb, interrogatin' her!"

"But Nathan, I've already said I'm sorry! I—"

"Sorry, sorry, sorry! Yeah, you'll be sorry all right!" Pushing his mug to one side, he leaned towards me, until his heavy, handsome face was only inches from mine. "You want to know how it happened, don't you?" he whispered. "Who did it. How it was done, and why. Well – what business is it of yours? That's what I'd like to know!"

"Nathan, have you been drinking?" For, although the Nathan *I* knew was always an amiable drunkard, there didn't seem to be any other explanation for this aggressive behaviour – and, in spite of his earlier insistence that he was only being good-neighbourly and checking up on me, I still wasn't at all sure why he'd chosen to come round here tonight, to harangue *me*. "Nathan, I'm sorry, but I—"

"You will be." Nathan grimaced. "Like I said before, sorry is just what you're going to be!"

"Nathan, please!" I'd had enough of this. "I can see you're upset, but I don't like being threatened, not even in fun. So if you've finished your coffee . . ."

"Very familiar with that Oxford man, ain't you?" he interrupted. He regarded me with distaste. "Took him all round the village, didn't you? Up Castle Copse, across the fields, over the glebe. Even brought him to our Jael's party! Didn't care about Simon's feelings then, did you? Didn't care about old Simon at all!"

"Oh, Nathan!" At last, at long last, I understood what this was all about. In an admittedly tactless, blundering and roundabout way, Nathan was expressing his concern for his friend. He'd seen I was on good terms with Nick Singer, completely misunderstood the nature of the Oxford set-up, and had assumed I was Nick's mistress, that I was flaunting him in front of Simon just to make him jealous and upset.

Reassuringly, I smiled. "Nick is just a friend," I explained. I met Nathan's gaze. "There is nothing what-soever between Nick Singer and me! We happen to live in the same house, that's all, and we certainly don't—"

"Oh, shut up." Nathan glared at me. "I don't want to know," he growled. "I ain't interested in anything you gets up to with that bugger, whether he screws you or you fucks 'im."

"Nathan, please!" Now, I was very offended. Even if Nathan *was* drunk, there was no reason for him to talk to me like that. I stood up. "I have a lot to do tomorrow," I began, coldly, "and I'm sure you'll be making an early start, so I think you ought to be off. If you've finished your coffee, that is?"

Glancing into his mug, I saw that he had. So, collecting

the mugs to take them over to the sink, I made the terrible mistake of turning away from him.

I never even heard him get up. But then, suddenly, my arms were seized in a pincer-like grip and twisted behind my back. Before I understood what was happening – before I could even think about scraping my heel down his shin, or elbowing him in the solar plexus – the rope was being tied around my wrists, so tightly that it burned my skin. The kitchen door was jerked open, and I was hustled out into the night.

My terror almost choked me. But, all the same, somewhere at the back of my mind, a little voice was assuring me that this was all a joke. That my assailant *must* be drunk. Or drugged. At any rate, he wasn't in his perfect mind. For God's sake – I had known him since he was a child! We'd been at junior school together. He and all his brothers and sisters were as familiar to me as my own family . . .

"Nathan!" At last, I found my voice. "Nathan," I pleaded, "please stop fooling around! Why are you doing this to me?"

He made no reply. Instead, he dragged me across the paving stones outside the back door, past the scullery window and into the wash-yard. I tried again. "Nathan," I wailed, "you're hurting me! Look, I know I upset Reb. I daresay I've hurt Simon's feelings, too. But I've never injured you, so why—"

"Shut up!" he hissed. "Shut your mouth, an' keep walking. Or it'll be the worse for you!"

I did as I was told. We stumbled a few steps further, and then we were in a dark and dismal corner, where the pipes came down from the guttering on the roof and emptied into a big, old-fashioned grated drain. Nathan pushed me into a squatting position. Then, he tied me to the pipes. My hands useless behind me, all I could do was sit there, while he tied knot after knot after knot. Dozens of knots . . .

I know, I know, I should have kicked him then. Screamed at him, spat at him, butted him where it would hurt! But, although I cannot quite believe it now, it never occurred to me to do any one of those things.

I'd slipped into victim mode, I suppose. I've read about this since, and apparently it isn't unusual, people who've been attacked say one just does. All I can advance in explanation of my own passivity is that surprise, confusion and terror stultified me.

Nathan finished his looping and tying. He stood back, glared at me, turned on his heel. Then, he strode off into the night.

I couldn't decide if I was relieved or not. As I stared after him I thought, he will come back, won't he? But did I want him to return? What would he do then? Take out the weapon he'd obviously forgotten to bring with him this time, and kill me?

Surely not! Although if he left me here all night, he wouldn't have to do the deed himself, because by the morning I'd have frozen to death.

Ten minutes or so after he'd melted into the darkness, I began to hope that this was it, that he wasn't going to return, after all. If I hadn't been so scared and so bloody cold, I might have found my situation laughable, even, for I was beginning to feel like somebody in one of those silent films, where the girl is tied to the railway line, and the villain stands gloating, waiting for the train.

Appreciating how ridiculous this whole thing was, I began to feel a little braver. I tugged at my bonds. Feeling some of the knots sliding on the cheap nylon rope, I experienced a sudden surge of elation. Now, I would get away!

But then, I realised it was no good. By jerking on the rope, I was only pulling the big knots even tighter. If I wanted to escape, I'd have to squirm and wriggle free.

As I tried to do this, as I chafed my poor wrists and felt rope burns sear my flesh, I tried to fathom what this was all about.

The best explanation I could come up with was that Nathan must be trying to protect somebody. To this end, he needed to scare me. But *whose* secret was he guarding? Who could be in danger because of me?

It had to be a member of his family. Who else could be so important to him that my life seemed to be of no consequence?

No consequence at all?

Chapter Nineteen

There was no point in shouting. No one would have heard a thing. The Larches stood well back from the road, which was much too far away for a casual passerby to hear anything yelled from round the back of the house. The grounds were extensive, and surrounded on all sides by tall, sound-absorbing hedges of hawthorn and yew.

If only I could get up, I thought. If I could stand and jig about, get my circulation going, I might be in with a chance of coming through all this!

I tugged again at my bonds. Then, I had a brain wave. If I could slide the ropes up the pipe, I decided, I might be able to struggle to my feet. But after I'd slid them up just a few wretched inches, I hit the bracket which fastened the drainpipe to the wall. I sat down again, with a bump.

I wanted to cry. I wanted to sob and howl, I wanted to scream that this wasn't fair, that nobody should have come here, to my own house, for God's sake, and done this to me!

The tears welled up, threatening to spill over. But, I didn't actually cry. Some instinct for self-preservation forbade it, told me I needed to conserve my strength. I had to sit here quietly, I understood that, and see this horrible business through.

But it could have been worse, I thought, as I sniffed the

219

air. For, although it was cold, it didn't sear my nostrils, nor was I exhaling clouds of steam when I breathed out again. It was the end of November, sure enough. But there did not *have* to be a frost.

I was out of the wind. My dressing gown was old, but far more serviceable than the one I'd left in Oxford. My father had always favoured thick, woollen, horse blanket affairs complete with braided edging and wide, chest-protecting lapels – and now I blessed him for it. This woolly antique would keep out much of the cold and damp.

Nathan *would* come back, to let me go. After all, he could not actually want me to die, could he? Surely not! What had I ever done to him or, more to the point, what did he think I knew, that he should wish to silence me forever?

Nothing. Nothing at all. All I'd done was make Rebekah cry. But this reflection did not really comfort me, for Nathan loved his little sister dearly, and would have deeply resented any injury done to her, that poor helpless creature whom all the Cassons protected with the possessive feroc-ity of a pride of lions guarding their weakest cub.

"When he comes back," I decided, "when he's sobered up and realises what he's done, he'll be all apologies, and I'll try to explain. He might be uneducated, but he's certainly not stupid. He's bound to understand why I'm so anxious. He wouldn't want a killer walking free any more than I do."

I stared into the darkness, straining my eyes and ears. The night was full of chittering and rustling and the shuffling of little feet in the damp, wormy undergrowth, but all I could see was blackness. My own feet and hands were frozen. I could not feel them any more.

I was so tired. So sleepy. I closed my eyes.

*   *   *

The cry of some night creature, either hunting or being hunted in its turn, was what roused me. Blinking wretchedly, I stared all around, trying to focus on whatever it might be.

I saw only the garden, bathed in cold, white light. For, since I'd slept, the clouds had been mostly blown away, the moon had risen, and there were thousands of stars in the velvet black sky.

I wondered what the time was. Could it be early, still? Or was it late? *Very* late? I had absolutely no idea. But then, as I gazed across the silvery lawns, my heart almost stopped beating. He had come back! Nathan was here, in the garden. Had he come to release me? Or to finish what he'd started, to end it all for me?

Or *was* it Nathan? This person was making his way across the flower garden. Straying now and then from the wide gravel path, he or she was moving erratically up and down, sometimes stooping, sometimes crouching very low, but then moving on again.

I stared hard. Now, I could hear the person muttering. This was ridiculous. Convinced I was hallucinating, I shut my eyes. When I opened them again, I reasoned, the person would have disappeared. But no. When I looked again, the person was moving closer to me.

A shred of dark grey cloud, steered by the wind, crossed the moon's pale face. The garden grew almost as bright as day. Then, with a start, I realised who the midnight rambler must be.

Jael was in my mother's ornamental herb garden, pulling up plants wholesale, or so it seemed, and shoving her spoils into a plastic carrier bag. I was so pleased to see another human being that I completely forgot she was supposed to be my enemy. I called, or rather croaked her name aloud.

221

She spun round. Guiltily, she started, staring into the black hole of the laundry yard. Panic seized me then, and I thought, what have I done? What if Nathan was trying to protect *her*? I'm in more danger now than I ever was!

I wished, how I wished I had kept my mouth shut! After all, there was a chance, a very small chance admittedly, that I could have squirmed free of my bonds, raised the alarm, called the police . . .

It was too late. She'd seen me and, frowning, she made her way across the lawn and stood before me where I crouched, helpless, cold and very much afraid.

Realising I was tied to the pipe, she pursed her lips in puzzlement. Or was it scorn? In any case, when she reached out to touch me, I almost fainted. "D-don't!" I managed to stammer, at last. "Oh, God! Please don't hurt me! I was only trying to . . ."

But then I tailed off, sobbing.

Jael dropped her plastic bag on the flagstones. "Good grief," she murmured, crouching down. "Heavens above, Lin! Whoever did this?" Peering at the cat's cradle of rope, she shook her head. "Hold still," she whispered. "Try not to wriggle, it'll make it harder for me."

So then, instead of hurting me, she began to unfasten my hands.

"W-what are you doing here?" I asked, as she tugged at the loops and knots.

"Doing?" Again, she pursed her lips. For a few moments, she seemed to hesitate, and I supposed she was concocting some tall tale. But then, she shrugged. "I was picking some of that there yeller stonecrop," she muttered. "Stonecrop and saxifrage, I wanted. They needs to be gathered by the light of the full moon, see. Otherwise, they don't have no power."

"Power?" I gaped at her. But then, I understood. "Oh, Jael!" I wanted to laugh out loud. I would have done, if my frozen face had let me. "Poor Jael, you silly, superstitious . . ."

That last word came out all wrong. Sispishishus, it sounded like to me. Jael frowned again. "Yeah, I know it's wrong," she admitted. "I know it's bad, to be stealing, like. But a few bits of stonecrop – I never thought you'd mind."

"Of course I don't mind!" I was sobbing again, but this time with pure, unadulterated relief. "Oh, Jael!" I repeated, wanting to kiss her, to hug her, then to kiss her all over again.

But there was no time for any of that. Instead, I sat slumped as Jael worked on, as she undid the final knot, tossed the rope aside, and slid her arm around my waist. Then, she helped me struggle to my feet. "Let's get you into the house," she said.

She took me into the kitchen. She opened all the doors of the range, then sat me down beside it, with my feet on the fender, for all the world like a chilled spring lamb brought in out of the rain and sleet. Then she made me hot chocolate, which she fed me on a spoon.

"Who was it?" she asked quietly, evenly.

I stared at her. "D-don't you know?" I managed to stammer, at last. For, feeling was returning to my frozen hands and feet. The blood was trying to push its way into the narrowed veins and arteries, not succeeding very well, and I was in considerable pain. "You mean you don't – you weren't following him?"

"What are you talking about?" She shook her head. "Come on, Lindsay," she whispered. "I can see you're shocked and upset. But don't look at *me* like I tried to do you in!"

"I'm sorry." Wearily, I sighed. "It was Nathan."

"Oh." Jael shrugged. "I see."

"You see, but you're not surprised. Jael—"

"I didn't know! Honest to God, I never thought he – well, what I mean is, I can't account for his coming round here and doing this to you. All I can say is, he seems to have been under a lot of strain recently."

"What?" Nathan, under strain? Come on, I thought, pull the other one, it's got little silver bells on. For, as everyone in Hartley Cross knew perfectly well, Nathan Casson was one of the most laid-back, easy-going individuals on God's green earth. "What sort of strain?" I enquired.

Jael did not reply. Instead, she offered me more hot chocolate. Gratefully, I sipped. Then, "Jael?" I prompted.

She sighed. "He's mostly okay," she murmured. "Most of the time, he's like the rest of us, just rubs along. Has a drink, spends a few quid on the lottery, wins a tenner now and again – he gets by. But now and then, things get too much for him, and he breaks out."

"Breaks out?" I repeated. I met her gaze. "You know, don't you?" I said.

"I know what?"

"Please, Jael!" For now, I was certain. Jael was no murderess, it was true. But although she herself might be innocent of any crime, those she was protecting were guilty as hell. "Jael," I whispered, "you know everything. Why Nathan's got it in for me. Why Simon is behaving so strangely, all over me one minute but ignoring me the next. You know who killed Louis Dyer, too."

"Your hands are like blocks of ice." Jael stirred my drink. "Come on," she prompted. "Have your chocolate. I ain't put nothing in it, promise."

"Jael, you must tell me!"

"Tell you what?" She shrugged. "I dunno what you're going on about, and that's the honest truth, so help me God. You're still in shock, seems to me."

I understood. I would get nothing out of her that night.

She had filled the big kettle, put it on to boil, and now she found a couple of the ancient stoneware hot water bottles which my mother had kept in the cupboard under the sink. Carefully, she poured scalding water into each. "Come on," she encouraged, helping me to my feet. "Let's get you to bed. Don't worry, I'll sit up. I'll make sure you're all right."

"But what about your husband?" I objected. "Isn't he expecting you back, and doesn't the baby need—"

"Don't you fret about none of that." She gave me a gee-up and make the best of it grin, which was quite unlike her usual lazy smile. "In a minute or so, I'll give old Neil a ring. Tell him I'm staying here with you."

"But what will you say?"

"Oh, I dunno." She thought for a moment. "That I called in to see you, I suppose. That I couldn't get no answer, and when I come round the back, I found you'd had a bit of a turn." She met my gaze. "I reckon that's just about the size of it."

"But—"

"Don't get yourself all upset." Obviously, she could still sense my fear. "Don't worry about our Nathan, either. He won't bother you again. Neil'll see to him."

"Oh."

I could hardly keep my eyes open. So tired that I actually felt sick, I ached all over and felt horribly dizzy, too. Had I been doped? In spite of Jael's assurance to the contrary, I wouldn't have put it past her to have laced my chocolate.

But, all the same, I let her take me upstairs. I let her tuck me up with a hot water bottle against my back and another at my feet. I let her sit down beside me, to watch over me whilst I slept.

The following morning, I woke late to see clear blue sky between the half-drawn bedroom curtains. Behind my back, somebody was smoothing my duvet. For a moment, I thought it was my mother, and was about to tell her to leave me alone. I wanted a lie-in today.

I blinked, then yawned. I still felt very groggy. Had I slept right through the night? Or had those dreams, which I could still half remember, in fact been reality? In the early hours of the morning, when it was just beginning to get light, had somebody really shaken me awake? Made me sit up, and drink some warm, soothing liquid, which tasted of lemons and spice?

I rubbed my gritty eyes. There were sleeping tablets in the bathroom cabinet. My mother had been hooked on Mogadon. I wouldn't have put it past Jael – for, of course, it *was* Jael who had drawn the curtains back and invited in the day – to have had a little poke around the place.

My nurse came round to the other side of the bed. She crouched down beside me. "How do you feel this morning?" she enquired.

"Okay, I suppose." I rubbed my eyes again. "All things considered, that is."

"I reckon you'll live." Jael grinned. Then, she helped me sit to up. She buttoned my nightdress up to the neck, she smoothed my hair out of my eyes – made me decent, as my grandmother would have put it. "You've got a visitor," she told me.

"Oh?" I didn't want Nathan Casson anywhere within a mile of my house! I didn't want his apology, his explanation – whatever – either. "I don't want visitors," I muttered, sliding down into the bed.

"You'll be pleased to see this one." Jael turned towards the door. "You can come in!" she cried.

So then the door opened and Nick Singer, looking creased and a bit sheepish, entered the room. "Hello," he said.

"Right, then." Maternally, Jael beamed at us both. "I'll let you two get on."

"Don't leave me!" Panicking, I grabbed at her hand. "Jael, don't go! You mustn't go—"

"You'll be all right." Jael smiled benignly. "Nick here'll look after you."

"But . . ."

"Like I said, you needn't worry about old Nathan. Neil's seeing to him! But if he *should* come round here, yelling his head off an' carrying on, Nick'll soon sort *him* out!" Flirtatiously, she eyed Nick Singer. "Big strong fella like Nick, he could deal with our Nathan any day."

"I suppose." I felt too weak and confused to argue, so I let it be. Jael slipped out of the bedroom. Seconds later, I heard the front door slam.

Nick stood at the bottom of the bed, idly glancing all around. Although he was familiar with the rest of the house, he had never entered this room before, never been allowed to see this time capsule of my childhood, my collection of china horses, my ancient teddy bears and dolls, my Enid Blytons and Judy Blumes in neat, colour-coded rows. This morning, all lay exposed to his critical gaze, and I didn't like that one bit. "Why are you here?" I enquired, not very cordially.

"I was summoned, wasn't I?" He shrugged. "Jael rang me, see. At the lab. No, she hasn't been going through your handbag. She noticed you'd left my number by your phone."

"But why did she ring *you*?"

"She said you needed me." Nick rubbed his eyes. He stifled a yawn. "So there I was, just about to come off the night shift and looking forward to a nice, big breakfast, when one of the porters comes to look for me. "You got a phone call," he says. "The lady reckons it's urgent." I thought somebody had died."

"But what did Jael say?"

"Just that she thought I should be here." Once more, Nick rubbed his tired eyes. "She didn't go into details."

"But you came, anyway."

"As you see."

"Why?"

"Why not?" Again, he shrugged. But he did not elaborate further.

"Nick?" I prompted.

"I dunno, really." He smothered a second yawn. "Look," he continued, "I'm a bit tired. Been up all night, and that. So if it's all right with you, I'll grab forty winks."

"Be my guest." I regarded him narrowly. "But the bed's not made up."

"I just need to catch up on my sleep. I'm not bothered where." He grinned. "Upstairs, downstairs. Lyin' across the threshold here, if you want – whichever you prefer. Can I get you anything?"

"Such as?"

"Something to eat? To drink?"

"I wouldn't mind a cup of tea," I replied.

He went downstairs, reappearing five minutes later with a mug of tea and a packet of Bourbon biscuits. I ate some biscuits, drank my tea, then lay back against my pillows.

The goal posts had shifted yet again. Nick and Jael were the conspirators now. Bossing me around. Dosing me with herbal sedatives, or whatever. Having private conversations with one another, giving me orders . . .

Nick took my mug. "Go back to sleep now," he told me.

"But I'm not tired," I objected. "I'm not sleepy at all, I—"

"Well, *I* bloody am!" He scowled at me. "Look, today we're gonna get to the bottom of all this. But you can't do nothing without me. So for once in your life, just do as you're told."

He glanced towards my bookcase. "You don't actually have to *sleep*," he muttered. "Read one of them Secret Seven books, if you prefer." He walked towards the door.

"Nick, where are you going?"

"To get some sleep, like I said. If that's all right with you?"

I didn't comment.

He left the room, and two seconds later I heard him stump downstairs.

I didn't think I'd sleep again. But, when I closed my eyes for a moment, a light doze must have become a deep slumber. I woke again at half-past eleven, feeling much better and greatly refreshed.

I washed quickly, then dressed in jeans and a couple of thick, woollen jumpers. I walked into the drawing room to find Nick lolling on the sofa, three or four unwashed cups on the side table at his elbow, and garlands of computer print-out festooning every piece of furniture in the place.

"This is all very Christmassy," I observed.

"Yeah, isn't it?" He shoved a small avalanche of A4 to one side. "Sit down," he invited.

So I did.

Nick looked at me. "How do you feel now?" he enquired.

"Much better, thank you."

"Good." Gravely, he nodded. "You look much better, too."

"I doubt that very much." I shook my head. I was beginning to wonder if the events of last night had all been a bad dream. "Nick," I began, "I don't know what Jael's been saying to you, but the fact is—"

"You ain't safe to be left alone, that's what the fact is. You need—"

"I don't need a babysitter!" I interrupted. "Nick, don't misunderstand me. I'm obliged to you for dropping everything at the lab, for coming over here today. But—"

"Don't think I came just because Jael asked me to." Nick was frowning at me now. "I think you ought to tell me what's going on," he said.

"But I *did* tell you."

"I need to know everything. I don't want just the edited highlights. I ain't got attention deficit disorder, I can follow a story the whole of the way." Glancing away, Nick looked down at his hands. "But if you think it's none of my business, just say the word, and I'll go back to Oxford straight away. This very minute, in fact. Then, you and the Starkadders can sort out your differences in private, and the best of luck to you."

He turned back to stare at me, his eyes bright and hard. "You'll need a bit of luck, believe you me."

He was right. But, more than that, I felt I owed him. So I explained. As best I could, anyway. I told him how I'd upset Rebekah. How I'd spoken to Simon, with whom I was getting on very well these days, how I'd told him I was convinced Rebekah knew who had murdered Louis Dyer. How I'd had a night visitor, who had – perhaps – tried to silence *me*.

"But I expect *you* think that's all very funny," I muttered. "The fact that I was trussed up like a chicken, I mean, and tied to the wall. The fact that I sat there like an idiot, waiting for somebody to come and let me loose."

Nick said nothing. Instead, he grimaced. Because, I supposed, he was trying not to laugh. "Well, it *is* funny," I conceded, as I blinked away a tear, which had unaccountably welled up and was wobbling precariously on my lower lashes. "That sort of thing hasn't happened to me since I was seven years old. Not since my brother and I used to play Cowboys and Indians, and we—"

"I don't think it's funny," interrupted Nick. Gravely, steadily, he looked at me. "Okay, so it was a childish thing to do, and I can't imagine why he bothered. But I don't find the idea of somebody hurting *you* funny at all."

"Oh." I shrugged. "He's obviously protecting someone," I concluded, picking at a thread of upholstery, then twisting it round my fingers, miserably. "He thinks I'm on to them, and wants me silenced."

"You reckon?" Nick shrugged. "I dunno about that."

"What's your explanation, then?"

"I don't have one. Yet." Nick stood up. "Bastard," he muttered.

"Who's a bastard?"

"What?" Nick stared down at me. "This Simon guy."

"I don't wish to discuss Simon."

"No, I don't suppose you do." Nick shook his head. "You say you're getting on well with him these days. But do you think there's a chance that you two might get back together again?"

"Nick, I *told* you . . ."

"Yeah, you did. Right, then. Let's have some lunch. Then we'll go and call on Mr Nathan Casson."

"Oh, Nick! Do you think that would be wise?"

"Well? What do you suggest?" Nick raised one eyebrow. "That we go to the police? Great idea. The inhabitants of this Godforsaken little dump are famous for co-operating with the police."

"But Nick, he's so big! He's strong, he's—"

"He's out to lunch, definitely." Again, Nick shrugged. "Yeah, well – there're two of us this time. You go for his knees."

We ate some lunch. Or rather, Nick did. He devoured sliced white bread, processed cheese and some chutney of dubious provenance which he'd found at the back of the larder. Meanwhile, I drank three cups of tea, and worried a Bath Oliver to death.

We got into the car. The idea of confronting Nathan Casson was making me feel quite sick. But this time, I told myself, at least I had Nick to hold my hand. I was properly dressed, I was rested, and I was prepared.

However, gloom soon descended again. So what, I'm rested, I thought, as we drove down Ruddle Pit Lane, past Jael's immaculate cottage and garden, and out into the open countryside. So what, I'm prepared, I murmured to myself, as we made our way down rutted tracks towards the seedy little bungalow by the glebe, which was the place Nathan Casson called home.

It was Nick who kept my spirits up. Nick who stopped me chickening out completely, and simply running away. "That family, they're like the bloody Mafia," he muttered, as we drove over potholes and through mud and mire. "Talk about *Cosa Nostra* meets bleedin' *Cold Comfort Farm!*"

"They're very clannish," I agreed. "They look out for one another, certainly."

"It's unnatural, the way they go on." Nick glanced at me. "I mean – *you* got a brother. But you don't spend your life in his pocket, do you? I doubt if you ever have, even when he lived in the same house as you did."

"Well, *we* were never very close. We don't even see each other nowadays." I shrugged. "We haven't fallen out or anything. We've just sort of drifted apart, I suppose. Nick, I never asked – do you have brothers or sisters?"

"Two older sisters." Nick shrugged, too. "They're okay – quite nice girls, actually. But we don't have a lot in common."

"What do they do?"

"One's a hairdresser, in Ilford. Got her own salon these days. Top rank stylists from all over, half a dozen local kids on youth opportunity schemes – everything. The other's a gangster's moll."

"Go on!"

"It's true!" Nick grinned. "She's a kept woman. Terrible, I know. Especially in these enlightened times. But she *is* kept by Avi the Aardvark, so you have to make allowances. I suppose."

I mulled this over. Then, Nick was at it again, I realised. Teasing me. Having me on. "She's kept by whom, did you say?" I enquired, to see if he could remember.

"Avigdor Stein. He's a crook." Again, Nick grinned. "He runs – now let me see. A debt-collecting agency. An escort service. A whole string of massage parlours, all over the South East. But he's into illegal liposuction these days. Alternative medicine, as well. That's his biggest racket right now."

"You do have interesting friends and relations," I observed.

"Not half so interesting as yours. Homicidal maniacs, religious fanatics, manic-depressive alcoholics – you name it." Nick shook his head. "Avi's quite a good bloke, really. Offered me a holiday job last summer, as a minder – a grand a week, all found. Pity I was busy at the labs. But he said, no worries. Any time I need to earn a few quid."

"Oh, well. If you mess up your research, it'll be something to fall back on."

"That's what I thought." Nick nodded. "I'm dead unfit at the moment. But if I lift a few weights, pump a bit of iron, I expect I'll do. Eventually."

"I'm sure you will," I agreed.

I relaxed against the back of my seat. If it came to a punch up, I reflected, I could always get behind my friend.

Chapter Twenty

Nathan was not there. As we walked round the bungalow, a shabby, lime-washed building constructed primarily of breezeblock and cement shingle, it became clear that there had been nobody at home for days.

For the place was as silent as the tomb. The blinds were down, and the ragged curtains all drawn tight. Two free-sheets, delivered by unusually intrepid newsboys, were shoved half-way through the letterbox, and dog mess lay mouldering in furry grey sausages on the tiny area of scrubby lawn. A copious scattering of large bones, supplied no doubt by Baines Brothers and probably well gnawed by Nathan's big black hound, made the place look like some sort of voodoo temple yard. But, to my relief, our local Baron Samedi himself was nowhere in evidence today.

Taking after his father, Saul, Nathan ran a sort of business patching up old wrecks and insurance write-offs. Several of these sorry vehicles, in various stages of renovation or decay, littered the muddy scrap-yard which was the closest Nathan came to having a garden. But there was no work in progress this afternoon.

"Where else might he be, then?" asked Nick, who was eyeing this whole ramshackle set-up with unconcealed distaste.

"I really don't know." Through a hole in the tattered blind, I peered into the kitchen. It looked even more neglected and disgusting than the one at Ferry Road. "Staying with a brother or sister, perhaps? Maybe he's gone to see his girlfriend. She lives in Worcester, I believe." I turned back to Nick. "The dog's not here. So he must mean to be away for a day or two, at least."

"Right." Nick started to walk back to the car. "Let's get on."

"But where are we going?"

"Well – for a start, do you know what this girlfriend's name is?"

"I'm sorry, I don't."

"Have you any idea where she lives?"

"None at all, I'm afraid."

"Then we'll just have to do the rounds." Bumping and jolting over the ruts, Nick reversed out of Nathan's muddy driveway. "So where shall we try first?"

I thought about it. The sensible answer was, of course, anywhere and everywhere. Mentally spinning a coin, I decided that Nathan was far more likely to be working than holed up in a brother's or sister's house – so, "he might be at Weobley's Yard," I suggested, at last. "He helps Jack Weobley break up wrecks, you see. For stock car racing, and spares."

"That's the same Jack Weobley who advertises in the post office, is it?"

"Goodness, aren't you observant?" Impressed, I nodded. "Yes, that's the one."

"Right." Nick revved the engine. "You'd better give me directions."

So I did, reassuring myself that if we should find Nathan at Jack's place, he wouldn't dare start anything there.

Jack's somewhat illiterate postcard had always been in the post office window, for as long as I could recall. These days it was curled and faded, the card yellowing, the ball-point writing grey with age. "Old Car's Wanted," it proclaimed. "Any Condition. Top Prices Paid. Cash Wating!!!"

I believe he offered a tenner a wreck – the scrap value, if that. But since he and Nathan were old mates, and often drank together in the Rose at Ashton Cross, I daresay the price of a pint was all Nathan expected for helping Jack. If, indeed, he ever got paid.

As for Weobley's Yard, this was really a field, in the middle of nowhere. Littered with wrecked cars, written-off lorries and all manner of other rusting junk, it was a local eyesore which numerous campaigns for its closure had completely failed to eradicate. In fact, it looked even more extensive and decrepit today than it ever had during my childhood in Hartley Cross.

We finally found Jack Weobley in the dilapidated double-decker bus which was also his workshop, rubbing green slime on his hands to clean them. Obviously, he was about to go home for his dinner.

"Sorry," he said, when I told him whom we wanted to see. "Never set eyes on the bugger once, this side of Monday morning." He grinned, then winked. "I reckon he's gone to ground, if you're askin' me."

"Why do you say that?"

"Well, the fact is, last Wednesday I saw his brother Daniel in town. *He* was tellin' me old Nathan's got this girl at the moment. Lives in Worcester, I think he said. The family's dead keen to meet her." Jack tapped the side of his nose. "But old Nathe, he's keepin' her to hisself."

"That's wise, perhaps," I observed.

"Yeah, *I* thought that." Sagaciously, Jack sighed. "They're a funny lot, them Cassons. Well, old Nathe's okay, but some of 'ems definitely not right in the head! So look, if he does call in, shall I ask him to give you a bell?"

"No, that's all right. It's not very important." I shrugged, then smiled. "I might catch him in the Lamb and Flag this evening, anyway."

"Right you are." Then, Jack shook his head. "I was ever so sorry to hear about your mum," he began.

"Oh. Thank you," I murmured, turning away.

"She can't have been all that old?"

"No, she wasn't." I didn't want to talk about my mother, so now I began to walk back to the car. Jack and Nick followed me.

When I got into the Escort, Jack crouched down and peered into the interior, examining it with a connoisseur's eye. "Give my love to Marjorie and the children," I said, as I fastened my seat belt.

"I'll do that." He grinned. "Nice little runner you got here," he remarked, nodding at Nick.

"It's okay." Nick turned on the ignition.

"Escorts this old can sometimes be a bit dodgy, though." Jack narrowed his eyes. "Ever get any problems with that there clutch?"

"No. None." Nick put the engine into gear. "Be seeing you, mate. Watch how you go."

Jack withdrew his head just in time, for Nick reversed at speed, then accelerated out of the yard.

"Where to next?" demanded my chauffeur, as we rolled in first down the one-in-six which was Highwayman's Hill and the local accident black spot.

"Babylon," I replied.

238

"You what?"

"It's a dairy farm, over Hampton Harcourt way. Nathan sometimes services the milking machinery, for Mr Greenwood there."

"How many miles to Babylon?"

"Only two. Then we could try up at Offa's Dyke House. He works for Major Harding at this time of year. Chopping logs, and that."

"Versatile little bugger, isn't he?" Nick glanced towards me. "Are you okay?" he demanded.

"Yes, fine. Why?"

"You're dead pale. I expect you're hungry."

"No, not really."

"Well, I am." He gestured towards the glove compartment on the passenger side. "Give us a Mars Bar. Have one yourself, too."

Nick ate his Mars Bar – a king-size one, of course – and also kept an eye on me, to make sure I ate mine. I did. But then, of course, I felt really sick. "There're some cans of Coke on the back seat," said my companion. "Reach us one over."

"God, your diet." I shook my head in disgust. "You'll be dead and buried long before you're forty."

"Yeah, well – we all gotta die some time." Nick slurped Coke, then wiped his mouth on the back of his hand. "Here," he continued, "just this once won't kill you."

I took the can. I had a gulp. The Coke washed away the taste of Mars bar, but I felt my teeth decaying almost spontaneously.

"Look, Nick – I'm sorry about this." It was half-past three, and the light was failing fast. We'd been to Babylon, to Offa's Dyke House, not to mention five or six of the

239

other farms or private houses where I knew Nathan and his brothers sometimes found work on the side.

Despairing, I sighed. "Those are all the places I can think of," I admitted. "But there are bound to be others. Dozens of them, in fact! He could be anywhere, I'm afraid."

"I see." Nick shook his head. "So this is how it all works," he muttered. "Your actual black economy, I mean. Tell me, is everyone from Hartley Cross on the fiddle?"

"I don't know." I shrugged. "I expect the people in the new houses out on the executive estate have proper jobs. *They* pay their income tax, I suppose."

We spent the rest of that fading afternoon wasting more petrol, more tyre tread, and lots more time. But, to my surprise – and, I must add, relief – Nick did not seem to be getting annoyed. He seemed calm. Relaxed, even. When we stopped for a think – or for me to think and to let him have a rest – he leaned back in his seat, stretched, yawned, then laughed out loud.

"What's the joke?" I enquired.

"*We* are." He rubbed his eyes. "I mean – just look at us! Here we are, in a clapped-out old banger, chasing this shit-head all round the county, all by our little selves. If we'd really wanted to find the bugger, we should have rung Avi. Asked him to get a few of his hard men up here. In fast cars, and with mobile phones."

"I don't think so." Nervously, I glanced at Nick. "When we do find him, you – you will be careful, won't you?"

"Careful?" he repeated.

"I mean, you won't do anything silly. You'll just talk to him, and—"

"Yeah, I'll talk," said Nick. He met my gaze. "Don't

240

worry. I'm going to talk to that sod like he's never been talked to before. In the whole of his stupid life."

Reaching for his six-pack, he cracked open another can of Coke. But then, as he offered me the first glug, our eyes met again. "You *are* all right, aren't you?" he murmured, his voice gentle, and kind. "Only you don't look all that grand."

"I'm okay," I told him. "I promise you. I'm fine."

"Good." Carefully, he placed the Coke can on the shelf above the dashboard. "All this business – well, it can't be very pleasant for you."

"It's not." I shrugged. "But you're helping me to cope. In fact, you're a regular knight in shining armour these days!" I attempted a brave little smile. "Nick, I meant to say this before. I'm really grateful for what you've done. I do appreciate—"

"I don't do this shining armour stuff routinely, you know," he interrupted.

"You don't?" I teased.

"No, of course I bloody don't!" He leaned towards me and then, very lightly, very fleetingly, he kissed me on the cheek. "I think we ought to get on," he said.

But Nathan had so many part-time jobs, so many casual employers, so many mates and so many pals whom he occasionally helped out, that it would have been impossible to check up on them all. Officially, of course, he was unemployed. So, he had to report to the unemployment benefit office from time to time. It occurred to me now that this might be his day for signing on. If that was indeed the case, he would have gone into Hereford, where he'd no doubt cash his giro, then spend the money on lottery Instants. Or in a city pub.

All the same – Nick and I spent the rest of that afternoon

on a scenic tour of Herefordshire. Everywhere, we drew the same short straw. Nobody had seen Nathan. Everybody offered to tell him we had called. But nobody knew when they expected to see him again.

We arrived back at Hartley Cross tired and dispirited. The last of the daylight had long seeped away, and I was most definitely not looking forward to the night. "He could be up at Simon's place," I hazarded, as Nick indicated to turn into my driveway. "It's not very likely, I know. But he just might."

"You reckon?" Nick glanced towards me. "Toiling in the master's vineyard, eh?"

"What?"

"Ploughing the young squire's lonely furrow."

"What *are* you talking about?"

"Forget it." Nick turned the car round, towards Brougham Gate. "Would you say you had right of entry there?" he enquired.

"Well – I suppose so," I replied.

"You don't need to knock on the door, then. You don't have to stand around in the rain. Well, perhaps you ought to crash about a bit today, is all I'm saying. We don't want to embarrass anybody, do we?"

"No, of course not." Puzzled, I frowned at him. "But Simon and I have always—"

"You'll need to give me directions," he interrupted. "I don't actually know the way."

We drove through the village, turned up the lane towards Brougham Gate, then made our way up the weedy drive and parked on the gravel sweep. Getting out of the Escort, we slammed the doors loud enough to wake the dead, then crunched over towards the house, which was all in darkness.

Nick stared around him, peering into the gloom. He'd left the Escort's headlights on, and I could see he was now taking it all in. The decrepit house, the derelict barn with mess and rubbish piled anyhow outside, the overgrown, unkempt grounds – he could not help but notice the air of general desolation and decay. Even in the gloomy twilight, he could see the whole operation was falling apart. "What a tip," he muttered, scowling in scorn.

Suddenly, a light shone like a beacon, from a downstairs window at the side of the house. "Well, at least Simon's in," I observed, brightly. If he was in a good mood, if he was actually speaking to me this evening, that would be something! In fact, it would go a long way towards cheering up an absolute bitch of a day. I smiled up at Nick. "I could do with a cup of tea," I observed.

"Let's go and cadge one, then," he murmured. But not at all enthusiastically.

As Nick had realised, I had *carte blanche* to walk straight into Brougham Gate. But, as I'd also tried to explain, I always minded my manners. So today, we walked round to the side of the house, where I tapped politely on the kitchen door.

We waited. We waited some more. But then, as nobody seemed inclined to come and let us in, I opened it. We both went inside.

Nathan and Simon were sitting at the kitchen table, turned away from me. Nathan's black labrador lounged by the fire. Always a friendly animal, today he barked his usual raucous welcome and thumped his tail on the floor. "Hello, Caesar," I began, as he bounded up to greet me. "Good dog! Well, what are you—"

"Lindsay!" Spinning round in his chair, Simon beamed

– no, he positively *glowed* – at me! He waved a dripping can of Jack Smith's Special in my general direction.

He frowned. But this was only because he was trying to focus on his visitors. Then, "Lindsay *and* friend!" he cried, triumphant. "Come in, come in!"

I glanced towards Nathan. He didn't seem inclined to second Simon's invitation. In fact, he didn't seem to wish to acknowledge me at all. Shoulders humped, head bowed, he slurped noisily from what looked like a full can.

They were both well and truly ratted. This was hardly surprising, I suppose, because if appearances were to be believed, they had been going at it all afternoon. Empty cans rolled around the filthy kitchen floor, had been kicked or lobbed into the scullery, or crushed and tossed into the passageway beyond.

Strangely – for he was more often than not a somewhat depressive sort of drunkard – tonight, Simon Dyer was grinning from ear to ear. It was Nathan, the invariably happy sot, who slouched, glowering. Who then, squashing an empty can with unnecessary violence, tossed it cursing into the kitchen sink. Lurching to his feet, he blundered drunkenly past my companion and myself. Then, wrenching open the door, he swore a command at his big black hound, and off they both went, into the murky twilight.

"Poor Nathan. He's not at all happy tonight." Still grinning broadly, Simon shrugged what was perhaps intended to be a polite apology for his uncouth friend. "Sit yourselves down, then," he invited. "Dick, Rick – grab yourself a beer! Smoke?"

"No, thanks." Nick was already on the threshold. Then, before I could stop him, he went after Nathan, following him across the gravel sweep. "Here, buggerlugs!" I heard him shout, as he disappeared into the gloom, "I want a word with you!"

Simon gaped at me. "What in the world's going on?" he demanded, amazed. Struggling to his feet, he leaned against the kitchen table, clinging to it like a man in a shipwreck. "Lindsay?"

"I wish I knew." At a loss myself, I could only stare back at him. "But Simon, do *you* have any idea why Nathan should want . . ."

I was talking to myself. For, even as I spoke, Simon left the house. He, too, disappeared into the darkness beyond.

I stood there, bewildered. All around me was a horrible, frightening, eerie stillness, and I shuddered in dread. For, to my mind, there is nothing as alarming as dead silence. Especially when one is already afraid!

But then, I heard something which chilled me to the bone. Nathan's dog was barking in anger. In rage, even! So now, fear for Nick, not to mention curiosity on my own account, meant I could stay indoors no longer. Fastening my jacket, winding my scarf around my neck, I ran out of the house and into the night.

The barking was coming from the garden, from the area where the herbaceous borders had once been, but where these days burdocks and thistles stood tall and proud. I could hear Nathan now, cursing and swearing like a trooper. But then, to my intense relief, I heard Simon's voice, and this was cajoling and placatory.

There was just enough light from the kitchen for me to see my way. So, following the sound of the voices, I crept cautiously down a gravel path which led away from the house. Night had fallen in earnest by now, and with it had come all the terrors of darkness.

But then, as I felt the sweat trickle between my shoulder

245

blades, as the hairs on the back of my neck prickled spikily, the moon appeared between two banks of cloud. Now, the silver brightness of moonlight lit the landscape like a blessing, almost as clearly as the sun did by day.

I finally found them, dog and all three men, in the former kitchen garden. Long since disused, nettles grew in the raised beds, and docks as tall as I was sprouted everywhere. Nick had cornered Nathan. His escape cut off, my former assailant stood at bay, his back against a high brick wall.

Easily as heavy as Nathan, Nick was a little taller, too. But Nathan was broader, with a rock solid centre of gravity. Sodden with drink though he was, now he stood four-square, defying Nick and swearing, incoherent but furious all the same.

"I want an explanation, right?" Nick's clear Cockney baritone rang like a bell, into the winter darkness. "I want to know, first, why you scared Lindsay half to death last night – and second, what the fuck do you think you're playing at here?"

Nathan scowled at him. "Fuck you, too," he growled. Then, he turned to glare at me. "Been out for the day?" he enquired. His formerly belligerent glower became a sneer. "Been having it out in the open? Like what you used to? Eh?"

"You want me to stick one on you?" demanded Nick. He clenched his fists. "You want to have your stupid head kicked in, is that it? Because if you do—"

"Why don't you just bugger off back 'ome?" Nathan wiped his mouth on the back of his hand. "Go on, Mr University Professor. Sod off back to Oxford – or wherever it is you come from! Because I tell you now, nothing here's got *anything* to do with you, and if you—"

"But I think it has," retorted Nick. "I—"

"There's your tart," interrupted Nathan, grinning. "You must be blind and daft to fancy that! But – I suppose she's willing. Fact is, she'd prob'ly pay *you*, so—"

"Nathan, please!" This came from Simon. "For God's sake, it won't help—"

"I seen her." His grin fading, Nathan ground his teeth in rage. "When she was just a kid, no tits nor nothing, I seen her! In her school shirt! Lyin' on her back, there in the barn! Beggin' for it, the dirty little bitch, just like a—"

But then, Nick hit him.

The blow wasn't hard. He didn't use his fist. Instead, he gave Nathan a slap, of the kind a harassed parent might give a persistently naughty child. Not that I'd ever slap a child across the face, you understand, but you get the idea. It was intended to shock, to frighten, not to injure, not at all. Even the dog understood that.

But although the assault on his master did not provoke the dog into attacking Nick, it certainly galvanised Nathan. He stared. He trembled. He stroked his face, wonderingly. For a moment, I thought he might even cry, for his eyes had grown unnaturally bright.

Then, "Sod you!" he yelled, as the first tear brimmed, then spilled over. He glowered at me. "You can look, you little slut!" he cried. "Yeah, you can look, with your big cow eyes! But that's about all you can do, ain't it?"

I stared at him. He was actually crying now, shedding big, drunken tears. "You come back here!" he sobbed. "You don't care, do you? You don't give a shit what you do to Simon! You're nothing but a whore!"

"How dare you!" Astonished, I glared back at him, and was about to give as good as I'd got, when suddenly I was aware of Simon, standing by my side.

247

I heard his sharp intake of breath, his groan of despair – and then, "Oh, Nathan!" he whispered, "don't! Please, don't say anything more!"

As it happened, Nathan couldn't, not even if he'd wanted to. For Nick had him by the throat. As I watched, appalled yet fascinated, he drew back his fist, obviously intending to hit him hard this time.

But Nathan did not mean to be thumped by Nick. He shook his assailant off, ducked under his arm, and ran off into the moonlit night.

Chapter Twenty-One

The echo of breaking glass came from some cold frames smashing as Nathan trampled them, in his clumsy, drunken haste to get away. For a moment, I wondered if he were going to ground, meaning to hide in the overgrown wasteland which was all that remained of the once lovely pleasure gardens of Brougham Gate. But then, as I listened to his retreating footsteps, I realised he must be making for the house.

Nick was nowhere to be seen. I supposed he had run after Nathan, whose dog could be heard barking like a mad thing, somewhere in the dark. I hoped the labrador wasn't anywhere near Nick. Whilst I was reasonably confident of his ability to deal with Nathan, a great, black hound bent on defending its master from assault was a different proposition all together.

Just as on the previous evening, the cloud had mostly blown away, and the moon sailed like a chariot across the starry, indigo sky. Although it wasn't yet six o'clock, it was extremely cold, and although I was sensibly dressed tonight, I began to shiver. Then, I became aware of Simon again, standing just a few feet away from me. He was muttering, moaning – crying, almost. A maudlin drunkard incarnate, he was sinking in a slough of self-pity and despond.

Obviously, he wasn't going to follow the other boys. But then, he'd never liked rough games. Finely-boned and slender as he was, punch-ups and fisticuffs had never been Simon's thing.

"Shall we go back to the house?" I suggested. After all, I reasoned, the poor creature must be deep-frozen by now. Clad in light cotton chinos, a thin summer shirt and that horrid old cardigan with burn marks all over the pockets, he was barefoot and jacketless, too. "Simon?" I prompted, gently. "Shall we go—"

"What?" As if he'd only just noticed I existed, he stared at me.

I repeated my suggestion.

He shook his head. "I can't go back there," he muttered. Then, as if his legs had suddenly given way beneath him, he sat down with a bump, on the cold, damp earth. Hugging his knees, he hung his head, and began to cry.

I didn't know what to do. But, if Simon didn't want to move, I certainly couldn't force him, so I sat down beside him, shielding him from the wind as best I could. I waited for his sobs to subside. After a few minutes, they did.

"What did Nathan actually mean just now?" I asked, as he rummaged in his pockets for a handkerchief, then gave up and wiped his face on his sleeve. "Simon, what—"

"I'm sorry?" He dabbed at his eyes. "Sorry, Lin? What did you say?"

"He said I didn't care what I did to you. He even called me a whore! Simon, you must tell me! What am I supposed to have *done*?"

Simon shrugged. "It's obvious, isn't it?" he muttered.

"Not to me, it isn't!"

"Then I'll have to spell it out for you." Simon turned away. "I'm supposed to be in love with you," he said.

My blood froze. "B-but you're not?" I stammered.

He shrugged.

I thought I would faint. But I didn't. Somehow, keeping my voice level – reasonable, even – I spoke. "Look," I began, "we're grown up now. You don't have to pretend! We both know how much we—"

"No." Simon buried his face in his hands. "I'm sorry, Lin," he whispered. "I never wanted to hurt you! But no, I was never in love with *you*."

It took a few minutes, certainly, for that last sentence to be processed and interpreted, for the literal meaning of Simon's words to sink in and be replayed inside my head. "But you used to say," I began, stunned, "we used to go, we had – are you telling me it all meant *nothing*?"

"I-I'm afraid so."

"Oh." I felt hot, cold, sick to the heart. "So it *was* you," I whispered. "You and Jael, all along."

"Jael?" Simon lifted his head. "What do you mean, it was Jael?"

"You and Jael were having an affair. You—"

"God!" Simon shook his head. Deep down in his throat, he made a croaking, choking sound, which I supposed was a sort of mirthless laugh. "There was only you," he muttered. "Believe me. I was only screwing you."

"Why?" I asked. I was outside myself now. Cool, calm and rational, this other self wanted an explanation. I knew that tears and breakdown would come – of course, they *must* – but they would have to wait. "Why, as you so eloquently put it, were you screwing me?"

"To please my father."

"Your *father*?" I repeated. I stared. "But—"

"The bastard." Simon ground his teeth. "I can hear him now! 'Go on, you little faggot,' he'd say. 'Prove it. Prove you're a man!' So I did. I fooled everybody. I even fooled Nathan! I had to be drunk, I admit it – but I even fooled you."

I gaped at him. Then, the full import of what he was saying finally struck home.

I thought I would die. Of shame, of mortification, of disgust. I wanted my mother! I wanted Nick. I wanted to go home again.

But then, as my world fell apart and crumbled round about me, the sound of breaking glass rang through the darkness. Simon started, then jumped up, and soon he was running towards the general direction the noise.

After a moment's delay, I followed him.

The part of the garden in which we eventually found ourselves was a former nursery area. South-facing and sheltered by day, at night time the raised beds and melon frames were bleakly overshadowed by rotting store sheds, great, tall trees and high, brick walls. Helpless, I stared into the gloom. I couldn't even see Simon now!

Finally, I groped my way towards a wall. Even the rough brickwork was somehow comforting, and I started to feel my way along it, hoping it would guide me out of here. For, in this part of the garden, the darkness was almost tangible, and I was very much afraid. "Nick," I hazarded. "Nick? Where are you? Answer me, for God's sake . . ."

"He's dead." As I gazed blindly into the blackness, a hank of my hair was suddenly grabbed and twisted, forcing my head back against somebody's great, hard hand. Then, before I could even think about squirming free, I was in an agonizing arm lock, my scarf was choking me, and what felt like a blade was at my throat.

"Your fancy man's snuffed it," hissed Nathan, the foulness of his drunken breath making me flinch involuntarily even closer to the blade of the knife. "He's back at the house, like the other bugger. He's—"

"Let her go." The voice was soft, pleading. Looking to my left, I saw Simon standing two feet away from us, his body silvered by the moonlight. Thus dramatically outlined, he looked as if he were on a stage. "Please, Nathan," he whispered, "please believe me. She doesn't know! You'll gain nothing by killing Lindsay, she doesn't even suspect—"

"Doesn't she?" Nathan pulled the scarf tighter, choking me. "Make up your mind!" he cried. "Decide, once and for all! Do you want this skinny little bitch? Or do you want me?"

Chapter Twenty-Two

As Nathan waited for Simon to reply, and as I stood there petrified, afraid that whatever answer Simon chose to make would condemn me to death – or at least to serious injury – I suddenly became aware of the warm breath of some creature, steaming through the wool of my glove.

Alarmed, I jerked my hand away. But then I realised it was only Caesar. Nathan's black labrador, always my friend, was snuffling and drooling around us, and clawing at my trousered legs. He wanted me to take his forepaws. To rest them on my shoulders. He wanted to give me a kiss.

But Nathan cursed him roundly. "Get down, damn you," he muttered, pushing the animal aside. "Sit! Now, stay!"

It was then, as my captor tried to shove his devoted beast out of the way, that I realised he had not been lying. Nathan had indeed been back to the house. My eyes had adjusted to the gloom and, daring to glance down, I saw that the weapon held tightly in Nathan Casson's big, calloused hand was one of Louis Dyer's old gardening knives, which were kept in a drawer in the scullery. I could just discern its brass-bound wooden handle, and its hanging loop of dull green twine.

My peripheral vision – or perhaps it was only my terror

– also suggested that the blade was black. So, was it rusted? Or bloodied? If bloodied, by whom? Had Nathan *really* murdered Nick Singer? Had my friend tried to help me only to be done to death by this madman, who now had the same blade at my own helpless throat?

I could see no way out of this. No way at all. Yes, I'd been to self-defence classes, I knew exactly where to hit and where it hurt, but I could not fight Nathan Casson! He didn't know the rules, he was bound to fight dirty and, big and bulky as he was, he'd have overpowered me at once. I could not disarm him, certainly. If I tried to break free, the chances were he'd cut my throat, by accident if not by design.

Despair washed over me in a black, tidal wave. The tears welled up. To stop them overflowing, I closed my eyes.

When I opened then again, it was to see Simon staring at me, but I could not fathom the expression on his face. Then, however, he spoke. "Please let her go," he said, quietly, reasonably. "Come on, Nathan. She's nobody! Nothing whatever to do with you and me!"

Nathan merely grunted.

"She was the means to an end, that's all." Dismissively, Simon shrugged. "Okay, so I chose Lindsay – but she could have been anyone. Any girl in the village, in fact! She was a smokescreen. A blind. But that's *all* she was."

"Oh, yeah? So why was she all over you?" Far from letting me go, Nathan held me even closer then. The scarf choked the breath out of me once again. "I *saw* you!" he cried. "I come back, and I saw you! Had your head on her shoulder, you did! Yeah, *and* she was huggin' you, strokin' your hair!"

255

Then, his voice became low. Dangerously low. "So now," he muttered, "decide. Which of us do you want?"

"You, of course!" Simon's cry was passionate, imploring. Tearful, even. "I've never wanted anyone but you!"

"You don't want to fuck *her*?"

"Of course not! I don't even want to know her!"

"Liar." Nathan spat that word across the void like a gunslinger challenging the local deputy, whom he was confident would never have a chance. "Why'd you invite her round here, then? Why'd you ask her in, why'd you fancy a nice little natter, all about old times? You don't want to know her? Balls to that! All best pals you was, when *I* come round!"

"But—"

"She'd practically moved in! There was her and our Reb up to their elbows, clearin' out your scullery! Doin' your bloody washing up!"

"I invited Lindsay round for coffee. That's all, I swear it. She and Rebekah offered to wash a few dishes. They—"

"Yeah?" Nathan sniffed. "So why'd she come back 'ere in the first place? She'd been gone ages. Years! Why'd she want to come back to Hartley Cross?"

"For her mother's funeral. You know that!"

"Funeral was weeks ago. Why'd she hang around?"

"To wind up Mrs Ellis's affairs. To deal with her estate." Simon's voice was quavering now. "Sh-she needed to sort out her mother's things."

"So why'd she bring her fancy man, then?"

"Lindsay can take anybody she likes to her own house!" Suddenly, Simon seemed to rally. "Don't you understand?" he cried. "I *don't* love Lindsay! I never did! Her private life is her own business."

"Yeah, well. Maybe." Partially convinced, perhaps,

Nathan sniffed. "All the same – she shouldn've interfered. Stupid, she was, to interfere. So now, I doubt if she'll *have* a private life much longer. Fact is, I doubt if she'll have any life at all."

"Give me the knife, Nathan." Simon's voice was soft, caressing, low. "Please?"

"You want it, you come and get it," Nathan replied.

So that was it. I was doomed. Despair is tangible, you know, and now I felt it, smelled it, savoured its bitter aloe taste. What a waste it had all been! I'd spent the past six years – more than six years – chasing rainbows. Destiny had been laughing its little cotton socks off at me.

But if, in a way, I deserved what was coming to me, Nick's fate was another matter entirely. What *had* Nathan done to Nick? Treacherous and stealthy though he was, surely a gormless great ape like Nathan Casson could never have outwitted my clever, ingenious friend?

It's true what they say. There are no atheists in trenches and now, for the first time in years, in a decade or more, I began to pray. "Please, God," I whispered, "let Nick not be dead! Let him find a way out of this mess! Let him come and help me!"

I could hardly believe it when my prayer was answered. Answered straight away, in fact. How's that for service, I thought, as the next thing I heard was Nick's own voice. "Simon?" he cried. "Simon, what the hell are you doing out here?"

I stared in disbelief. I don't know what I'd expected – but it certainly wasn't this! For, Nick sounded languid. Relaxed, and really rather bored. "Simon," he continued, "are you trying to catch your death, or what?"

As I gaped, Nick Singer came strolling towards us. Then, he was standing in a shaft of moonlight, an unlikely apparition in scuffed denims and his old navy jacket, which I'd last seen lying in its nest of Coke cans and old Mars bar wrappers on the floor of his car.

"Come on, Simon," he continued, "let's go back inside! Bloody freezing out here, it is."

"What did you say?" Turning to stare up at Nick, who was easily twice his size, Simon's astonishment was plain for all to see. "Where did you come from? I thought—"

"Nick!" Alarmed – terrifed, in actual fact – I cried out to my friend. "Oh, Nick! Please be careful! He's got a knife! He—"

"What's that?" As if he'd only just realised Nathan and I were standing there – which might indeed have been the case, since we were in deep shadow – Nick frowned. Then, "shuddup, Lindsay," he drawled. He draped one arm across Simon's shoulders and, as he did so, he directed the merest flicker of a wink towards me. "She natter all the time when she was your bird?" he enquired.

Simon looked dazed. "W-what do you mean?" he stammered.

"I was asking if the little cow was as gabby back then as she is today."

Then, I understood. I breathed out again, but this time I exhaled not a shuddering gasp of terror, but a careful sigh of relief. Simon had cottoned on, too. "Yes," he agreed. "Yes, I suppose she must have been."

"All the same, ain't they?" Matily, Nick grinned. "What *I* say is, show me a woman what knows how to keep her legs open and her mouth shut – and I'll show you a cat as windsurfs."

"Right," agreed Simon, grinning back. "Don't get me wrong," he added, quickly. "I mean – I *like* women! For the most part, I reckon they're okay. But—"

"You'll never beat a good night out with the lads."

"That's right." Simon, bless him, actually managed a leer. "Couple of pints, a decent Indian takeaway—"

"We'll have to have a jar sometime," interrupted Nick. "Just you and me. Have a game of pool, yeah?"

"Great," agreed Simon, nodding vigorously.

Nathan had been silent throughout all this. I can only suppose he was bemused. He could certainly see Nick was making a pass at Simon. Whilst one hand was thrust casually into his jacket pocket, jangling his loose change, with the other he was actually stroking Simon's shoulder. From where I was standing, Simon looked as if he were rather enjoying it.

I could feel, I could almost hear Nathan's heart, thudding noisily against my back. His breath rasped in my ear. Evidently, he didn't know what on earth to make of this. But then, at long last, he finally found his voice. "Here," he growled, "you get your dirty hands off of 'im."

"What was that?" Nick stopped jangling coins. "He say something?" he asked Simon, but still grinning, and still hugging Simon tight.

Don't overdo it, I thought. Please, Nick – don't muck *this* up! You're not doing one of your experiments now. It's my life on the line here!

But, whatever happened next, one thing was certain. I had definitely been marginalised. Nathan's attention was distracted, and soon he might even forget he was holding *me*! Trying to pace myself, I watched Nick like a hawk, waiting for a signal, a nod perhaps, a sign that I might risk trying to wriggle free, to make a run for it . . .

Slowly, agonisingly slowly, the minutes ticked by. By now, Simon and Nick were nattering like a pair of old women at the local launderette. Nathan would soon tire of it, surely? He must! He would, please God, push me away and attack Nick Singer instead?

"You get away from here much?" Nick was asking then, as he slid his hand up and down Simon's upper arm, from elbow to shoulder, back again. "Get out of Hartley Cross, I mean?"

"Not often," replied Simon. He shrugged. "You see, transport's a problem for me. I—"

"*I* got a motor." Nick winked. "Tell you what, we could go for a ride. Tomorrow, that suit you? We could make a day of it, we—"

But that did it. Nathan let go of my hair. The knife was no longer at my throat. For, with a growl of jealous fury, he launched himself at Nick – who let Simon go, and prepared to defend himself against that wicked, flashing blade.

But, in his haste to attack Nick, Nathan had forgotten where he was. More to the point, he'd forgotten all about his dog. Told to sit, the animal had obeyed, and throughout all this recent palaver he'd been hunkered down, bored and restless, at his master's feet. "Get out of the way, bugger you!" cried Nathan, who suddenly found his progress checked by a great, black mound of canine flesh . . .

I suppose the dog meant to obey. But, as he tried to manoeuvre in what was a very confined space, he bumped against his master. Caught off balance, Nathan stumbled. Flailing for a hand-hold, the knife he was still grasping slashed through my coat sleeve, grazing my wrist.

I screamed. The dog barked. Nathan cursed again. Then, something warm and wet was pouring over my feet, and I thought, oh great, the wretched dog is peeing all over me. How very much in keeping, how beautifully symbolic of everything else that's happened here tonight! But then, as I stood there, a heavy body slumped awkwardly against mine. A low, agonized groan made me shudder, and I heard – or rather, felt – Nathan Casson collapse against my side.

Had he suffered a heart attack, I wondered blankly, as I realised he must be hurt. Badly hurt, at that. But then, glancing down, I saw my light green wellingtons were black. The warm, wet liquid flowing all over them was blood. For, the broken glass in the ancient cold frame, next to which he had been standing, had sliced through Nathan's calves like butter, and both his legs were literally gushing hot, crimson gore.

Nausea rose like a wave, overwhelming me with both terror and disgust. For a long moment, I was speechless. But then, "help!" I wailed, or rather croaked. "Nick! Simon! Help me!"

It was like being leaned on by a mountain. I did my best but, try as I might, there was no way I could support Nathan's whole weight alone. Also, it was so dark that even though my eyes were slightly better accustomed to the gloom than they had been a while earlier, I could not see anything in this murky corner. I was afraid that if I moved, I too would fall, perhaps slicing *myself* open on shards of broken glass. What was more, the stupid dog still crouched there, greedily lapping his master's blood.

Hours seemed to go by. But then, to my inexpressible relief, I felt my burden being shifted. Nick had recovered first, and now he was manoeuvring Nathan away from me, dragging him into the patch of moonlight where once, aeons ago, he and Simon had stood.

As soon as he was clear of the broken cold frames, Nick let the body crumple, to slump on to the muddy turf. "Get his legs up!" he cried, as Simon stood there immobile, pale, speechless – and helpless – as a ghost. "Come on, move! Look, chuck us that old box there. Get both legs higher than his head. Gimme that cardigan, now!"

Simon did not move a muscle. Threading my way through the murderous, broken frames, I reached the safety of the wide grass path, then passed Nick the wooden box. Together, we lifted Nathan's legs on to it.

Nick whipped off my scarf, which he bound around Nathan's right shin. Jerking off one of Nathan's shoes, he yanked off a sock, then improvised a bandage for his left leg, too. "For God's sake, Simon!" he muttered, as he worked, "you could at least go and call an ambulance!"

"What?" Simon looked dazed. "What did you say?"

"The phone, you stupid bugger! Go and use the phone!" Nick's eyes met mine. "Oh, for crying out loud! Lindsay? *You* go!"

So, I ran to the house. Fortunately for me, the phone was where it had always been, tucked away in a sort of mock Tudor, cigarette kiosk affair, just inside the entrance hall.

I made the call. I'd never dialled 999 before, and I felt as if I were in a play, I was amazed when somebody actually answered me. Then I hurried back to the scene of the accident. "The ambulance is on its way," I gasped. "They say it is, anyhow."

"Thank God for that," muttered Nick. He glanced towards Simon, who was keening and moaning to himself. "So what're we gonna do about that bugger there?"

"I don't know," I replied. Helplessly, I shrugged. "Shall I go and fetch him a coat?"

"That might be a good idea."

For, somehow, Nick had persuaded Simon to give up

262

his cardigan. Torn into strips, this had become a series of additional bandages and makeshift tourniquets, inexpertly applied. "I dunno if that's okay," murmured Nick, as he saw me stoop to examine his handiwork. Helplessly, he shrugged. "I never done any first aid. He might get gangrene or summat. If the bandages are too tight . . ."

"He doesn't seem to be bleeding as much as he was, though. Surely that's a good thing?" I stood up straight again. "I'll go and find some coats."

Back at the house, I grabbed an overcoat from a peg in the scullery, and an old tweed jacket from a hook on the kitchen door. Returning to the scene, I laid the overcoat over Nathan's prostrate form.

I offered the jacket to Simon, but he only glared at me, so I draped it around his shoulders. Angrily, he shook it off again. Please yourself, I thought.

Tea. I'd been a Girl Guide and I remembered now, that was what we needed. Hot, sweet tea. I turned to go back to the house a third time. But then, my legs seemed to give way beneath me, and I more or less collapsed on to the ground.

I tried to get up again, but, suddenly, everything seemed too much for me. Someone else should come, I thought. Somebody else must take over now. "I wish the ambulance was here!" I wailed.

"So do I." Nick was as pale as paper. I prayed *he* wouldn't faint. Nathan's dog had crept close to me, and I hugged it gratefully, both for comfort and for warmth.

So the four of us sat there, like a tableau. Simon crouched by his lover's body, shivering in his shirt sleeves, and weeping like a beaten child. Nathan had passed out. Or at any rate, he was silent. Nick sat by himself, his hands clasping his knees, his eyes staring vacantly into space. I snuggled up to the dog, which whined and whickered miserably.

I willed the ambulance to arrive.

Chapter Twenty-Three

The ambulance took more than half an hour to reach Brougham Gate. When it did finally arrive, the men admitted cheerfully that they had lost their way at least twice. Then they bemoaned the fact that they'd been called away from a Scrabble championship, back at base. Their rivals would certainly beat them now.

Perhaps they meant to defuse a fraught, tense situation. Perhaps they wanted to calm us all down, to lessen our obvious fright.

"In any case, it always looks more than it is," observed one of them, eyeing the sticky black puddles of blood, which seemed to lie everywhere. "Right, then. I'll just go and fetch my stuff. We don't need back-up," he told his mobile phone, walkie-talkie or whatever it was, which crackled importantly on his lapel. "Give you an update in two, three minutes, okay?"

Meanwhile, his friend was checking on the casualty. "Well," he murmured, impressed, "you did all the right things. Like keeping him warm, I mean, and reassuring him that we were on our way. Whoever did the bandaging made quite a good job of it! There's very little coming through either of these dressings here."

He grinned up at Nick and me. "He'll need a transfusion, though. No doubt at all about that."

So, very carefully, the men lifted Nathan on to a stretcher. Sliding him into the vehicle, one of them covered his face with a plastic mask, while the other took the patient's blood pressure and monitored his vital signs, nodding and smiling perfectly complacently.

"Okay then, Control. We're coming in." The paramedic took off his stethoscope, then put it away. "You can't every man Jack of you come in the old bus," he added, as if he thought we were all about to clamber inside.

"We'll take one of you," said the other, "but that's all."

"Go on, Simon," I muttered.

So, Simon climbed aboard. "You a relation?" demanded the ambulanceman. "Or just a friend?"

"A friend," murmured Simon, sniffing and knuckling his eyes.

"So what happened?" Encouragingly, the paramedic grinned. "Bit of horseplay, was it? Got out of hand?"

"That's it." Mechanically, Nick nodded. He glanced towards Nathan. "Do you reckon he'll be okay?"

"Sure he will. He looks a bit off-colour now, I grant you. But by tomorrow, he'll be as right as rain." Again, the paramedic grinned. "He's lost a pint or two, for certain. But – big bloke like this. Young, healthy, no heart problems – he'll be fine. Don't worry."

"We'll be taking him to the Infirmary, not the General," added the other man. "But give it an hour or two, before you ring. He should be up on the ward by then." He looked from Nick to me. "Here – you two all right, are you?"

"I think so." I tried to smile, and I suppose that, in the end, a sort of grimace must have creased my face. "Yes," I assured him, "we'll be okay."

"You get inside, then. Make yourselves a nice, hot cup of tea. Right?"

"Right," I agreed.

"Be seeing you, then." The men closed the doors. The driver started the engine, and off they went, into the quiet night.

Nick and I were left standing in the darkness, in front of the great, looming hulk of Brougham Gate. To my great surprise, for I hadn't remembered that shock tends to come and go, I found I was feeling calmer now. Perhaps this was because Nathan was physically out of the way?

Nick, however, was shaking like the proverbial aspen leaf. "Come on," I murmured. "Let's go home."

He did not move.

"Nick?" I slipped my arm through his. "You saved his life," I whispered.

"You reckon they'll give me a medal?" He glared into the night. "I wish I'd kicked his great fat head in."

"You don't mean that."

"Yes, I bloody do!"

"You're in shock." Gently, I tugged at his arm. "Let's go home," I repeated. "Then we can get warm, and have a hot drink, like the ambulance men said."

"I could do with some brandy. But I expect the shop's shut by now." Nick kicked a stone across the path. It bounced off a shard of broken glass. Then, he turned to look at me. "You okay?" he demanded.

"I think so," I replied.

"Good." He shrugged, then sighed. "You look all right."

"I'm probably suffering from delayed shock, just the same. In a minute, I'll collapse in a heap."

"Let's get back to your place, then. You can collapse in comfort there."

We didn't dare drive. So, very slowly, we walked back to my house. Nathan's poor dog, bemused and perplexed, trailed wretchedly after us. "Come on, Caesar," I encouraged, patting my thigh. "Come home with me. You can have supper, too."

"You're stark raving bonkers. You know that?" Nick glared at the hound. "That stupid mutt nearly did for you! But now, I suppose you want to feed it *boeuf à la mode*, then tuck it up in bed."

"He's had a shock as well, poor thing." I stroked the dog's smooth, satin head. "I'll put him in the conservatory, if he bothers you."

"He don't bother me," growled Nick. "But *you* do!"

"Why, what have I done?"

"Oh – nothing." Nick began to move a bit faster. "Let's get home. I really need that cup of tea."

Ten minutes later, we arrived at The Larches. I left my disgusting wellingtons in the garden. As I padded into the kitchen, however, I realised that my trousers were also covered in blood, which had soaked through my tights and was drying patchily against my skin.

My beautiful scarlet jacket, brand new that previous September, was ruined. One sleeve was slashed and shredded, and the shoulder yoke was torn beyond repair.

"Did he actually get you?" demanded Nick, as I rolled up the sleeve of my jumper, to check on my own little wound.

"Yes." I dabbed at it with my finger. "But it's just a scratch."

"That's what people say in films. Before they drop down dead." Taking me by the elbow, Nick propelled me across the room, until I was standing directly underneath the light. Lifting my hand, he examined my wrist. "It doesn't look too bad," he conceded.

"He only just caught me," I agreed.

"You ought to wash it, though."

"I will. After I've fed the dog, that is." I smiled up at him. "Why don't you put the kettle on?"

"First, we're going to wash your wrist." Morosely, he glowered. "For God's sake, Lin! You don't want tetanus, do you?"

"I suppose not."

So now, Nick led me over to the sink. He ran hot water into the bowl, washed his own hands, then tore off several sheets of kitchen towel. He bathed my cut under running water, then he dabbed it dry. "You don't need a plaster," he murmured.

"No," I agreed.

"But it could do with some antiseptic. You got any Savlon? Or TCP?"

"I'm afraid not."

"Oh." Considering, he looked down at me. "Suck it for a few minutes, eh? While I make the tea."

We drank our tea. We even ate some biscuits. By now, Nick had stopped shaking. He was even on speaking terms with the dog, talking nonsense to it and stroking Caesar's warm, silken ears.

"We must go and see Jael," I told him.

"I know," he said.

So, we got up from our chairs. Nick shrugged on his jacket. Then, as if I were disabled, he helped me on with my old gardening coat. "Are you all right?" he enquired.

"Nick, you keep asking that!"

"I need to make sure, that's why."

"I'm fine, honestly." I thought, it's true. I *am* all right.

For I was beginning to realise that Simon's declaration – that he didn't love me, that he'd never loved me, that he'd used me, that I'd been merely the means to an end

– which should have precipitated a breakdown, had instead been a release. It was as if the prison gate had swung open. The gaoler had gone. I was standing at the door of my cell, and wondering if I dared cross the threshold into a whole new life . . .

Nick and I walked down the drive, our feet crunching on the dead leaves crisped by an early evening frost. It was going to be extremely cold tonight. "You got some gloves?" asked Nick, as we went past the church.

"Yes, but they're filthy. I'll put my hands in my pockets," I said.

"You should do your coat up, too. Here, let me." He fastened my buttons. "It'd be a shame to catch your death of cold, after all that's happened tonight."

"Perhaps," I agreed. "But I don't think—"

But Nick had turned away. "Come on then, mutt!" he cried, glaring at poor Caesar, who was following at a polite distance, unable to decide if his company would be appreciated – or quite the reverse. "Pick your feet up, you stupid hound!"

Caesar grinned. At once, he came bounding up to us, to slobber joyfully all over Nick's hand. "Sod off, bugger you," muttered Nick. But amiably.

Jael knew something was up. Although she lived at the other end of the village, at least a mile from Brougham Gate, and although the ambulance hadn't driven past her cottage, although there'd been no sirens or flashing lights, her sixth sense had warned her to expect visitors.

As we walked down Ruddle Pit Lane, we saw her through the kitchen window of the house. Sitting quietly in a rocking chair, she was knitting what looked like a baby's jumper, in a bright tomato red.

As soon as I tapped, she came to the door. She ushered us in. "Simon or Nathan?" she asked me.

"Nathan," I replied.

"Is he dead?"

"I don't think so. The ambulance men didn't seem too concerned. They said to ring the Infirmary, in a couple of hours' time."

"What about Simon?"

"He's okay. He went with Nathan, in the ambulance."

"So that's that. It'll all come out now." Jael covered her face. Then, silently, she began to weep.

I looked at Nick. He raised his eyebrows, shrugging an enquiry, as if to ask, what should he do? I pointed to the kettle.

How do other nations cope, I wondered, what do foreigners drink in times of crisis if they don't drink tea?

Jael heard the water running, and took her hands away from her face. "Tea's in the jar marked sugar," she whispered, her voice thick with tears. "I keeps meanin' to change 'em round, but I ain't quite got me act together yet, so I—"

"Jael, please sit down!" I sat down myself, in the chair opposite her. "Do you want me to tell you what happened?"

"Please," she murmured.

So I did. Whilst Nick made a pot of tea, I explained what had taken place that evening, over at Brougham Gate. Then, I had a question of my own. "Who actually murdered Louis Dyer?" I asked her. "Jael – *was* it Nathan?"

"Yes, course it was Nathan," she replied.

"But why? Why did he have to kill an old man?" I met her tearful gaze. "Why did he have to do it so cruelly, with the piton and mallet, and why—"

"I don't know!" cried Jael. "We ain't exactly discussed it over lunch, have we? I dunno why he did it that way!"

"I think you do." I looked straight at her, into her beautiful grey eyes. "He wanted the police to think you were the killer. It was Nathan's little joke, wasn't it, to point the finger at you?"

"No." Steadily, Jael met my gaze. "You're completely wrong about that," she said.

"But—"

"Lin, you must believe me – I'd never even *heard* of that business in the Bible, with the tent peg an' all. Not before Nick here mentioned it, anyway!" She glanced towards Nick. "When me and him was sitting up with you last night, he told me that old story about the king's general and the woman in the tent – an' *he* wondered if the killer done it that way to suggest the murderer might be me."

Jael sighed. "But I reckon it was a coincidence. Nathan just wanted to do somethin' nasty and definite. To make sure old Louis was really dead."

"How can you be so sure?"

"Oh, God – Nathan don't know his Bible like that!" Miserably, Jael sniffed. "The fact is, he can hardly even read. Dad used to take a strap to him, to make him learn his letters – but Nathan never got past *Janet and John at the Seaside*, all the same.

"They got a name for it nowadays, haven't they? Dyslexia, is it? But when our Nathan was little, it was called being lazy, and he got the belt."

"Poor Nathan." For, in spite of all he'd done, I was moved to pity then, for the clumsy child who'd been beaten for idleness by a bigoted, dictatorial father, and written off at school.

I glanced all round the immaculate kitchen. "Where's

272

Neil?" I enquired, not really expecting him to emerge from a cupboard or descend from the ceiling, but I did wonder.

"I sent him out tonight." Expressively, Jael shrugged. "He's been mopin' about the house all day – he's on short time again this week, see – so I told him to go over and sit with our Daniel for an hour or two. They're gettin' up a darts team, for the Old Rose."

"I see." I looked again round the spotless kitchen, which was chock-a-block with brand new gadgets, including a state-of-the-art dishwasher which I was quite certain hadn't been there the other day. "He seems to do quite well, for all that," I observed, ashamed of myself for digging, but feeling the need to know.

"What?" Jael frowned. Then, she understood. "Oh, I see what you mean," she said. "Blimey, Lin – Neil's wages at Baines Brothers didn't pay for any of this!"

"Oh? But—"

"Three-fifty an hour, plus a bit of overtime if you're very lucky. That's all them skinflints up Baines Brothers pays!" Nervously, Jael giggled. "We won some money, see," she whispered. It was as if she were confessing a dreadful, an absolutely terrible sin.

"On the National Lottery?" I prompted.

"The Lottery?" Jael was appalled. "We *never* does the Lottery!" she exclaimed. "But Neil's got half a dozen Premium Bonds. Had 'em since he was a babby, never won a dicky bird. Then, last year, one of 'em come up trumps."

"I see." I smiled. "Congratulations."

"Thanks." Beseechingly, she gazed into my eyes. "Don't spread it about, will you? If our Dad knew, he'd be up here goin' on about the sin of gambling, preachin' hell fire an' damnation, an' I don't know what all! One of these days, Neil's gonna stick a proper shiner on the old bugger. But I'd rather it wasn't just yet."

"I shan't tell anyone," I assured her. "Why does Neil still work for Baines Brothers?" I enquired.

"I told you before. He loves those poor beasts." Eloquently, Jael shrugged. "Yeah, he eats meat hisself. Yeah, your pigs and cows and sheep, they all gotta die somehow. Some day. But, as Neil says, there's no reason why they shouldn't go quick and painless, like. Decently, and with dignity."

"I see." I supposed there was a sort of logic in that. "What did you do with the rest of the cash?" I asked her.

"Most of it's invested. For the babby, like." Jael dabbed at her eyes. "Poor Nathan," she sniffed. "He's never had much of a life! What with our Dad always going on at him, sayin' he was lazy and stupid and slow. Then him growing up and realisin' he wasn't ever gonna be one of the lads. It must've been a big relief, findin' out old Simon was the same."

"But why was that such a problem?" I asked, puzzled. "Jael, why—"

"It's not illegal, it's not wicked, it doesn't make you blind. Yeah, I know all that." Again, Jael shrugged. "But, I ask you! Our Dad and Louis Dyer – nasty bastards the pair of them – can you imagine either of the buggers bein' happy for a son of theirs to be gay? *Can* you, Lindsay?"

"No," I admitted. "No, I can't."

"Then there was that blasted will." Jael sighed. "I can hardly credit it, even now, but the fact is Nathan and Simon believed what Louis said. I remember the night Nathan come home after seeing Simon about it. They'd been fishing or summat, then they'd gone back to the Gate.

"Nathan was furious. Stark, staring mad! He got me in

274

one of the outhouses, said Louis had told Simon he was bein' disinherited. That the old man was goin' to leave everything to me. But Nathan said he'd kill the bugger before that happened.

"I *told* him it was a joke! That Louis was winding Simon up, like he always had, and to take no notice of the silly old fool!"

"I see." I looked down at my finger nails. "You and Louis," I began, carefully. "He was . . . ah . . . very fond of you. He made no secret of that."

"He had a crush on me. That's all." Remembering, Jael shuddered. "We was never lovers," she insisted. "God – *I* don't go for old men! Even rich old men. I never have."

"Who else knew?" I asked. "About the murder, I mean?"

"Your Mum suspected, I'm sure." Jael frowned. "But, well – she never liked me. Never liked any of us, in fact. One day, I remember, I saw her in the shop. She give me such a look! As if to say, I know all about it. So don't think it's a secret, girl, because it ain't.

"That's why she sent you away, of course. To keep you safe from Nathan. He was so jealous of you, being Simon's girlfriend, an' all."

"But there was no need for Nathan to be jealous!" Bewildered, I shook my head. "Surely he realised that?"

"He'd seen you, though." Suddenly, Jael blushed. "He'd watched you when you – well, you know what I mean."

"Yes." I blushed, too. "I know."

"Right." Jael turned to look at Nick. "So how about that cup of tea, then?" she demanded.

I had forgotten all about Nick! For a moment, I blushed even redder, I'm sure. But then, I rallied. "Those chickens on the lawn," I murmured. "The dead pigeon on my

275

mother's grave, the sheep's head in my car – what was the point of all that rubbish? To scare me away?"

"I suppose so." Jael sipped her tea. "It's not really rubbish," she observed, mildly. "If you know what you're playin' at, it's very powerful stuff."

"Really?" I narrowed my eyes at her. "I know you were in my room that time," I told her. "I smelled your perfume. What were you up to in there?"

"Only making sure you'd be safe."

"You were casting a spell, you mean?"

"If you like." Jael shook her head. "But *I* know what I'm doing, see."

"Really?"

"Yeah, really!" Offended, Jael frowned. "When I was a kid," she explained, "our Mum often used to send me round Mrs Samson's – you remember Mrs Samson, don't you? Lived in the cottage down Glebelands way – to get some of her special rub, to put on Reb's chest. Well, after a bit, I got interested in the other things she did, with plants an' charms an' that. She taught me all sorts of stuff."

"Then you taught Nathan?"

"Not really." Jael sniffed. "But he soon found out about it. Then, he used to take the piss. Threaten to tell our Dad I was dabblin' in witchcraft an' the black arts. He knew I'd get the strap.

"So, I had to tell him all about it. Well, I told him this and that. He wanted to know all the nasty stuff, of course, about castin' spells an' puttin' curses on people – which ain't what it's about at all!" Jael shook her head. "But that business with the chickens and the sheep – I never discussed anythin' like that. He must've been watchin' some stupid film, I reckon. He's always been childish," she whispered, starting to cry again.

For a minute or two, Nick and I let her weep. Quietly, we sipped our tea. Then, "perhaps we should be going," murmured Nick. He looked enquiringly at me. "Shall I go over and fetch Neil?"

"I'll be okay." Bravely wiping her eyes, Jael managed a smile.

"What shall we do with the dog?" I asked, glancing towards Caesar, who sat quietly by the stove.

"I'll keep him for now." Jael looked at Nick. "There's some rope in the wash house," she said. "Would you go and fetch it for me? Then I can tie 'im up in here tonight. He can open doors, see, an' I don't want him wandering about all over the house, looking for our Nathan. Frightening the babby, an' that."

"I'll get the rope, then." Nick got up. He went out.

"He's a nice bloke," observed Jael, as we heard Nick's footsteps on the cinder path.

"Yes, he is," I agreed.

"Tell me to mind my own business. But you let him slip through your fingers, you'll regret it." Jael looked wise. "Men like Nick – well, they don't grow on trees."

"You're so right." I tried to smile. "They normally just swing from them."

"Lindsay!" Jael frowned. "*I* like him," she said, simply. "I like him very much."

"He rather likes *you*," I told her, as Nick came in through the kitchen door again.

Chapter Twenty-Four

To this day, I don't know how I managed to stay so calm. I can only imagine it was because I thought I was in a dream. I didn't feel any of this was really happening. I suppose I was also suffering from delayed shock.

At any rate, as I write this account, six or seven months after the events themselves and in the safety and comfort of my room at 26, Ferry Road, my hands shake. I make silly typing mistakes, and keep hitting the wrong function keys. I wish Nick would come back from the lab – he's been there since six this morning. I hope Tessa brings that coffee soon.

As we walked home again that eventful winter evening, Nick was very quiet. He didn't make jokes, he didn't tease, nor did he maunder on in that whimsical, rambling fashion which I'd come to know and – almost – love. I realised that, for all the time we'd spent together recently, Nick Singer was still an unknown quantity to me.

We passed the church. We crossed the road. I massaged my eyes. "I'm so tired," I yawned. "In fact, I could sleep for a week!"

"You're not the only one." Rubbing his face, Nick glanced down at me. "Are you hungry?" he enquired.

"Hungry?" I thought about it. "Yes," I replied, "I suppose I am. A bit."

"I'll make you a sandwich, then."

At that moment, I realised, there was nothing I'd have liked better than a crumbly cheese sandwich, on nice brown bread. "You're just like my mother," I told him, as we made our way back up the drive.

"Oh?" He grinned. "Go on with you. I'm sure your poor mother wasn't like me at all."

"No, she wasn't really." I thought about it. "You're my knight in shining armour, then. That's what you are."

"It's a pity armour rusts," he said.

We had reached the house by now. "Nick," I began, as I searched my pockets for my keys, "let me say this. Don't interrupt, and don't make a joke of it."

"Get on with it, then."

"Thank you," I said. "Just thank you."

"My pleasure," he murmured. As I found my keys, he took them from me. He opened the front door.

"Why didn't I see?" I asked him, as he stood aside to let me go in. "Why didn't I realise? For God's sake – they were always together! We used to call them William and Ginger, they were so close!"

I shrugged off my coat. "I thought it was just hero-worship. The poor, slow kid admiring the rich, clever one. Because Nathan was always hanging around Simon. Pretending to punch him, giving him sweets he'd stolen from the minimart, taking him fishing with his big brothers and casting lines for him. My God! It was staring me slap in the face!"

"But *you* don't have a suspicious nature." Nick draped both our coats over the banister, then took my hand. He led me into the bright, warm kitchen. "You're one of nature's

279

innocents," he continued. Shaking his head, he smiled at me. "That's what's so refreshing about you. You're almost permanently surprised."

I wasn't sure if I liked that. It made me sound rather childish. Thick, even. "Last night," I began, firmly changing the subject, "you decided to confide in Jael. Why?"

"Because I could see she was on your side."

"Really? *I'd* wondered if she and Simon were in it together."

"*What?*" Nick was playing with my fingers now, sorting them out, counting them, turning them this way and that. "No chance," he said.

"But how did you know?"

"How could I not know? Jael might fancy herself as the local sorceress, but she isn't wicked, nor is she insane." He looked into my eyes. "You let the fact that she's so gorgeous cloud your judgement. I suspect you always have."

"But—"

"She's just an ordinary woman, you know. Remarkably level-headed, considering the company she keeps."

"Maybe." I shrugged. "I suppose I only ever saw her beauty. But, Nick, how did you know about Simon?"

"I saw him watching you, that's all." Raising my hand to his lips, Nick turned it over. He kissed the palm. "It was the night of that awful party, when he and Nathan were rat-arsed. Simon came to the door of the sitting room, and stared at you.

"Then, all of a sudden, Nathan appeared – and he was watching Nathan instead. I've seen that look before. On the faces of women in pubs, usually. They've been flirting with the barman, or whatever, an' they know the old man's gonna knock them into the middle of next week when they get home."

"But," I objected, "Simon hadn't been flirting with anybody. He ignored me all evening, in fact. That's why I was so upset."

"Yeah, maybe. But it was the look on his face that convinced me. He was scared, but excited. He'd upset his friend – I've got no idea how, of course, perhaps Nathan was pissed off because Simon had had you round for coffee that time, and it was still festering, I dunno – and Nathan was going to make him pay for it. Simon was dying to get home – but dreading it, too."

"Why didn't you mention any of this to me?"

"You'd have been furious! You'd have told me to mind my own damned business, and to keep my great big nose out of your affairs."

"Yes." I bit my lip. "I suppose I might."

"There's no bleeding *might* about it!"

"I suppose not." I looked up at him. "You *are* clever," I said.

"I'm not. I'm just observant, that's all." Nick shrugged. "It's my training, I suppose."

"What do you mean?"

"In any sort of research, you have to know roughly what you're looking for. Well, that's obvious, of course. But you must leave your options open, too.

"I could see you were – how shall I put it – very involved with Simon. But he didn't seem at all bothered about you. At first, I thought it must be an ordinary one-sided infatuation. I'm sorry, Lin. I'm not trying to upset you, honestly. But you must admit it's the sort of thing you see all the time. I told myself it was none of my business, anyway.

"But then, when I was down here another time, I couldn't help but notice – well – things. I was puzzled,

I suppose, so I began to speculate. To let my mind wander."

"But how did you know Nathan was Simon's lover?"

"I didn't *know*. Even after the party, I was still guessing. To be honest, I thought it might be one of the other Casson apes. Nathan was just watching out for one of his brothers, sort of thing."

"But then?"

"Later, I realised Nathan was always *there*. Popping up like a bloody jack-in-the-box, following you around. The jealous lover to a T, in fact."

"I've been so stupid." Ashamed of myself, I sighed. "Now you've explained, it's all so crystal clear!"

"I don't think it's *that* obvious." Nick shrugged. "But tunnel vision's certainly a killer. It was Pasteur who said – at least, I think it was Pasteur, it was one of those clever foreign bastards, anyway – in the field of experimentation, chance favours only the prepared mind. One must always have a prepared mind."

"I suppose one must."

"One must also have an early night." Yawning, Nick shook his head. He let go of my fingers. "You go on up. I'll tidy away in here."

I looked round the kitchen. It was certainly a bit of a mess. But that didn't matter. "I think you should come up, too," I said.

"You do?" he murmured, kissing the top of my head. "I don't know about that."

"Don't play hard to get, Singer. It really doesn't suit you." I raised my face to his. For, although I'd been blind, although I'd been stupid, I knew at least one thing for certain.

I would sleep well tonight.